Who You Are

MURPHY BROTHER STORIES, BOOK 6

JENNIFER RODEWALD

WORDS THAT EDIFY
Rooted Publishing

ROOTED PUBLISHING

Contents

H E WASN'T GOING BACK, and that was final. And he didn't regret it.

Brandon Murphy had made up his mind long before the second semester of his sophomore year in college had drawn to a close. What a horrible end of the school year that had been. Even now, months later, Brandon felt the thick weight of it as a black ball of lead in his gut.

How could Tyler do what he'd done? Brandon still could not reconcile any of it. And Becca? How could she have . . .

As the now-familiar surge of electrified resentment zipped through his limbs, Brandon positioned a section of log and gripped the maul. Eyes focused on the target, he lifted, then swung. Steel cracked against seasoned pine, wood splintered, and pieces flew, exposing white heart stained with streaking blue. A hint of satisfaction stole the resentful energy. For a moment.

There would be more to come though. Experience over the past few months had proven it.

He took evasive action, pressing his body into driving-work mode. He had a mound of wood to split and the abundance of energy to do it. If he kept to a hard, rhythmic pace, he wouldn't have to think about Tyler, still secreted away at some rehab facility—a truth that was, in fact, *un*thinkable. If he pushed his muscles hard, he couldn't allow his mind to wander over the collapse of an older brother he'd so hugely admired, and all that Tyler had lost within one short year. He couldn't feel the emptiness of disappointment, nor would he have to wrestle with the frustration toward heaven.

How could any of it have happened though?

Brandon kicked away the accumulation of split wood littering the base of his stabilizing log and gripped another piece to be sundered. Harder. Just work harder. Stop the thoughts. Ignore what pricked. He did so, until sweat soaked the black roots of his hair and seeped into his eyes, until he was panting and in need of water, stat. For an hour? Maybe that and a half more.

With a careless nudge, he lifted the bill of his hat, swiped away his sunglasses, and ran the long sleeve of his denim shirt over his soppy forehead. He dropped the weighted head of the maul, a satisfying thud against forest floor, and let the handle slip from his grip. It leaned into the pull of gravity until the diminishing pile of work yet to be done caught its full descent with a knock of wood on wood. His aluminum water canteen waited where he'd left it on the last break, the lone watcher of his labor sitting on the open tailgate of his late-nineties Ford pickup. As his breath evened out, he leaned on that tailgate, tipping the metal to his lips.

Cool water wet his lips, slid down his throat. Small, escaping rivers washed away stray bits of slivered pine and dust as it dribbled down his chin. And his thoughts returned to the exact place Brandon wished them not to go.

Why Tyler?

Why did this bother *him* so much? Hadn't his nearest older brother let him down before? Surely he must have . . .

This, though. Opioid addiction? From Tyler? So entrenched that he would steal to find his fix? So buried in it that he would turn away from the woman he loved? How did this happen? How did the slippery slopes of life sneak up on one so . . . so good?

And why did it devastate Brandon?

He's recovering, Brandon. Go see your brother. This was Mom's bidding. Brandon had refused.

Men are only men, son. Even the best of them. This is why all need to be saved. Dad's quiet words held truth, but not enough to penetrate Brandon's hard frustration. After all, hadn't Tyler already been saved? A professing believer since the age of seven, Tyler had been the one to explain Jesus's gift of salvation to Brandon himself! Older brother led younger brother in the sinner's prayer for redemption when Brandon had been six.

What did one do with the fall of a saint?

In Brandon's case, hide from the world and lose himself in work. Perhaps eventually that would make things better.

CHAPTER ONE

(in which Megan knows the reason why)

A LMOST Three Years Later

Megan Alexander pressed her ear harder against the open space on the wall between the shelves. Convenient that Daddy's office was right next to the family library. This was not the first conversation she'd ever eavesdropped on, but it was certainly the most important one. At least to her—to her future and happiness. Regarding that, her blood surged with heated betrayal. How could Daddy?

"Is this a threat, Mr. Alexander?" Marcus's incredulous voice cracked.

Daddy could do that to anyone—intimidate them until they felt they were a twelve-year-old wimp up against the mightiest of dragons.

"Threat?" Daddy chuckled. "Marcus, you ask your father if I make threats." The bulging pause hung intentional, and Megan pictured Daddy's pointed, brow-raised glare. "It's as good as done. Official papers amended. You go through with this little scheme of yours, and she'll not see a solitary dollar. I haven't spent my life building all of this to see my daughter swept into your world of conceit, entitlement, and greed. She's more than you've measured her to be."

A throat cleared. "Seems a mean thing for a father to do to his only daughter."

Exactly. That was exactly what this was! Mean! Megan's fist curled as she hugged herself tight. *How could you?*

All she'd ever wanted was to be happy. This was the way to it—Marcus Kensington was the key to the prayer she'd first whispered as a nine-year-old, one perpetually repeated over the past thirteen years: *God, please make me pretty and popular so I can fit into this world. So I can be happy.*

And hadn't God done His part?

Megan was beautiful, and she wasn't of the fake-humble sort who pretended she didn't know it. Her face and form had unlocked the gates to the rest. The popularity she knew must lead to easy happiness—the envy of all in her wealthy circle. That was the only way to it in this world—the world of wealth and immense social struggle that was the unseen, unspoken side of the coin.

Her family was new money. New to this world that not even Daddy, in all of his vast wisdom, understood. This world Daddy didn't particularly love, but his simple invention that apparently improved the turkey hunting sportsman's life immensely had plunged them into. A world that had knocked Megan around hard during her elementary years, leading her to mutter that defining prayer.

Make me pretty and popular. So I can be happy.

She'd been right too. Being pretty and popular *had* made things easier. So much easier. And her ticket to maintaining the smooth-sailing, happy life had crossed her path six months before. Marcus Kensington was the son of long-standing money. He was also, at twenty-seven, the best-looking eligible bachelor within Megan's elite social circle. Or, more accurately, the circle of which Megan existed on the fringes. Marcus would fix that—on his arm, she would finally be wholly adopted into this world of high society. Ushered into full acceptance.

No one would dare to remind her of her family's humble beginnings if she was Marcus's bride. They wouldn't call her turkey-girl anymore.

"I beg you to reconsider," Marcus's low voice sounded desperate.

"Do you?" There was a hint of mocking in Daddy's. "Why?"

Another break. Megan fingered the rock on her left ring finger. Three carats of brilliance wrapped in a double halo of pink and white diamonds, all set in in gleaming platinum. It was extraordinary, as had been Marcus's proposal. A carriage ride through the heart of old town. Private dinner at Neiman's—private because Marcus had bought out the entire restaurant for the evening. Lilies at the table, surrounded by tealights flickering in the semidarkness. And the man who could secure Megan's prestigious future, going down on one knee.

"You are the loveliest of them all," he'd said smoothly, his blue eyes holding hers with a gleam. "I knew from first glance I must have you. So promise me forever, Megan. Promise you'll be mine."

It'd all been out of a dream.

"You're using her." Through the wall, Daddy's flat accusation burst though Megan's reverie. Just as he had the night she and Marcus had gotten engaged. What a letdown that scene had been.

"You're what?" Daddy had thundered. "Did it not occur to him to ask me first?"

"Oh, Daddy." Megan had brushed him off with a wave of her hand, blissfully unaware of her father's true and fervent disapproval. Sure, he'd not been thrilled with Marcus taking her out for the past few months. But

that was just Daddy being a daddy. All protective of his daughter. But surely now, with a proper engagement, Daddy would see that Marcus was serious and that he made Megan happy. He could secure her future happiness.

"Megan," Daddy had barked, startling her out of her heady stupor. "He's not a good choice."

"Why on earth not?"

"He's selfish, Meg. A pretentious snob who will always, only, look out for himself."

"He isn't. Look at this ring! It's a Tiffany's, for goodness' sake. That's generous, isn't it?" And beautiful. Already the envy of every single one of her girlfriends. Livy Isaacson most of all—her bestie had gushed and squealed, as a friend should.

One brow slid up into Daddy's forehead, and he looked at the ring as if it offended him. "It's territorial branding, nothing more. A dog does the same thing to a tree."

"Daddy."

"Megan, you need to trust me on some things. You've been sheltered—apparently too much. I know what goes on beyond your view. I know the Kensingtons, both Marcus and his father. This is not a life you want. Not the life I want to see you shackled in."

What should have been the happiest night of her life had ended in tears. Daddy could be so obstinate! And why was he so judgey? Just because the Kensingtons were old money and maybe didn't accept the Alexanders on first arrival? Pfff. They were cautious, that was all. There was nothing wrong with being cautious. Anyway, didn't Daddy understand that her marriage into that family would bind up all the frayed edges in that situation?

And whatever did he mean by choosing that word *shackled*? What a way to view marriage!

"This is a mistake, Mr. Alexander." Megan could picture the fire in Marcus's midnight-blue eyes, and she wanted to cheer him on. "Mark my words, Buck. This move is one you do *not* want to make."

See, Daddy. He wants me.

"You may stick with Mr. Alexander, should it ever be necessary for the two of us to communicate again. And who's doling out threats now, boy?"

Silence.

"I've said what I called you here to say. You can go." Daddy's tone waved Marcus away, as if he were a schoolboy being firmly dismissed.

"And if I marry her anyway?"

Bless Marcus, he would fight! Megan nibbled on the edge of her lip, a smirk working on the corner of her mouth.

"You heard what I said. Megan will always be my daughter. *Always.* But the rest . . . "

"Then it's settled."

Megan sighed as she sagged against the wall, held upright by the cool wood paneling. Had she been afraid Marcus would call off their engagement? Ha! Daddy was wrong. And surely this was all just a test anyway.

Happiness was not lost after all.

Footfalls clapped against the wood floor on the other side of the wall, followed by a swish and then a hard smack of the office door. Megan pushed off the paneling and stood straight, running her damp palms down the legs of her designer jeans. Looking down, she caught the glinting center stone as it stole the chandelier light from the middle of the room and claimed it as its own.

No, happiness was not lost at all. She grinned at the beauty winking up at her, and when the footfalls stopped at the opening of the library doors, she looked up, ready to fly into the arms of the man she would marry.

Those blue eyes landed on her with such hard force her feet remained planted. Marcus did not smile. He did not beckon her to him. Nor did he speak. He simply shook his head and then walked away.

All her happiness followed after him. Gone. Daddy had ruined everything.

***

I doubt you need me to write out the reason—you already know. I will need the ring back. -MK

Two days later, Megan stared at the note, written in hurried script, penned in black ink, on a plain scrap of paper, folded into quarters. Nothing remarkable about it—a simple memo, as if for his office assistant, reminding her to do something mundane. *Schedule lunch . . . call a client. . . end the engagement.*

Give back the ring.

Nothing remarkable at all.

Shoulders curled as if that could protect her heart from the cruelty of hopes shredded, Megan lowered onto the edge of her bed. The dark words blurred as she read them yet again, hot tears burning her eyes. She focused on his flippant signature. *MK.*

Marcus Kensington. *Megan Kensington.*

Not to be. *Thanks, Daddy.*

"Megan?" Mom's voice came hesitantly from the doorway of Megan's room.

Molten iron cooled in her chest, becoming rigid.

Mom didn't sense the wall erecting within her. "Meg, my love, what's wrong?"

Megan lifted her chin, slowly turning daggers of resentment onto the woman who had ever only been her number one fan. "What's wrong?" She fixed a glare on her mother. "How could you let Daddy do it?"

Tipping her head to one side, Mom stopped mere feet from Megan, her expression all sympathy and understanding. "Your father felt it was best. There was no persuading him. But it will all come right, Meg my love. Once you and Marcus are married, I'm sure he'll—"

Megan thrust the pathetic note toward her mother, nearly smacking the slender, well-maintained woman in the gut. Startled, Mom fingered the page, then lifted it from Megan's grip, eyeing her daughter with dread.

It took less than a second for the rosy pink to drain from Mom's cheeks. Her mouth pressed firm, brows drew in tight. "Then your father was right. As he usually is." She sighed, shoulders drooping. "Oh dear, how I'd hoped . . . "

"Hoped what?"

"That Marcus would prove himself to be a better man."

"A better man? Mom, that's insane! How could you hope for me to find better? Marcus Kensington is the center of everything!"

Mom lowered onto the bedside, one hand cradling Megan's shoulder. "That does not mean he is a good man, Meg. Though clearly I had thought . . . " Another sigh, then a shake of her head. "Surely you know —"

"What I know is that Daddy ruined my life!" Megan shrugged off her mother's touch. "The most eligible man in our circle asked *me* to marry him. And now he wants his ring back! Because *my father* threatened him!"

"Threatened?" A light chuckle escaped Mother's lips. "Oh, my dear girl, that's a little dramatic. There was no real threat."

How could this woman laugh? This was nothing funny at all. Megan turned away, focusing her hard stare on her balled fists. "He said he'd remove me from the trust."

"And that's a threat?" Mom moved so that Megan could not escape eye contact, and then lifted her brows. "If Marcus loved you, just *you*, why would he care if your dad took away your trust fund, hmm? He's a capable man with his own fortune, isn't he?"

Could Mom be so simple? Sure, Mom was a little bit on the . . . the all-is-bright-and-rosy side—sometimes ignorantly so. But. Megan kept in a growl, but not the bite. "Because it makes it painfully obvious how much Daddy doesn't like him. What man on earth would want to marry into that?"

"Oh, there are plenty of men who possess the sort of fortitude for that. Besides, your dad didn't turn him out, didn't say you would be disowned. In fact, I believe your father made it clear that you will always be his daughter, always wanted and welcome in this home, no matter what you did. He simply removed the financial gain you possessed. And I thought sure that his doing so would make Marcus's true intentions clear." Again, she sighed, her body sagging low. "And I guess it did."

"There is no man on the planet who would endure such an insult, Mother."

At this, Mom snorted. "Megan, as much as I adore you, and I know that you are a smart young woman, full of potential and fire, I must admit, your father has been right for some years. You, my daughter, are a touch ridiculous. And a little on the side of ignorant, if you want the full truth. I have spoiled you too much."

Megan drew back as if her mother had slapped her—which had never once happened in her life. "What?"

"This life we've created for you has made you blind."

"I can see perfectly. I can see that Daddy has been mean, and now you! *You!* Mother!" Her sure confidante and the woman who had always, *always* been her champion. What had happened in the last few days?

Weeks, had it been? Yes, weeks, actually. While Daddy made his opinion of Marcus known, Mom had cooed and eased tensions, as she did so well. But she had also worn a look of . . . doubt. When did Mom begin doubting her?

Gently clasping Megan's flailing hands, Mom pressed them into the small space of mattress between them. "You are young, and the world you know is small. Megan, you must trust me for the truth of this: there are better men out there. Men who will not care whether or not you come with an Alexander trust. Men who would love you for better or worse, for richer or poorer. Your dad felt it necessary to put it to the test—and now we all can see why. Marcus Kensington is not that man."

Megan drew her hands away and crossed her arms. "He is the cream of our circle. Within that, there is no better. Ask any single young woman."

One eyebrow lifted on Mom's face, the look of the unpersuaded. "Then beyond that."

"And how will that happen?" Megan lived in the trappings of wealth, and everyone she'd ever met was assaulted with that truth. From her clothing and jewelry to the vehicles they owned. Her very education proclaimed prestige. Was she to figure out how to go incognito?

Did she even want to?

No. She liked her life the way it was. She'd particularly liked it with Marcus Kensington in it. Life with him would be easy. Happy.

Resentment surged hard.

"I have an idea." Mom's proclamation came suddenly, and when Megan lifted her gaze back to meet her face, she found the woman's stare had wandered toward her massive window. Megan followed it.

Beyond the glass panes, a sprawling garden lay dormant in late-winter's rest. Snow dusted the evergreens. Tall grasses bowed to the ground, their reds and browns a feather contrast to the blue greens and white. In a few weeks, life would spring new, beginning with a low carpet of crocus. Then the daffodils . . .

Thoughts that should have cheered. Instead, Megan felt only bitter disappointment and anger at the man who had caused it. She turned back to her mother.

"What idea?" Megan wasn't sure she wanted to know, unless it was a way to win Marcus back and have Daddy bend his iron will to hers. What were the odds of that?

Most certainly not favorable.

"Let me think on it some . . . " Mom said.

"First tell me what it involves." Mother was the quirky sort. The type who didn't simply *explain* how a flower grew, but, grabbing her daughter by the hand, made sure she was an *eyewitness* to the entire process. Seed to stem to bud to blossom . . . Megan had copious amounts of drawings and photos documenting the whole educational experience. And not just of that.

The courting and nesting practices of great horned owls.

The molting process of a cicada.

The growth of bacteria.

Megan had witnessed much of what nature and science had to offer. And she usually thrilled in it.

"You will see for yourself, Meg." Mother smiled and then leaned to press a kiss to her forehead. A new scientific experiment had germinated in her mind. A predictable response, but still unclear.

Megan swallowed. This time, she did *not* want to see for herself. "See what?"

"That there are better men in this world." She curved a hand on Megan's cheek. "Much better men. I promise."

And how on earth was Mom going to prove that? Megan had a nagging sense that she'd better buckle up.

CHAPTER TWO

(in which Brandon reads a strange letter)

"**B**RANDON."

He stopped, boot footed, on the tile floor of the mudroom. As he often did on a Friday night, he'd eaten at his parents' long, wooden table. These days there were usually only four of them seated—Mom, Dad, Brayden, and himself. It felt odd, even now, after several years of having the family simultaneously grow and slim down. More than half of the seven Murphy boys were married and had families of their own. Only the younger three were single: Tyler, Brayden, and himself. But Tyler was often gone too, off telling the world about living abundantly even after deep disappointment. And Brayden would soon be gone again as well, off to finish his college education.

Which Brandon hadn't done.

Three years post that decision, and Brandon still didn't regret it. Even if he also still wrestled with the sense of aimlessness that had been a partial catalyst in that decision.

"Can you stay just a bit longer? Maybe walk with me down the road?" Mom slipped her arm around him, turning her bright-blue eyes up to his face. Silver had replaced most of the sandy blond in her hair, but she still kept it most often swept back in a simple French braid. The years of mothering seven rambunctious boys, of running a house full of noise and activities, and of building her own business out of passion and creativity had marked her face with lines at the corners of her eyes and near her mouth.

Mom was aging.

Brandon hadn't noticed up until that moment. But she wore the years with joy and dignity. With loud laughter, enthusiasm, and hope. Couldn't he be more like her? After all, this woman had raised him. Why did he feel trapped within a heart that yearned for delight but found mostly visionless frustration?

He clapped silence over the thoughts that would surely visit him again later. Squeezing her shoulders, he nodded. "A walk it is. Should I grab your coat?"

With a soft pat on his chest, she turned away to snatch the garment herself. He opened the glass-paned front door and held it wide as she followed him out. Having zipped up, she then led the way down the deck stairs that landed on the front drive. Together, they walked the length of the driveway, and when they came to the road, Brandon turned left. Mom looped her arm through his as they continued.

"I love late winter. Everything on the cusp of new beginnings."

He chuckled. "You love every season, Mom."

"That's true." She leaned into him. "And why shouldn't I?"

"Winter is cold. Lots of snow up here."

"Beautiful white blankets." Her voice smiled. "Glitter set off by the evergreens."

"My mother, the blogger."

"My son, the lone woodsman. How does he not appreciate these small gifts?"

That nicked, though he knew the words were spoken good naturedly. Brandon led her on without a response.

"Brandon?"

"Yeah, Mom."

"You're not happy."

Air emptied from his lungs, and he dared to glimpse her upturned face. Her gaze was all loving concern.

"I'm just . . . " What, exactly? *Stuck. Lost. Wondering if my life will ever matter.* He mentally glanced over his brothers' lives.

Matt, happily married and waiting expectantly for his second child. He was a tree farmer, and by all appearances, thrilled with his life. So he should be. Jacob had discovered real, lasting happiness after losing everything. Connor, who had chosen honor and sacrifice, had been blessed with the love of his life and a son whom he adored. Jackson also had his own family —a beautiful wife, who worked with their mother now, and two adorable kids. Tyler . . . Tyler had failed epically. Then got back up. Perhaps of all of them, Tyler had become the most successful, at least by the world's standards. And Brayden was killing it in school. Full academic scholarship and well on his way to becoming the first medical professional in the family. And hopefully, ironing out the spiraling path he'd tread during their late-teen years.

They were all so . . . alive. Doing well. Happy.

And Brandon?

"I feel like you're waiting for life to start." Mom spoke into his unfinished statement. Nailed it.

Brandon sighed. "Seems like the gun should have gone off a while ago." Maybe it had and he'd missed it. Should he have finished college? Then what?

Mom rubbed the firm muscle of his upper arm. Then she stopped, pulling him to a halt with her. "I've got a letter back home that is a little on the strange side. It's from an old friend—she sent it over two weeks ago. At first I thought to laugh it off and move on. But these past weeks, her request keeps floating in my mind, and you along with it."

Did this relate to his stalled life?

Tipping her chin up, she searched his eyes. "I'm going to send it with you tonight. Read it. Pray over it, will you?"

Brandon felt his brow pinch. "What does it say?"

Her work-rough hand curved over the stubble of his jaw. "You'll see." That strong hand drifted away. "Brandon, we've always called you the bold one. Perhaps only such a heart as yours could take on what has been asked."

A touch of frenzy lit in his chest at her odd words.

"But I'm not telling you to do it. Only that I keep thinking you might —though, to be honest, that seems bizarre."

"I really wish you'd just tell me what this is." Why was his heart thumping with dread? Was Mom suggesting he sign away his life? Maybe donate a kidney? Fly to Africa and dig wells?

By the serious gaze she held on him, all seemed like a possibility. Strangely, as he considered the call to some great unknown, the panic quieted.

Maybe he hadn't missed the start gun after all.

Perhaps his life had been waiting for this exact thing. For whatever was contained in the letter. The knotted muscles in his shoulders eased, and he even felt the relief of a small grin lifting his mouth. "Okay, Mom."

"Okay?"

"Yes. If you think I should consider whatever it is. I trust you."

Mom bit her lip and turned her look from his face to the forest of pines and spruces at his back. That moment of peace evaporated as he watched her expression.

She was not at all sure about this thing.

***

Brandon set aside the folded sheet of stationary. The page was heavy and smooth, no run-of-the-mill big-box-store purchase. The monogrammed initials embossed in gold at the top read AMA in swooping script. Personalized stationary, and expensive at that. A thing of the past, and also of the wealthy. Beneath that a greeting, and then what followed had been surprisingly direct, condensed, and shocking.

He shouldn't have stared at it so long. Now the inked words, penned in perfect, graceful cursive, bearing the marks of careful intentionality, had branded themselves in his mind.

Who would make such a request? It was crazy! This was the twenty-first century, for heaven's sake. And America. People didn't do things like this. Did they?

No. They didn't. People didn't even write things out by hand and put them in the mail, let alone pen such a thing. It was too audacious to be real. Too . . . absurd.

He reached for the page again—this was at least the dozenth time. This go, however, he'd find the prank in it. There had to be something tucked within those curving connected letters that would hint at a joke.

Ah! Yes!

This had to be Jackson's work. Jackson, the master of practical jokes. Jackson, the man who, if anyone, had the ability to shake a brother out of his doldrums. Maybe Mom had put him up to it? Perhaps she had grown worried about Brandon's extended life funk and had commissioned something to shake him up. That was plausible, wasn't it?

Letter between finger and thumb, Brandon took in the words again.

This is unusual, I know. But as the saying goes, desperate times . . . My Megan is a good girl, but she is blind in some places, and I fear she'll be taken and the worse for it. I know your young men are solid people of God. I know because I have done my research. And if you'll recall, I'm particularly good at research. Buck and I have prayed over it, and he has given me the go-ahead to ask this of you.

I leave this in your hands, my friend, knowing that your heart is in your sons as mine is in my daughter. It is an imposition, and I am well aware of it. But if such a knight is in your household and available, would you be willing to send him?

Six months is what we're requesting. Six months of what would amount to a trial engagement that would have a twofold effect, or so we hope. First, that Megan would see better, know better. Second, so that the man seeking her now (and others, because we know there are several raptors circling the nest!) would no longer see her as easy prey and would turn that scoundrel's attention away.

Six months. And perhaps, by God's good favor, a future beyond that?

A mother and father could pray so, couldn't they?

You forever have my admiration, Helen, no matter your answer.
As always, your Christian sister,
Anna M. Alexander

Nothing of the style bore evidence of Jackson's work. Nothing. Then again, Jackson was the master.

But would Mom participate like this?

In the morning, before setting out with his chainsaw, axe, and maul to cull a private acreage of dead timber standing as kindling waiting to fuel a wild blaze, Brandon would go and find the truth. Demand Mom tell him. And then force himself out of the murky blahness he'd been swimming in.

He didn't know how to accomplish that last part.

Once again, the letter landed on his bedside table, and Brandon reached for the Bible Dad had given him upon his high school graduation. *Never go anywhere without your sword, son. And never make any decision without seeking wisdom.* Hand to shoulder, eyes leveled on Brandon's, Dad had spoken solemnly, and the words had sealed upon Brandon's mind.

Word of God in hand, he shut his eyes and directed his mind toward God. *Approach God's throne of grace with confidence, so that we may receive mercy and find grace to help us in our time of need.*

The verse in Hebrews came easily to mind. He had reached for it often enough over the past few years. Needy man, apparently.

I need wisdom, Lord. Is this for real? And if so, is it from You?

Stillness settled over him as Brandon stretched long on his bed and waited. No definitive answer drifted over him. Only quietness. Strange, that in that silence, Brandon felt the struggle grow within him, the one that had pressed upon him fiercely ever since he'd quit college to become a woodsman—it thrashed harder. The quicksand of melancholy had claimed him, and though he'd fought against it, prayed for release from it, the daily bleakness sucked him in further.

What was he supposed to do with his insignificant life? Why did disappointment weigh him down like a millstone? When would he be cut free?

The struggle, the questions, felt dark and empty and lonely. Brandon opened his eyes, focused on the Bible in his hands, and flipped to the bookmark he'd stuck in the Psalms.

He leads me beside quiet waters.

Yes, the waters were quiet. Too quiet.

Doldrums.

Was it yet time to get up and leave the quiet waters? Was the letter an invitation to new pastures?

Lord, shepherd me...

Brandon finally slept, though fitfully. No audible answer had come. But by the morning, after a not-so-restful night, he'd made up his mind.

One way or another, it was time to leave the quiet waters.

CHAPTER THREE

(in which Megan and her dad strike a deal)

A FINE MIST BLANKETED the hillside as the sun eased itself into the new morning. Gauzy white swirled at the base of evergreens, a sight of mystery and of beauty. Longer, warmer mornings had come, the seasons sliding one to another.

Trust in the Lord and do good. That particular line from the psalm had draped itself in his mind over the past few days.

Brandon wasn't often a philosophical man, but as he strode around his parents' home toward the backyard, he wondered if this stunning mystery of life changing right before his eyes wasn't God's personal message to him. As was that verse.

He hoped it. And feared it.

He rounded the house and came to the back side of Mom's greenhouse. Glancing through the tall paned windows, he found her bent over her wooden table, working. Faint sounds of a soft piano piece drifted from the interior through the glass, the movement of music gentle and lovely. The arrangement Mom was midway through creating was full of the earliest spring blooms of yellows, whites and peaches, and structured evergreen boughs. A celebration of changing seasons.

Mom was an artist, for certain. And by her face, wreathed with unmistakable joy, she entered into her craft as if it was worship. And so it was, Brandon realized.

How to live in such a way?

Brandon stood at a distance, fingering through his mind for answers. He'd lived under her roof for twenty-one years, had claimed her as his mother for two more beyond that. How did he not know her secret? It certainly wasn't that life was always easy and beautiful. Just in the past handful of years, he'd witnessed firsthand that it was not so. She'd writhed with heartache for Tyler, every bit as Brandon had. But she'd done so with hope. With some kind of otherworldly, soft joy that lived through it, in spite of it. A joy that was ready to embrace Tyler when he'd emerged from the darkness, stronger, better, and more complete for his brokenness.

Brandon hadn't.

He'd wrestled hard with disillusionment and bitterness. Even now, a few years past the darkest part of Tyler's failure, with his relationship with the brother he'd been closest to and had admired most, Brandon still struggled with the heaviness that had shackled him when Tyler went to rehab.

Mom took the blows of life with hope. Brandon knew the source of it— Jesus Christ, *the hope of glory!* But knowing and *knowing* apparently weren't the same. Truthfully, he envied his mother. And his father, who never seemed to falter. And Tyler, who came to full—well, nearly full— restoration. The Shepherd had guided all of them through the dark valley, and now they were safely in green pastures again.

Lord, am I simply blind? If so, help me to see. Take me out of this melancholy...

The sound of footfalls on forest floor drew Brandon out of his head. He looked toward the back of the yard, where the long-used trail up to the ridge began. The scuffle of dewy fallen leaves, brown and damp from snowmelt, and whisper of swishing pines announced a traveler before he stepped into the mowed grass of the yard.

Tyler.

Brandon turned and grinned. "You're home," he said when his brother was near enough not to shout.

Tyler nodded, hands stuffed into his windbreaker's pockets. "Late last night."

"How was this trip?"

"Good. Only fell five times."

How life had changed. Tyler-Tarzan had never fallen before, and he'd prided himself on it. When he did fall, it was hard, and it had nearly been the undoing of the man Brandon had idolized. For a time, it seemed Tyler would never get back up again. One fall had defeated him.

But not for good.

"You prevailed," Brandon said.

"Yep."

"And speaking?"

"It went well, I think. Did you pray for me?"

"I did." And he had. Always did when Tyler went on one of his climbing and speaking expeditions. God was using his brother's accident and subsequent opioid addiction for good. That was something to rejoice in, wasn't it?

Why so downcast, oh my soul? Put your hope in God! Brandon's silent recitation of the psalm poked a hole into his gloom.

Tyler motioned with his head toward the flagstone bench tucked into one of Mom's flowerbeds. "You don't usually stop in before working."

Brandon followed him, and the pair sat on opposite ends of the stone. "No, not usually." He leaned to pull the folded letter from his back pocket, stared for a moment at the linen stationary in between his fingers, and then passed across the space toward Tyler. "I'm glad you're here though. What do you make of this?"

Eyeing Brandon for a beat, Tyler took the letter, opened it, and scanned the neat penmanship. His brows raised high with every line passing under his gaze, lips parted. When finally he looked back at Brandon, Tyler's expression was full shock. "Who is this Anna Alexander?"

"Apparently a friend of Mom's." Brandon rubbed his neck. "Mom gave that to me last night . . . "

Tyler's brows folded. "Mom wants you to consider this?"

"Yes."

"That's . . . surprising." Tyler looked over the words again. "Remember how upset she was when Connor proposed to Sadie?"

"Exactly." Brandon glanced over his shoulder at the greenhouse. Mother still worked away, unaware of her sons and their discussion. "Do you think this is one of Jackson's pranks?"

Tyler's attention followed Brandon's, and he studied their mom. "Mom wouldn't do that to you right now, Brandon. Not with . . . "

Not with him fighting this . . . thing. What was this darkness?

With a small nod, Brandon retrieved the letter from Tyler's hand, studied it yet again, though he didn't read the words. Didn't need to.

"What will you do?" Tyler asked.

Brandon drew a long breath. It was crisp and full of musty fallen leaves and fresh pine. "You know in the Bible there's that story of Jacob wrestling a man all night?"

"Yeah . . . "

"And he wouldn't let the man go until he blessed him?"

"Right. Changed his name and the way he walked for the rest of his life."

Brandon didn't know why he'd thought of that, why he'd brought it up.

"Are you wrestling with God, Brandon?"

Heat suddenly stung his eyes. Was that it? This weight wasn't a millstone, but it was Brandon wrestling with God? Why? Because he lacked vision. He wanted, desperately, direction. Blessing.

Brandon shrugged, then focused his attention back on the letter. "I think I'm supposed to do this." He waved the page. "Is that crazy?"

Tyler sat back. "A little." Then he grinned. "But so is a man climbing with one leg."

Both men chuckled softly. God was not beyond doing crazy, was He? Brandon shifted to slide the letter into his back pocket again. "Mrs. Alexander is asking for six months. I'm supposed to help Matt with his addition before that time frame is up."

"I can do it." Tyler volunteered without hesitation.

Brandon eyed him. "Becca lives in Pleasant Valley. She and Lauren are best friends."

A touch of red bled through the dark beard covering Tyler's face, but he held a steady gaze on Brandon. "I know."

"Have you reached out to her at all?"

"No."

"Why?"

Tyler's face turned toward the forested hillside beyond the grassy space, his dark eyes misting. "I'm a coward, I guess."

"Do you still love her?"

"Always." The simple, naked truth, stated unashamedly. Again, Tyler looked at Brandon. "I'll go for you, Brandon, if you think you're supposed to do this crazy thing."

Quiet settled between them. Comfortable and easy. Estranged brothers who had been restored. Brothers who had wrestled with hard things between them and had walked away changed.

Perhaps not all struggle was a curse. Not in the end. But Brandon wasn't the philosophical type.

He stood and stretched. Tyler did as well. A gust raced from the hillside, rustling leaves on the ground and swaying evergreen boughs, bringing with it a taste of snow. Change.

It was settled then.

Brandon would tell his mother, then write back to this Anna Alexander and set out to do something crazy. Hopefully, on the other side of it, he'd walk away changed.

***

"Meg, we need to talk."

Five more ominous words Megan could not think of as she sat beneath a spotless window in a splash of yellow sunshine on the window seat in the library, scrolling through Pinterest for evening gowns on her phone. Knowing the standard—phones were to be set aside during what was supposed to be human-interaction time—Megan slid the tech in her palm onto the windowsill and tucked her feet beneath her.

"Am I in trouble?" She met her mother's eyes. But not Daddy's. She hadn't yet forgiven him, though it'd been three weeks since he'd threatened the man who was supposed to be her fiancé. And was she supposed to forgive him so readily? Megan thought not.

"No, my love." Mom smiled for both her and Daddy, which might have been presumptuous, as Daddy didn't even try to summon such an expression. "But we have some news."

"News . . . "

Daddy lifted a straight-backed chair from its position near a bookshelf and dropped it in front of Megan's perch on the window seat. "An arrangement," he said gravely.

Megan's tummy clenched, and she immediately disliked whatever it was her parents were about to say. She squeezed her hands together and gazed unflinching at the man she'd spent most of her life outright adoring.

Had he always been this overbearing? She hadn't thought so. Always this unrelenting? Only in business matters, which was why they'd moved from the lower-middle-class suburbs to this elite community some fifteen years before. Daddy had invented a new turkey blind, and the hunting world had gone crazy over it. It was a stroke of genius, and paired with Daddy's keen business instinct, had vaulted the Alexanders into this world of luxury.

Megan was grateful. And yes, she'd idolized her daddy all her growing-up years. Right up until she'd overheard him pushing Marcus out of her life. That little incident was still a smoldering resentment in her gut, and to that moment she'd yet to speak more than a simple *yes* or *no* to him. She turned her attention to Mom, whose smile gleamed with enthusiasm, as it always did when she was about to embark upon a discovery.

Heaven help them.

"Your mom came to me with a suggestion." Daddy pressed back into the chair. "To be honest, I thought it was farfetched."

"It's an arrangement. An experiment maybe. And it isn't farfetched. People have been doing it for centuries, and often it turns out beautifully."

"What was farfetched?" Megan asked slowly.

"This plan." He rubbed his chin, his confidence suffering a wavering moment. That cleared quickly. "Arrangement."

What on earth was this *arrangement* they kept speaking of? "Could one of you just tell me what you're talking about?"

"An engagement."

Megan choked on her own spit. "I'm sorry?"

An engagement? As in, an engagement, engagement? One intended to end at the long end of an aisle in the middle of their large church in front of a pastor and everyone else?

Couldn't be.

"Yes. An engagement, as in betrothal."

Betrothal! Who used that word? Who did this thing? This was . . . ridiculous. A tiny chuckle bubbled from deep within, growing steadily as she fiddled with the idea Mom had just spit out. It was completely, thoroughly, and utterly ridiculous.

Farfetched indeed. They were teasing her. Trying to pull her out of the sulk she'd indulged in the past weeks. Convinced of it, she tossed her head back and laughed outright. And then looked back at her parents.

Mom's grin held, fully delighted. Daddy remained calm. Dead. Serious.

One last coughing chuckle left her chest, and then panic set in. They were not joking. Daddy definitely was not. Her heart came to a painfully hard stop as she looked into his determined eyes.

"How could you even think—" she stammered.

"You apparently lack good judgment," he said, as if he was stating something as obvious as the current weather. *It's dreary outside.*

His words were a hard sting, a slap across the face. "Daddy," she whispered, heat pricking her eyes.

"Marcus is a leech." Daddy's voice bit like a serrated blade. "You refused to listen when I gently warned you before his proposal. You ignored me by accepting his gaudy, pompous ring. And these past few weeks, you have sulked like a spoiled child over my intervention. Accused me of unloving injustice. You insist that what I did out of sincere love and thoroughly informed concern for my *only* daughter was mean and unfeeling. That *I* am the selfish man in this. I cannot conclude anything but that you lack good judgment, and important life decisions are not safe left in your fumbling hands." He didn't flinch in all that speech, though pain did seem to lurk in the recesses of his gaze.

She'd hurt him. Disappointed him greatly. And now he was striking back.

Did Daddy function that way?

Perhaps she *had* handled Daddy's actions with a measure of childishness. Maybe less flinging herself with dramatic sobs. Less of the silent treatment she'd followed that outburst with. If she'd employed rational argument rather than emotional tantrum. If only that, he wouldn't say such hurtful things. Do this humiliating thing.

What of her disappointment though? Could he really do this to her? "I won't marry some stranger."

Mom came to stand behind Daddy, her hands resting on his stiff shoulders, one small diamond on her left hand grabbing hold of the weak sunlight pushing through the window and reflecting it with cheer. "You won't marry right away. That is the arrangement—you are not trapped. Brandon has agreed to come, to live six months in the guest house, and to see how things go between you."

Megan focused on Mom's ring. It was simple, modest. Daddy could have upgraded that stone and the setting years ago. Why hadn't he? Perhaps he *was* selfish, and Megan was only just now seeing it. She looked at him. Still composed, steady. But yes, there was that hint of hurt in his unwavering stare. And she couldn't take it in.

She slid her attention back to Mom. "See how things go? What does that mean?"

Mom's radiant confidence cracked. "Well, to see if Brandon—you, the pair of you, can make a life together."

"A life *together*?" Megan's voice took flight, her grip on her panicking anger slipping fast. This was nothing but a selfish move on Daddy's part! He was controlling and mean. And Mom! Not trapped? What did Mom think an arranged marriage was, if not a trap? "You want me to agree to an engagement to a complete stranger with the full intent of marrying him? Are you insane?"

"I am not insane." Mom held her dignity, and Daddy shot Megan a heated look of warning. "I told you, there are better men out there. Since you are bound and determined not to listen to your father and me, we think it would be most effective to *show* you. And anyway, Brandon Murphy is not a complete stranger. You grew up together."

Brandon Murphy? Never heard of him. She had zero memories of such a person. "Grew up together when?"

Mom's chin shifted upward a touch—a sign that she might be a bit uncomfortable. "When we lived in Sugar Creek. His mother and I went to MOPS together. You and Brandon were a pair in the nursery."

"The nursery!" Mom was insane! "As in, we were in diapers?"

"Well, you were. I'm sure Brandon wasn't by then—he was nearly five, I think."

Madness! "Mom, I can't with this . . . " Megan pushed her feet out from under her and jumped from the window seat.

"Sit down, Megan." There was no room for refusal when Daddy used that tone. *Selfish, controlling man!* "It's done. There's no negotiation in it."

"You would just hand your daughter over like this? To a man you only knew when he was five years old?" Megan slumped back onto the seat. "How could you, Daddy?"

This father she hardly knew. Where was her gentle, generous father, who had doted on her? The one she'd simply adored?

"I trust Kevin implicitly." Daddy held her with that unwavering gaze, though now there seemed to be a touch of compassion in his look. "He is the most honest, godly man I've ever known. He showed me what it is to live Christ, an example I've never forgotten. I have no doubt that if there was something of concern in Brandon, he would say so."

"Who is Kevin?"

"Kevin Murphy, Brandon's father."

"And you think a father would say anything negative about his son?"

"If it was necessary to protect another, yes. Kevin would do that."

Megan blinked, releasing more tears. Her mind spun too hard to formulate more arguments. All she had was wild emotion screaming *no!* But that would only reinforce the claims Daddy had made against her.

She was *not* an irresponsible child who lacked good judgment.

A long, gaping silence ripped between them. Megan clenched and unclenched her fists. Rolled her lips together to keep from spewing her emotion.

Why would a man agree to this? What was wrong with this Brandon Murphy that he'd even consider this insane *arrangement?* Was he hideous? Socially inept? Stupid? Cruel? An opportunist?

He couldn't be anything good, of that Megan was certain.

"What if I can't stand him?" she muttered hopelessly. "Will you make me marry a man I loathe?"

Daddy's large, warm hand slowly reached and covered hers, his touch gentle. Fatherly. Loving. "Trust me to do good for you, Megan." His voice cracked with emotion. Why should he be fighting tears? "I am doing this in love, Meg. Because I want better for you than what you're choosing for yourself."

This did not feel like love. This felt all sorts of mean. Not only had Daddy driven away the man she had chosen to marry, but now he was demanding she marry another. A stranger. And this was Daddy's version of doing good? It made zero sense. Sobs shook her shoulders, and suddenly Daddy was on the seat beside her, strong, tender arms pulling her close.

"Six months, Megan. Try for six months," he said calmly. "And then at the end of that trial, you can dissolve the arrangement if you want. The trust will be yours, and you can choose whatever path you want. Just give me six months to show you something different."

She pressed into his shoulder, sniffing. Six months, and then not only could she end this arranged engagement, but she could take control of the trust that was not to be hers for another four years?

Daddy must be desperate.

His hold around her shoulders tightened, and he tipped his chin to speak low near her ear. "I want the best life for you. You're my daughter. How could I want less?"

There was love in that, even if he'd delivered a blade to her heart moments before. Was Daddy being mean, controlling, and selfish? At the moment, he was cradling her with strong tenderness. And he had given her a choice at the end of this bizarre experiment.

Six months, then.

Six months, and Daddy would see that she had good judgment after all. Six months, and he'd entrust her with her own life. Her world would then be set back to right.

She could endure this arrangement for six months for that.

CHAPTER FOUR

(in which Brandon meets Mrs. Knolls)

TYLER HAD STARTED THIS new tradition. It was practiced whenever the Murphys gathered in any number, not just on Thanksgiving—or any other holiday, for that matter. Brandon imagined it was practiced daily between Mom and Dad and the God of the universe, whom they loved, whether any of their seven sons and their extended blessings were there or not.

"Purple crocus dotting the brown forest floor," Mom said wistfully.

An item, moment, experience to number as a gift. Tyler had started it shortly after he'd been released from Seaside recovery. He'd learned it from . . .

Well, Brandon didn't know that one. But Tyler had learned it, practiced it, and the habit of looking for tokens of God's love in everyday moments seemed to have transformed his outlook. No longer did he lament the loss of his leg, the heartbreak in losing Becca Colson, and the downward spiral that had marked his senior year in college. No longer did he shake his fists toward heaven.

Tyler was redeemed, restored, and repurposed. And he marked moments with the things he could lift back up in gratitude.

"Boys who became men, steeped in the Word and seeking God's will." Dad spoke from across the table, the proud and tender gleam in his eye coming to rest on Brandon. "Men who are willing to do hard, unusual things."

A quiver trembled in Brandon's chest as his heart squeezed. Dad approved of Brandon's decision.

Dad approves of me.

That was Brandon's silent item added to those spoken gifts. It meant the world, and Brandon supposed that having Dad's nod was every bit as precious to all his brothers as well.

Big shoes, that man.

The practice circled round the tables, the large open front room boasting two of them for this gathering of the mass Murphy clan. No doubt all of them could count that as a blessing. Brothers and sweet sisters-in-law. Nieces and nephews. Overflowing love, loud and abundant laughter.

Thanksgiving indeed, even on Easter. Especially on Easter?

Brandon pondered what the holiday looked like at the Alexanders'. He couldn't help it—by next week he'd be with them. Figuring out how to do this strange thing that had been asked of him. He'd written back to Mrs. Anna Alexander, stating in unflowery terms that he accepted the *arrangement*, and when should he come?

After Easter, the lady replied, and thank you very much.

What would his life look like there? Clearly there was wealth, and Dad had confirmed that, yes, there was plenty in their realm. Mr. Thad Alexander—Buck to his friends, though Dad didn't say why—had made something of the two pennies he'd rubbed together. A stroke of genius in a single invention had vaulted the Alexanders into multimillionaire status.

That was a little intimidating, if Brandon was honest. So he didn't focus on that aspect.

What was it like to grow up an only child? As the second youngest of seven, Brandon was hard pressed to imagine—though doing so might be easier for him than one of the boys who had been born in the middle.

Who was this Megan Alexander? What was she like? He pictured a delicate beauty. Timid and in need of protection. Innocent and prone to kind smiles that would invite shady characters. At such ideas, a powerful surge of protectiveness welled.

And it continued, long after the meal was consumed, copious amounts of leftovers stored and put away, and even beyond the great exodus of his brothers who, with smiles and laughter and love and direction, shepherded their families from their childhood home to their grown-up lives beyond. Brandon pondered the mystery girl he'd agreed to a trial engagement with as he entered his small home tucked into the woods, all dark and quiet and lonely.

Megan . . .

Her name was on his mind, in his prayers, as he tucked into warm blankets and closed his tired eyes.

Megan . . .

His new future? Time would tell for certain. But it already *felt* certain to him.

***

Megan gathered nail polish, books, sheet music, and a notebook and pen. With order and care, she placed them in her bag, thought over the faces she'd visit today. A wispy smile eased the tense corners of her mouth. The dull ache in her head, often present these past few weeks, quieted.

At least in this she still maintained control. She was never more herself than on Tuesday and Friday afternoons. Thank goodness this was only Tuesday—that would leave her Friday to anticipate. By then she would likely need the escape more than ever—though previous to this week she didn't think of her visits as escape. She thought of them as . . . lovely. Like a stroll through Tim's gardens behind the Alexander home, particularly in the spring when the lilacs perfumed the air and the birds were a hallelujah chorus. She hadn't needed an escape back then. She could simply enjoy the loveliness for itself.

That was about to change. Brandon Murphy was about to impose himself on Megan's mostly lovely life, threatening her pursuit of happiness.

That very evening he was due.

And she'd prepared herself for battle. The man had no idea what he was getting into.

***

Brandon looked at the address penned on plain wide-ruled paper, the ink blue and the penmanship his mother's. *Mrs. Tilly Knolls, #38 Spruce Acres.*

"She won't know you from Adam, but I think she'll recognize my name," Mom had said. "I was just there last month, and she had a whole hour's worth of stories to tell me about when I was a girl. Give her the flowers—she especially loves daffodils—and if you need to, show her a picture of me on your phone. Oh! And you might need to use my maiden name to help jog her memory. Then give her the arrangement."

He looked over the large arrangement Mom had sent as he mentally reviewed her instructions. From Spruce Acres, the retirement home to which he'd just arrived, tucked into a knoll of blue-green trees currently showing off a glittering blanket of late-season snow, his four-hour journey would be down to only thirty minutes of traveling through a rather elite and quiet part of the world. What once had been owned by a wealthy rancher had been parceled out into thirty-acre parcels and sold as prime real estate. And prime it was. The combination of views unparalleled, lake nearby, and ski resorts within easy driving distance all were enhanced by extravagant homes beyond his imaginative scope.

The unease of being too small and unsuited for the life he was striding into clenched his gut. He was a meager woodsman—when boiled down to reality, he chopped firewood for a living. And liked it that way. Sort of. How could he ever be comfortable here? This bizarre idea had disaster splattered all over it.

Brandon shifted his mind from the discouraging thoughts, refocusing on Spruce Acres and Mrs. Tilly Knolls, Mom's elderly friend from her childhood, whom she asked him to visit.

Opening the door to his pickup, he braced both feet on the wet ground and stretched. Inhaling, he held the breath of fresh snow, then reached for the arrangement and strode forward to complete the favor. At the front desk, he gave his name and signed in, nodded to the woman who stared up at him rather gooey-eyed, and followed the hall signs to apartment 38.

Tilly Knolls was a tiny, frail woman in her late eighties. She had white wiry hair that apparently she still kept long, as it was neatly rolled at the base of her neck. Her blue eyes were bright and clear, and as she pulled her walker backward to allow Brandon space to enter, she smiled full.

"Mercy me, God sent a *manly* specimen to gawk at!" She cackled with delight. "I do not know who you are, young man, but come right in and let me stare at you a spell!"

Heat threatened to crawl straight up his neck and flood his face. Brandon chuckled nervously as he did as instructed, finding himself in the middle of a room that immediately felt too small. Scanning the tight environment, he set to action, first placing Mom's arrangement on the small round table in the corner. With a fast pivot, Brandon then made the four strides necessary to reach Mrs. Knolls's side, and taking her elbow, he escorted her to the midnight-blue recliner in the opposite corner of the table.

Unabashed admiration filled Mrs. Knolls's expression as she stared up at him. "I sure hope my memory decides it wants to remember you. Such a face!"

Brandon glanced away, a river of warmth winding its way into his face.

"You might as well tell me your name, good lookin'. Though I can't promise I'll know it five minutes from now. You'll likely have to settle for good lookin'." She cackled again.

He let his deep laugh roll. "Brandon Murphy, ma'am."

"Brandon Murphy. I like that. But I also like 'good lookin'.'" She patted his arm. "Ohhh, and muscled too! Do you get this from a gym, or are you a man who does physical labor?"

The flames consuming his face! This woman, though she looked neat as a pin, was as brash as they came. He liked her immediately. "I swing an axe every day, and by the end of it, I'm too tired to think of a gym."

Mrs. Knolls's smile was all little-girl starstruck and as bright as a fresh layer of snow. "Do you know, my new boyfriend, I used to be an artist?"

"I didn't." Should he mention now why he was here? Perhaps bringing Mom into this conversation would distract her from—

"I even sketched nudes."

Brandon gulped.

"If the darn old arthritis hadn't stolen the talent right out of my fingers, I'd ask you to strip right now."

Holy moley, what had Mom set him up for?

Stepping backward, Brandon cleared his throat. He looked everywhere but at the eighty-some-year-old ogling him right then, and his panicked search landed on the arrangement. With a desperate gesture intended to shift Mrs. Knolls's attention, he pointed to the display on the table. "My mom sent this for you. She asked me to deliver it to you since I was going to be in the area."

"Your mom? Do I know her?"

"Yes. I'm sorry." Relief was a cool sweat replacing the burn of embarrassment on his skin. "My mom is Helen Murphy. You were a neighbor when she was a girl, and she visits you every so often."

"Helen Murphy . . . " Her thin silver brows puckered.

"Helen Chase? That was her name before she married my dad."

Those brows flew up. "Helen Chase! Oh! Young man, Helen Chase was the orneriest little girl you ever met. Do you know her?"

"Yes, ma'am. She's my mom."

"Your mom?" Her angular chin tipped to the side. "Who are you?"

"Brandon Murphy."

"I don't think I've ever met you. Oh! But my, you're good lookin'!"

Goodness' sake, this was . . . interesting. "Thank you, ma'am." He gestured back at the arrangement. "My mom said you like daffodils, and she wanted you to know she was thinking about you."

"Your mom . . . Wait. You just told me about that, didn't you? What was your name again?"

"Brandon. Helen Chase is my mom. She wanted you to have this." Again, he directed Mrs. Knolls's attention to the table.

This time the woman looked there. "Oh my, how lovely. Do you know I love daffodils?"

A relieved sigh emptied from Brandon's lungs. "No, ma'am. I'm glad to hear it."

Pushing her walker, Mrs. Knolls aimed her fragile steps toward the table. "Well, this is just lovely. So kind of you to bring me flowers, young man." She'd stopped at the table, studying the beauty of the outdoors brought in. In her careful study, Brandon could see the artist lingering deep within and knew she'd been telling the truth. He wished, for the moment, that she could still hold a pencil.

Only for the arrangement though. The fragrant gathering of slender evergreen holly—bright-red berries, apple-green foliage of boxwood, and deep blue green of juniper—spilled gracefully over the burlap-covered tin Mom had used for the container. All of it set off the cheerful yellow of daffodils.

Blue eyes looked up at him, took him in the same way she had just done the flowers, and then giggled. "It's been a long time since I've had a strapping man call on me. Like a boyfriend!"

Heaven help him.

"I sure do wish I could still draw."

Oh no. "Perhaps in small bits?" He rushed to distract her again. "I can see about finding you a sketch pad, and you could work on a sketch of the flowers?"

A sassy cock of her brow warned him that he had not been successful.

He rushed to fill the silence before she did. "Mom says to tell you she'll be this way in a couple of months."

"Mom?"

"Helen Chase."

She threw her head back and laughed. "Do you know what that little girl once did to my laundry?"

"No, ma'am." Relief once again sagged through his body. "I'd love to hear it though." He nodded toward her recliner and then offered his arm.

Mrs. Knoll latched on to it, abandoning her walker, and Brandon guided her to her seat. He then moved the walker so it was in reach when she'd want it, and pulled a chair out from the table to sit on. "Tell me what Helen Chase did to your laundry."

"That little rascal!" Mrs. Knolls rocked backward and laughed. "She stole it right off the line! Tied my satin slips together and ran around the neighborhood with them flapping at her back like a cape. Called herself Helen the Great."

Brandon laughed, trying to imagine his mother as a little girl, thieving her elderly neighbor's laundry. "Did she ruin them?"

"Oh no. The little imp hadn't meant any harm. Never did. But I sure let her know that wasn't acceptable. She had to come dig dandelions out of my yard for that little escapade. Goodness, but that girl could find some trouble. Innocent as a summer day is long, but trouble. She was my little girl Dennis the Menace." As distant gaze overtook her laughter, and she looked beyond Brandon. Seeing the past, perhaps. For a long moment, she simply stared, and then the brightness in her eyes dimmed. A sheen glazed those blue eyes.

Her look settled back on him. "Who are you again?"

"Brandon, ma'am."

A small, almost sad smile smoothed her lips. "Brandon." She leaned back and closed her eyes. "Brandon Murphy, right?"

He smiled full, and unexpectedly the heat of tears pricked his eyes. "Yes, ma'am."

A contented sigh flowed from her small frame, and she reached out an arthritic-gnarled hand. Brandon leaned forward to grasp it, randomly noting her fingernails looked freshly painted. Dark pink, with glitter. Silently, he wondered who had done that for her and thanked them.

Her thin fingers trembled in his, but she managed a slight squeeze. "I'm glad to know you, Brandon."

"I'm glad to meet you too." He stood, her hand still in his, and closed the gap. Without reservation, he pressed a kiss to her hairline.

"Careful, I might mistake you for a boyfriend."

He chuckled, standing straight.

Her eyes fluttered open, and an earnest longing filled her look. "You'll come visit me again?"

"Absolutely."

"Soon?"

"I'll be nearby. I'll come as often as I can." He winked, and she giggled.

"The girls will be so jealous."

Brandon smirked. "Of the arrangement Mom sent, right?"

This time, her full cackle filled the room. "Yes. That."

He pressed her fingers and then stepped away. "I'll see you soon, then."

"Looking forward to it, good lookin'."

Brandon was still laughing as he pulled the door to apartment 38 shut. So caught up in his amusing visit, he didn't think to look if anyone else occupied the hall, so when he turned, he nearly toppled over a brunette beauty on a mission.

"Oh, I'm sorry." He gripped her shoulders to keep her from bouncing off him and onto her backside.

Jewel-blue eyes found his. And held. And then a pink blush filled her lovely cheeks. Brandon might have held his breath, but he couldn't know for sure. The moment felt surreal.

She moistened her lips. Pink. Soft. Then she blinked. Spell broken. Hugging a small stack of slim notebooks against her chest with one arm, she adjusted the strap to a canvas bag on her shoulder. "No harm done."

She then moved from his touch and nodded toward the door he'd just closed. "Is Mrs. Knolls awake?"

Look at me again . . . Brandon cleared his throat and scratched the back of his head. "Yes. She's awake."

"How is she today?"

"She's . . . " *Crazy. Funny. Delightful. Embarrassing.*

A gentle laugh floated from the jewel-eyed girl, a sound that Brandon immediately wanted to keep forever, as it somehow loosened the long-held knotted tension in his chest. "She's one in a million, isn't she?"

Brandon scanned the face that smiled up at him. Soft curves that tempted drew his eyes, skin that looked as velvety as bunny's fur. He rolled his fingers into his hand.

"Unforgettable."

The young woman nodded. "Have a good day." Ducking her head, she moved around him, knocked on the door to room 38, and then slipped from the hall.

He found himself alone and breathless. And wishing he'd gotten her name.

CHAPTER FIVE

(in which Brandon is in over his head)

MEGAN PASSED THROUGH THE stone archway of the small covered front porch and nearly danced through the frosted-glass paned double doors. In the entryway, the beautifully crafted, curving grand staircase to her right, her heeled boots clipped cheerfully on the gleaming dark-wood floors as she padded over to the pair of velvet-covered wingback chairs tucked into an arched nook. On one of them, she dropped her canvas bag, and on the other, she plopped herself.

Never failed. This assignment she'd once resented, and now loved, never failed to turn up delight from the very depths of her soul. And today . . .

She lay her head back, the soft corner of the wing cradling it, and shut her eyes.

And smiled. And smiled some more.

"Did you have fun?" Mom's happy voice caught her off guard.

Megan jerked herself upright and flung her gaze toward the stairway. There, her footfalls kept secret by the thick white run of carpet climbing the length of risers, Mom grinned down at her. A hand on the glossy nut-brown railing, she leaned, as if anticipating a wonderful story.

"You startled me." Megan's grin resurfaced. "But yes. It was fun. It's always fun."

A proud gleam lit Mom's expression. "I'm glad to hear it."

She could easily say, *So I was right.* But Mom wasn't that way. Though she'd been the one to push this project onto Megan nearly ten years ago, telling an almost teenage version of herself that she needed to be willing to serve others and she desperately needed to know life beyond her wealthy and spoiled circle. And Megan had argued with fits of tears and stubborn resentment at being made to do something so terribly uncomfortable. Despite those things, Mom wouldn't gloat. She simply delighted that Megan had found unexpected joy in it.

"Dinner is in an hour. And prepare yourself." Mom's happy face morphed into a mild warning. "Brandon will be there."

Ugh. She slumped backward. If there was one thing that could pop Megan's happy bubble, that was it. The needle to her warm delight. Worse, the sharp pin to the daydream that had been inspired—a hero, come to rescue her from her parents' plot . . . Perhaps the handsome grandson of Mrs. Knolls.

Why had she never seen him before?

"None of that." Mom stepped down the stairway, her voice chiding and determined. "You will welcome him into our home."

Megan released a ragged, and rather childish, sigh. Or groan. Whatever. "What sort of man agrees to this kind of thing, Mother?"

"The sort who has prayed about it and feels it's worth a go."

"You know for a fact he's prayed about it?"

All humor left Mom's expression as she landed on the wood floor, her arms crossing with certain authority and expectation. "Bring your charming self to dinner tonight, Megan. Not your obstinate self."

Megan peaked one brow. Mom matched the look, never once looking away. Obstinate much? Megan came by that trait honestly, from both her parents. Though Mom was a river of kindness and joy, both characteristics were fortified with a strong current of utter determination.

Well. Let the challenge commence. Megan had it well within herself to match that resolve. After all, she was her mother's daughter through and through.

Prayed about it? Ha! Brandon Murphy better look out.

***

Brandon sat forward on the edge of the well-padded chair, leaning into the table that stretched between himself and Mr. Alexander. Spread out on the surface of the space, a map of the Alexander property had been unrolled and weighted down.

"The guest house is here, boasting a fine overlook. That's where you'll stay." Buck Alexander tapped on a square icon located near the river. "The acreage, unfortunately, is riddled with dead trees. The clean-up project has been neglected far too long, and I have no skill in such things, nor the time to oversee it."

"My wheelhouse, sir." At least there was dignity in *that*. As to the rest of this, Brandon had been swimming in some serious questions about his sanity. "I'll see to it."

Across the way, Mr. Alexander's midnight-blue eyes appraised him, found something worth approving, and gave a short nod. "Your dad says sawdust is your natural habitat."

A chuckle moved Brandon's chest. This whole scenario would have been much easier if the Alexanders had simply brought him up for this task alone. And why hadn't they? This daughter of theirs must be . . . something. What exactly had she gotten herself involved with that would prompt Buck and Anna to such drastic measures? He once again imagined Megan Alexander—a delicate beauty, maybe shy and a little slow witted. Easy prey for unkind men.

As he conjured up an image of that, a recent memory pounced on it with keen force. Jeweled-blue eyes, glossy dark-brown hair, and a lovely face.

Who had she been?

Likely best he hadn't asked her. He couldn't dwell on *that* nameless woman when he'd basically engaged himself to another—only her name was known. Just not her face. As he pushed his thoughts toward Megan, a shadow of a figure caught his attention at the door to Mr. Alexander's sprawling office. Brandon turned his chin, wondering if Megan was about to make herself known. He hoped so—it would be a relief.

The figure—certainly female by the shape and form—slipped back into the wide hallway and then turned from sight. Ah . . . shy and frightened.

"Brandon?"

Brandon jerked his gaze back to the man he'd been in conference with for nearly an hour, and refocused. "I'm sorry."

"Overwhelmed?"

"By the job with the trees?" Best to focus on that part of this strange assignment. "Not at all. Where would you like me to start?"

"I'll leave that to you." Mr. Alexander gave the map under his hand another firm thump. "As to the other . . . "

"Megan?"

"This is a strange thing."

"It is."

"But you'll give it a try?"

Clasping his hands together, Brandon shrugged. "I'm here."

"And I can trust you?"

Seemed a late, though legitimate, thing to ask. Brandon straightened his posture. "I swear I won't do anything to hurt or dishonor your daughter. I'm honored that you would consider me a man you would ask such a thing of." As he finished, he wished again the little mouse of a girl had stepped into the room so he would finally know what he was into here.

"Your dad . . . "

Yes, his dad. There wasn't a man on the planet Brandon respected more —and that was true for all the Murphy sons. While there was pride in that, there was also weight. Heavy, sometimes strangling weight.

"Because of him, I trust you. Megan though . . . "

Brandon waited for several heartbeats. Buck Alexander said nothing more, though his expression carved with worry.

"Megan?" Brandon prompted.

Buck's lips became a hard line, and he let his focus wander. Brandon's gaze traveled as well. Over the expansive office that extended from this window-side nook. A massive desk claimed a large portion of the room. On the other wall, an impressive stone fireplace reached toward the dramatic nine-foot coffered ceiling, a blaze dancing orange, white, and yellow in its wide belly. A long leather sofa claimed the other end of the room, the set of built-in shelves behind it full of texts. Overstuffed leather chairs posted on either side of the sofa. All of it was equally impressive as it was masculine.

"Megan is stubborn." Mr. Alexander had apparently let the quiet go long enough. "And to be blunt, she's not thrilled about this."

Brandon brought his focus back to the man across from him. *Stubborn* didn't fit with his assumptions of a damsel needing his protection. He swallowed as dread clenched in his gut. "I thought . . . " He cleared his throat again. "I was under the impression that she . . . "

"Frankly put, she was livid when her mother and I told her."

Stubborn and livid. Great. That was perfect. "How did you convince her?"

"I'm going to be completely candid with you here, Brandon. As I would be with your dad."

Little late for that. Brandon swallowed again and then nodded.

"She was engaged before. Recently. The man was nothing more than a leech. A fortune hunter. Megan is to gain full control over a trust that will see her life very comfortable. When she refused to hear my warnings about this man she'd agreed to marry, I called Marcus here to spell out clearly what would happen if he wed my daughter."

This kept getting worse. "Which was?"

"She'd not get a single penny of it."

The blow! What had that done to Megan?

"Marcus walked away and within forty-eight hours broke things off with her."

And into this, he'd agreed to come? Lord, what had he been thinking! Trust the Lord and do good? This was a terrible idea.

Brandon turned his face toward the crackling fire, certain wild horror was written plainly on his expression. "None of this was communicated to me or to my parents." Had it been to them? Surely his mom and dad wouldn't conceal this from him, would they? His fists, tucked on his lap, curled tight. Not only was he entering a war waged between parents and daughter, but the daughter was apparently willful and foolish. A helpless damsel? Ha! More like a spoiled child.

He wanted no part of any of this.

"Brandon." The voice that spoke his name was firm and determined.

He looked straight at the man who had beckoned him here, and spoke flatly. "This is beyond me, sir."

"We asked for six months."

"You asked for a commitment. An engagement."

"Yes. But at the end of six months, if you feel you can't go forward with it, you are free to go. During that time, your housing and food, your every need, will be provided. And I have work for you to do." Again, he tapped on the map. "Legitimate, dignified work, for which you will be well paid."

There was that. Couldn't it be only that? Brandon's head swam, kicking through irritation and confusion. Was he still to do this? *Wisdom, God. What have I agreed to here?* "And Megan? What if she wants out?"

"At the end of six months, she has that option."

Did she? So this was simply a waiting game for her? "What happens if she wants out sooner?" As in now, because apparently she wasn't for this in the first place.

"I have outlined my expectations to her. She knows the costs."

The trust. That had to be the wager. Good heavens! This was a . . . game! A bet! He was enrolled in some sort of private version of . . . of *The Bachelor* or something. How had this even happened?

Brandon's jaw tensed until it hurt.

"I know what it looks like, Brandon. But you don't know what is at stake for her. In the long run. I love my daughter, and I can't bear the thought of her throwing herself into the life she was heading for."

If that was what she wanted, Brandon couldn't see that this would stop it. Delay it, obviously. But change her course? This was all ridiculously foolish.

"Meet her."

Brandon looked back at Buck Alexander, recognizing a touch of desperation now lurking in the man's voice. Yes, the man had to be desperate to put something like this into motion. And what did that make Brandon, exactly? After all, he was there . . .

"You're here anyway," the older man pressed. "You might as well."

He knew he scowled, but the man across the table didn't back down. And that desperation had seeped into his eyes. He did love his daughter, even if this idea was plainly misguided. A sigh emptied from Brandon's lungs.

He was there, that was true. And he'd already given his word, which did matter. Rubbing his neck, he looked at the map on the table.

There was real work for him to do. At least there was that.

Brandon nodded. He'd meet this woman-child. And then he'd disappear into the forest to cut down trees. At the end of six months, he'd go back home, knowing that at least he'd kept his word.

Hopefully by then this Megan girl would have outgrown some of her foolishness. If not for her own sake, for that of her father. Heaven help the guy who had to deal with such a girl for a lifetime.

Brandon wasn't going to be that man.

CHAPTER SIX

(in which the games begin)

OF ALL THE CRUEL tricks!

Standing in the middle of her expansive walk-in closet, Megan removed the apricot sweater she'd worn to Spruce Acres and flung it toward the hamper. As usual, her aim was pathetically wrong.

Mother had played her. Megan had no real idea how she'd arranged it, but sending Brandon Murphy to the retirement home—*and to Mrs. Knolls!*—like bait on a hook. It was an intolerable move. Using an elderly woman who typically couldn't remember a conversation three minutes after it'd been had to gain the upper hand? Just . . . cruel!

Oh, Brandon Murphy was gonna have it. Who played such schemes anyway?

Well, Megan wasn't fooled. No matter how good looking the man she'd bumped into was, she wasn't putty. *Why'd he have to look so good? The villain.* And no matter that he'd been visiting one of her favorite residents of Spruce Acres. And quite an impression he'd left too. Mrs. Knolls had practically swooned—and Megan had joined her in it!

How dare he intrude on her private world at the retirement center anyway. It was there that she was unbound to be entirely herself. There that she could laugh and listen and learn and never have the weight of eyes watching, sharp tongues ready and waiting to slice with barely whispered critiques. What Mom had insisted on being Megan's act of humble service had become her refuge and joy. And that man had just threatened it with his presence.

Certainly Mom thought that was all that it would take. Megan would be knocked silly by the sight of a well-built, good-looking man present in her favorite part of life, and then discovering it was the very one Mom had chosen for her, Megan would go quietly into that life.

Nope.

Two could play at this. And as for Brandon, caught in between Megan and her parents in this battle of wills? Any man who had agreed to this sort of scheme deserved what he got.

Chin set with a determined tilt, Megan focused on the clothing options. She always looked fantastic in white. Pure, snowy white contrasted with her dark hair and set off her blue eyes. She pulled her favorite cashmere white sweater from a shelf, smiling at the softness in her hands. So touchable, it was nearly irresistible . . .

A pair of dark skinny jeans or her dark pencil skirt? Hmm . . . what sort of man was this mercenary? She thought on the arrangement of holly and daffodils he'd left for Mrs. Knolls. Her elderly friend had raved about that —about how lovely it was and how thoughtful he'd been.

"Such a gentleman!" Her hands had clapped together and tucked under her chin, and the woman had grinned like a young girl in love.

A gentleman indeed.

Had he picked out the arrangement himself? Had it even been his idea? Megan drummed her manicured fingers against the floor-to-ceiling shelves neatly displaying her vast collection of designer clothes.

Brandon had been wearing a pair of dark, though obviously well-worn, jeans and a flannel button-down. Blue plaid. Marcus Kensington wouldn't wear such a get-up if naked was the only other option.

Jeans then. Dark skinny jeans.

Boots or heels?

He wore blue-plaid flannel.

Boots.

A determined smirk played on Megan's face as she dressed. When she stood in front of the mirror in her en-suite bathroom, she tapped a light-pink gloss on her lips and fluffed her beachy curls so they were just so. Touchably soft. Tempting. She tilted her chin this way and that, ensuring she looked her best.

And she did.

Hands on her hips, she nodded at her reflection. "Well then, Brandon Murphy. Let the games begin."

Irritation her fuel, she spun away, marched herself out of her room, down the stairs, and into the dining room.

The man she'd literally run into—and then wasted a whole afternoon daydreaming about—turned from the blaze at the fireplace at her entrance. Wide-eyed shock morphed in slow motion on his handsome features as he took her in.

Megan enjoyed every moment of it.

***

His legs nearly wobbled. He'd been sweating since he'd changed into "dinner" clothes after settling into the guest house a mile down the lane.

Now, after he'd turned around to gain his first glimpse of Megan Alexander, *his fiancée*, Brandon stood like a man who'd just been whacked on the back of his head. Utterly stunned.

Shut your mouth.

Brandon snapped his lips closed as he remembered to breathe. But it was hard.

She was *her!* He wasn't sure if he was pleasantly surprised or dangerously confused.

"Megan, nice of you to join us." Mrs. Alexander circled around the large table—set with white china and cut crystal glasses, one of Mom's arrangements displayed in the center—giving only the slightest hint of irritation as she approached her daughter. "I wondered if I needed to come find you."

Had she been nervous and that was the reason for her fifteen-minute delay? For some reason, Brandon hoped so. But as Megan appraised him with unabashed scrutiny, he doubted it.

"Here I am." Turning to her mother, she spread her arms out, palms up. "All ready to be traded away."

"Megan," her mother hissed.

The beautiful sprite shot a challenging look first at her mom and then directly at him. Behind Brandon, Mr. Alexander cleared his throat.

"Way to make a good impression, Meg." He stepped around Brandon and stopped in the space that separated the *couple*. "Brandon, my daughter, Megan. Megan, Brandon Murphy."

"The mercenary." She looked straight at Brandon, unflinching. Smirking. "Delighted."

Mercenary!

Every imagining of a wispy, tender, defenseless young woman went up in the flames of her obvious contempt. How could such a beautiful creature be so . . . so . . . venomous? And why the heck did she have to be the *very same woman* he'd bumped into outside of Mrs. Knolls's apartment?

Was she the same woman? She was identical to that lovely memory in face and form. But this unlikable *girl* in front of him? Nope. Couldn't be that doe-eyed, soft beauty who had summoned an immediate longing for connection from him. The only connection he had with this creature right then was the sort that demanded an immediate sever. The kind that screamed *run!* with perfect, chilling clarity.

He was supposed to be engaged to this? Not on his life.

She cocked a brow, and her chin, waiting for him to respond. He cleared his throat—wow, it was super dry—and pushed forward an open hand.

"Megan?"

Megan sauntered closer, her lovely face tilted at an irritatingly arrogant angle, and gripped his offered handshake. Hard. Brandon nearly flinched from surprise.

"Actually, we've met, haven't we?" One eyebrow slid up as she again appraised him head to toe. By her expression, she was not impressed. "Though you were wearing blue plaid earlier."

Dang! She was that same woman. Of all the horrible turn of events. He'd *liked* that girl. Why'd *this* snipe have to go and ruin it?

Brandon swallowed, feeling trapped. And hot. He tugged at the collar on the clean white button-down he'd changed into. "Uh . . . "

She breathed a contemptuous laugh at his pathetic response. How was he supposed to handle this? He'd had zero experience with this sort of . . . female. He'd grown up with only brothers, and when they'd married, they'd found *nice* women.

"You've met?" Her mother, scowling at Megan, stepped beside her father, still between the pair.

Megan turned an insincere smile toward her parents. "Well, not exactly. We bumped into each other at Spruce Acres earlier this afternoon." She then turned unsmiling eyes on him. Sharp and accusing. "What were you doing there anyway?"

Man, he needed to get away from the fireplace. He was going to overheat. Clearing his throat, he held her smoldering gaze. "I was delivering an arrangement for my mom."

"To someone at Spruce Acres?"

"Yes. Mrs. Knolls." He stepped forward, a scowl pinching his face. What was with this thinly veiled accusation?

"Your mother, who lives who-knows-how-many-hours away, wanted you to deliver something to a person living in *my* retirement home?"

His head snapped back. "*Your* retirement home?"

She folded her arms. "Espionage."

"What?" This girl was insane!

"It means spying, blue plaid."

"Spying?" Brandon blinked. And stared at her. Likely with a horrified look of firm dislike, because that was exactly how he felt. *Marry* this girl? Not for a million dollars.

***

"What are you doing?" Dad wasted zero time turning to Megan, a fierce look of near rage darkening his expression. The front door had barely clicked shut behind Brandon the mercenary when Dad lit into her.

Though her middle trembled at the thought of Daddy being genuinely good and outraged at her, Megan steeled herself, refusing to look away. "I told you both I was not *for* this. You brought him here. I see no reason to be nice to a man who would—"

"Nice? You were on the opposite polar cap from nice, Meg! At this point, common civility would be aiming pretty high for you. *Nice* is way out of reach. What was that display of . . . of spoiled brat?"

She flinched. Inside, she writhed. She'd always been Daddy's girl. Lived in the light of his adoration. To have him furious like this, at her, especially after the animosity between them for the past few weeks, was . . .

Daddy pushed his chair from the table as Mom reentered the dining room from seeing Brandon out. "I'm ashamed of you, Megan," he spat. "I have never been so ashamed."

. . . devastating.

Striding from the space, he left Megan alone with her mom in a wake of molten rage. Megan's gaze drifted from the spot Daddy had just occupied to where Brandon had sat across from her, looking more and more uncomfortable as the meal had worn on. She'd laid out her punches, snubbed his lack of education, his choice to work manual labor, and his general lack of ambition in life.

As if she had a right to talk.

"How exactly do you expect to fit in here?" she'd asked him pointedly near the end of the meal.

Clearly fed up, Brandon had tossed his linen napkin onto the table beside his barely touched meal and met her haughty look. "I don't. Nor do I want to." He held her in an angry stare, his dark-brown eyes full of disapproval, and then turned a softening look to her mother. "Thank you for dinner, Mrs. Alexander. I'm sure it was delicious. I'll see myself out."

That had been the final scene. The one she'd hoped for, because surely no man would stick around after that. It was her exit strategy from this horrible arrangement. Her plan to wrestle back freedom.

She'd won. Why did she feel so awful?

I'm ashamed of you, Megan.

Her dinner turned sour in her stomach.

"Do you think your father will give in so easily?" Mom slipped onto Daddy's abandoned chair, her tone more tired and disappointed than angry.

Megan's attention flicked to her. Easily? That display had taken all her wit and courage, not to mention the better half of her self-respect. She never wanted to replay it again.

"What will you do if your father decides it's time for you to be out on your own?"

"You're kicking me out?" Panic beat its way up her throat.

"No." Mom sighed, her unsmiling face turned toward her folded hands on the table. "But maybe it's time for you to figure out what your life would look like outside of this house."

"I knew what I wanted it to look like!" Angry tears made her vision hazy.

"As Marcus's wife?" Mom's brow pinched with frustrated defeat. "Have you heard that he's with Janie Stewart now?"

Yes, thank you for that rub of salt. She'd heard.

"Didn't take him long, did it, Meg?"

"What's that supposed to mean?"

"You just proved that you're a sharp young woman. I'm sure you can figure it out." She shook her head. "Though, I can't figure how a smart girl such as yourself can't see clearly enough to know which things she needs to let go and which things—standing right in front of her—she should grip with all her might."

Megan pressed her lips together. Not only did she feel like scum, both her parents were rapidly losing any shred of faith they'd had in her.

Maybe she'd taken the wrong approach.

Wearily, Mom stood from the chair. "Brandon's a nice man, Meg," she said quietly. And then she left Megan alone with the dying embers of the fire and her loud guilty conscience.

A pair of remorseful tears found their way down the sides of her nose, one and then the other. She'd lost the reins to her life. Perhaps she'd never had them in hand to begin with. There was apparently no good way out of this. Just through.

She'd go see Brandon in the morning. Ugh.

Hopefully he'll be gone by then.

Did she really mean that? It had been the point of her bad display.

If he wasn't . . .

Sigh. Then they'd see, she guessed.

CHAPTER SEVEN

(in which it is mutual)

"SHE'S A TERRORIST DISGUISED as a beauty queen. A siren who delights in demoralizing men one biting word at a time. I can't imagine what Mom was thinking." Pacing with blazing energy through the guest house he was to call his home for the next six months (not likely!), Brandon unloaded his anger on the phone, delivering an earful to Tyler.

"I thought Mom left it with you to decide." Tyler did not match his ire. "No arm twisting."

"Not helpful." Brandon's head throbbed unmercifully, and he stalked across the bedroom toward the connected bath, hoping that he'd find a supply of painkillers in some cabinet.

"Brandon, deep breath, buddy." Tyler's calm voice was fingernails on a chalkboard, fueling the crazy that Megan had already set ablaze. "You're not usually reactionary like this."

He wasn't usually dealing with a woman with a rabid personality. Sheesh, she was awful. A rich, spoiled woman-child who needed a good spanking.

"Listen, I know you're mad right now."

Brandon crammed a hand through his hair, wondering why he'd called Tyler in the first place. This was his moment of crisis, and instead of sharing outrage with him, or at the least sympathizing, his reformed big brother was barreling toward a pep talk. Brandon did *not* want a pep talk. "Mad? Mad doesn't touch it, brother. This girl is horrible. I was crazy to agree to this."

"But you did."

Three granite words that left Brandon pinned to this impossible arrangement. He had agreed to this.

But.

"I didn't know all the pertinent information. Namely, that Megan is a monster running around masquerading like an innocent girl."

Tyler chuckled. "Maybe you're taking it a bit far?"

Nope. Not even a little bit. And this wasn't funny. Brandon did not want to be tied to *that*. Not for six months. Certainly not for a lifetime.

"Brandon, sometimes people show the worst of themselves when they feel trapped."

Great. Recovery mumbo jumbo from the addict-turned-inspirational-speaker. Not what he needed. "Then I've seen the worst, and I don't want any part of it."

"You prayed about this. You told me yourself that you felt like you were supposed to do this. Like the way Connor was with Sadie."

"Sadie wasn't a pernicious snipe." No painkillers in the bathroom. For all the luxury this place boasted—plush furnishings, expensive-looking linens and towels, and hey! even a mint on his pillow—he thought surely there'd be something to make the drumline in his brain take a break. *Come on, man!* Brandon slapped the cabinet doors shut and stomped down the stairway and into the kitchen.

"Brandon."

Brandon searched cabinets, jerking doors open none too gently. He suppressed the need to growl. Anger broke free anyway. "When did I lose you, Ty? I always had your back, you know that? Even when Becca called that intervention, I had your back. I was so angry with her for you. And when she broke your engagement . . . Took me over a year just to see her and not feel mad. Because you're my brother, and she betrayed you. Where's your loyalty?"

"That was your poor judgment, Brandon." Tyler's response came low and quiet. Humble and full of regret. "Becca wasn't wrong."

A fresh jab of conviction made his night worse. Why had Brandon brought that up?

A long silence carved between them. Then Tyler sighed. "Brandon, I'm with you on this, okay?"

A bottle of off-brand ibuprofen stared back at him from a corner cupboard—a little shocking since everything else in this cushy place was name-brand expensive. *Jackpot.* He popped the cap, dumped two into his palm, and gulped the pair back in one swallow. With a smack, he set the bottle on the counter and turned back to the stairway. "So if I said I'm packing up and heading home at first light?"

"If you think that's what you should do . . . "

Something inside sank. A sure sign of *no, that wasn't what he should do.*

Of course it was what he should do! Any sane man would be tossing his bags together that very moment.

"Just make sure you don't leave room for regret."

Regret? Walking away from a girl who was sure to make him nuts? Who would regret that?

Tyler's voice filled the pause. "You've really only given this a few hours, you know? Sleep on it, Brandon. I'll call you in the morning."

Ugh. This was why he hadn't called Dad. All calm logic and unruffled feathers. He'd wanted someone who would be outraged with him. Tell him to hit the road and don't look back. Man, sometimes Tyler could be so disappointing. And right. Usually not both at once though. This was a first on that account.

"Brandon?"

"I'm here," he growled.

"I'm praying for you right now."

The knife of conviction twisted painfully. He'd not had a single heaven-directed thought pass through his mind that wasn't simply reactionary emotion since Megan had swept into that dining room and unruffled all his neat and tidy feathers. Reaching his room, he sank onto the king mattress, deflated. "Thanks, Ty."

"I'll call you tomorrow."

"Yeah." He leaned back onto the puffy California king pillow.

Tyler hesitated before he hung up, and Brandon knew his brother would stay up late praying for him.

It was humiliating, to tell the truth. To be on this side of a mess. Brandon had been pretty hard on not only Tyler when he'd ended up in rehab, but on a couple of his other brothers too when they'd found themselves in messes. Jacob, when he'd married Kate, a girl who only six months before had been dating their brother Jackson. What a long run of family drama that had incited. Brandon had resented both Jacob and Kate for it. Then there was Jackson, the brother who had confessed that he'd been drunk when he'd married Mackenzie, and worse, he and Mackenzie had been total strangers at the time. *What a stupid thing to do,* Brandon had thought. *How could Jackson do something so dumb?*

Huh.

Leaning back, Brandon tipped his throbbing head until it thunked against the silver upholstery of the headboard, wishing he could shut off both the thoughts streaming through his mind and the conviction slicing through his resolve.

He had a hard time with empathy in general. When others did dumb stuff, well, Brandon usually plunged into deep disappointment—bordering on resentment—with them. Being on this side of a self-inflicted disaster was new. He wasn't loving the experience.

With a heavy, resigned sigh, Brandon made an intentional effort to take his raging emotions captive. *What would you have me do here?* With that one felt prayer, the tumultuous sea of anger calmed. As if God had simply been waiting for Brandon to turn his attention heavenward.

The painful tension at his neck uncoiled, and Brandon drew in another long, this time cleansing, breath. Sinking down farther against that plush pillow, he laid a hand over his heart and let the release take him.

It was the first time in his life that a major issue—his or someone else's—didn't keep him up through the night. When he woke up to a cheerful golden light streaming through the unblinded windows, he was shocked. He blinked awake as the warmth of new day infused his face, realizing he still wore the dark-wash jeans and white button-down shirt he'd worn to dinner.

He'd slept hard and peaceful.

What did that mean?

***

"I've decided you do not have enough to do." Daddy sat calmly on the other side of his desk, the size of which always seemed like a full continent to Megan.

That was an unexpected intro to this before-the-sun-is-up meeting he'd demanded. Megan had complied easily enough to his summons, planning on forming some sort of placating apology—a week overdue, but she'd had to wrestle hard with her defiant pride about doing so. Finally, days since her initial rudeness toward Brandon at their first dinner, she was prepared to display some humility, Megan had rehearsed her apology as she'd trudged down the hallway.

She hadn't been given the opportunity to deliver it.

Still in her soft sweats that she'd slept in, Megan tucked her fuzzy-socked feet beneath her on the wide chair Daddy had directed her to upon her entry. She'd expected another lecture on her poor behavior that first night. Perhaps a demand for her to apologize to the man she was supposed to be engaged to, since she hadn't summoned one up all on her own. Megan *was* sorry she'd embarrassed her parents, but she still hoped with everything she had that Brandon Murphy would run back home as fast as those long, well-built legs would take him.

These first few days, it seemed he would not, as he'd been hiding in the woods, as told by her mom. Brandon didn't show up for dinner, though each night Shay had set a place for him.

That meant he was scared. Cowardly mercenary.

Megan figured this call-to-meeting was for her father to give a new command: apologize to that blue-plaid chicken so he'd show up to eat. But Daddy wasn't issuing that command. Did that mean Brandon had already broken the agreement? *Oh please, yes!* That begged the question though: Why hadn't he run yet?

"You need a job."

She met her father's unwavering look. "I volunteer at Spruce Acres. And I help Tim in the gardens."

His mouth tightened. "I am aware, and that you may continue. The rest of your time, however . . . "

This did not bode well. Megan braced herself.

"You will work with Brandon."

"What?" Megan spat the word like there was a bug in her mouth. So the engagement was still a thing? Did that make Brandon admirably tough or stupidly stubborn?

Megan assumed the stupid option.

Satisfaction played on Daddy's lips. "He's a lumberjack, and he'll be clearing the dead trees on the property."

Of course Brandon was a lumberjack. Megan suppressed the urge to roll her eyes. Blue plaid indeed. If he'd worn red, he'd be the living stereotype. Ridiculous man.

"What will I be doing with . . . " *The blue-plaid mercenary.* " . . . Brandon?"

"Whatever he tells you to do." Daddy raised one challenging eyebrow.

Megan crossed her arms. "What if he asks me to do something indecent?"

Shaking his head, Daddy rolled his eyes. "He won't."

"You don't know him."

"I know enough. *Brandon* is not the one I'm worried about."

That stung. She was his only daughter—his only child! How could Daddy prefer a virtual stranger over her? A quick-flash replay of that introductory dinner shot through her mind. There was that. Megan drew in a breath, studying the man who used to call her his *best girl*. Daddy's expression was granite, and without a doubt this wasn't mutable.

Hugging herself tighter, she dropped her gaze to that massive desk. "When am I to begin?"

"Immediately. We'll head to the guest house as soon as you're dressed. Wear clothes appropriate to work in, and you'll find a pair of leather gloves waiting for you in the entry."

He'd prepared for this. With one quick decision, Daddy had set this plan in motion. Was she forever to be directed by his will, never having a say in her own life?

When had Daddy turned against her?

"Don't pout, Megan. It makes you look like a spoiled child."

He was treating her like a child! She pressed her lips together and looked hard at him. Daddy returned that stare strength for strength.

"How long is this to last?"

Daddy didn't hesitate. "As long as you are engaged."

Did he have to say it like that?

"Get dressed. We leave in fifteen minutes." Daddy turned his attention to a stack of papers in front of him.

Megan wanted to shout at him about how unfair he was being. How mean and overbearing. But that yucky feeling held over from that now-infamous meal tabled her rising fit. Daddy was ashamed of her.

That mattered. More than she wanted to admit, it mattered.

Actually, it sort of broke her heart.

***

Standing on the front porch, enjoying the brisk chill of the bright morning as he took in the river view, Brandon sipped the sure-to-be overpriced coffee he'd brewed in the supplied kitchen. It smelled rich and nutty, but if he was honest, it was a little bold for his taste.

He'd get used to it.

Somewhere between scooping grounds into the French press and soaking in more of the promising sunrise on the porch, Brandon had made a decision: he'd stick this out. It wouldn't be that bad—the past few days he'd worked as if he'd been at home. Alone. Just him, the forest, and his chainsaw. If he could see this assignment as a job, he'd be fine. His word would be kept, and hopefully his sanity as well. Encounters of the unpleasant kind with Megan the monster could be kept to a minimum, and at the end of six months, she'd declare an end to it. She'd go her way, her trust intact. Brandon would head home with a paycheck for the job he'd complete by then. No regrets.

Win-win.

From the shelter of spruce and pine dappling the riverside, birds sang cheerfully, filling the sweet crisp air with hope and happiness. Brandon grinned briefly before taking another sip. He'd call Tyler in a few minutes, thank his older brother for talking him down the other night, and let him know he was staying. Then he'd ask about Becca—if Tyler had contacted his ex-fiancée yet.

The sound of tires on the gravel drive stalled that intent. Brandon guessed that the approaching vehicle would carry Mr. Alexander, and he was glad to have a verdict in hand before the man appeared. Buck had asked him to give it a week before making any solid decisions, and that had proven good advice.

Sure enough, Buck sat in the driver's seat of the Land Rover now parked in front of the carriage house. Calmly, Brandon tipped his mug to his lips again and then moved toward the wide steps centered with the house. He stopped short, however, and all peace shattered when the passenger door popped open.

Megan stepped out, her full scowl visible even behind her ridiculously large sunglasses. She aimed her look straight at him, and he had no doubt she was glaring, and then she smacked the vehicle door shut with a good *whack*.

Good heavens, first thing in the morning? His day took a nosedive, and he hadn't even finished his coffee yet.

Mr. Alexander motioned to Megan with his head—a *get goin'* signal— and then strode across the flagstone path and up the five steps to the porch. Megan followed, looking like a prisoner being led to the gallows. Exactly how Brandon felt as he turned his attention to Buck.

"Megan's going to be your assistant." Buck didn't waste a breath on pleasantries, just dug in straight to the awful point.

"My . . . my assistant?" This deal just kept getting worse. "What will she be assisting me with?"

Buck tugged his aviator glasses off his face. "The trees. Clearing the dead ones."

After setting down his half-full mug, Brandon balled his fists behind his back. "Sir." He cleared his throat, eyeing Megan. "I'm not sure you know what you're asking. What I do is hard work, and it can be dangerous."

Leaning lazily against the porch railing and still wearing those stupid glasses that nearly swallowed her face, Megan crossed her arms and tossed her head, as if waiting for a showdown she was anxious to see. And smirked.

That blasted woman-child smirked. One week of not seeing her had not been long enough.

"Megan plays tennis. She's quick on her feet, and her arms are surprisingly strong. She'll be fine."

Tennis? Was he comparing felling trees and chopping firewood to . . . tennis? Brandon held an incredulous look on Buck, who simply stared back at him, unflinching. Behind him, Megan examined her fingernails. Her perfectly manicured fingernails.

Buck at last turned back to his daughter, replacing his sunglasses. "I expect you to work, and I'll ask Brandon for a full report." Then he clambered down the steps.

Brandon glanced at Megan, finding she had looked away, shielding her likely pout from his view. Least of his concerns. He jogged down the steps and pathway after Buck. "Mr. Alexander, I really don't think this is a good idea."

"I do." He turned, hand on the car door.

"Sir, felling trees can be really dangerous. Seriously."

"Then I'd rather not have you out there doing it by yourself."

"I work alone most the time."

"Not here." He reached forward and gripped Brandon's bicep. Then leaned in, speaking lower. "It'll give you two time together. To get to know each other."

Perfect. Just perfect. That was exactly what Brandon was hoping for—more time with the Megan monster. He knew quite enough already, thank you very much.

"She's not as bad as you think," Buck muttered. "Usually."

Brandon couldn't help the doubtful raised eyebrow. Buck ignored it, clapped his arm, and climbed into his vehicle. "We'll expect you both for dinner at the house. Shay will have lunch waiting for you here at the guest house. Megan's too." He pulled the door shut, started the engine, and backed away. With a hand up, he was gone.

Brandon stared at the taillights, both hands on his hips. What was he supposed to do with a spoiled monster tagging along with him all day? One hand crammed through his hair and then anchored on his neck. This was never going to work.

"Scared?"

Hand still gripping near his collar, Brandon turned slowly.

Megan came off the railing, stepped to the stone piling that framed the top of the steps, and pressed a shoulder into that, her arms still crossed. "Is the big, strong lumberjack afraid of a little one-hundred-and-fifteen-pound girl?"

Terrified. Not of her though. For her—he might throttle her before the day was done.

"This is a bad idea." He dropped his hands and squared his shoulders, then made his way back to where she posted.

"Agreed," she said, finally pulling off those hideous glasses.

She did have pretty eyes. The brat.

"Good. You can stay here. Do whatever it is spoiled rich girls do with their lazy days. I'll pick you up when it's time for dinner."

"My dad will know."

"How's that?"

"I don't know how he does it, but he always finds stuff out. I think he's enlisted the squirrels as spies." She tossed her head again, likely to get that dark mane of loose hair out of her face.

Also pretty. Had she curled it? How did she expect to work with her hair blowing in her eyes? Foolish girl. Also, what was with her and this obsession with spies?

"You think you can cut down trees?" He knew he sounded like a patronizing, sexist jerk. Didn't care.

She stood straight, hands on her hips. "You think you can survive a whole day with me?"

"No. I can barely stand you now." He stepped nearer. Looming over her. "Let me make this clear, brat. I don't like you. I certainly don't want to spend any time with you."

"Why did you come here then?"

"I was led to believe you were a nice human who needed help out of a situation. Clearly that was a lie."

"I don't need your help." Her jewel eyes narrowed, and he thought she might snarl like the beast she was. "Let me make *this* clear, blue-plaid mercenary. I don't like you either. I think you're pathetic."

He'd never had a person tell him they didn't like him. It was a new experience—one he'd likely not enjoy the replay of later. Right then, however, all he knew was that he detested this woman-child and wanted her to go away. "Then it's mutual. There's no way on this planet you and I are getting married. Ever."

"Ever." She straightened, tipping her face up so they stood nose to nose.

She had a pert little nose that came to a point. He'd thought it was a cute little thing when he'd bumped into her at Spruce Acres. Before she'd opened her venomous mouth. Now it rather reminded him of a vulture.

"I wouldn't marry you even if I had no other options," she seethed, jabbing his chest with her finger. "Which, for the record, I do."

"Yes, I heard that." He pushed her hand away, a little surprised he hadn't turned to stone at her touch. "Men who would only tolerate you for your trust fund."

She flinched. Brandon stepped back, almost feeling bad. Almost.

Megan whipped away and scurried down the steps. "Let's get this over with."

Over with, right. As if that were going to happen. He had a strong suspicion this was not a one-and-done situation. He was going to be stuck with her all day every day for the next six months. He should have left that first night while he still could.

Thanks, Ty.

He stomped into the house, forgetting his half-full coffee mug on the porch railing, and smacked the front door shut behind him. *Lord, I've spent less than two hours with her, and I don't think I can take much more. What am I supposed to do with such a brat?*

Likely it wasn't heaven's answer, but all he knew was to go to work. Apparently with the monster.

Fine. If work was what she wanted, that was what she'd get. Hard, sweaty, break-her-stupid-acrylic nails work.

Who knew? He might enjoy seeing that. In any case, He wasn't going to be the first one down on this deal.

CHAPTER EIGHT

(in which Megan works and Brandon nearly laughs)

B RANDON STOPPED HIS BEAT-UP truck somewhere on the north property line of the estate. Megan wondered how he knew exactly where he was as he set the brake and wordlessly jumped out of the stinky vehicle. She also wondered how he'd survived a full day's drive in the thing. It smelled like gasoline, greasy fast food, and man sweat.

Yuck.

Almost solely for the reason of needing to breathe fresh air, Megan popped open her door and slid to the partially frozen earth. Standing at the opened tailgate, Brandon had already applied a pair of worn leather gloves, two times the size of her new ones, and was unstrapping the larger of two chainsaws he'd secured at the back of the truck bed.

"Can you see through those ugly things, or are they purely to display your vanity?" He didn't look up from the chainsaw as he talked.

"My glasses?"

His head came up, and he gave her a look that read *yeah, quick one.*

"Yes. I can see."

"Good. Keep them on. Tomorrow bring some safety glasses."

Megan rolled her eyes. She hoped not to be anywhere near this chainsaw brute tomorrow. "Know what? I'm just gonna find a cozy spot out of your way. Let me know when you're done." She could stay out of the way, pretend to scroll her feeds while secretly watching Brandon work. After all, he was a well-built jerk. She might as well get something decent out of this ridiculous situation.

She ran a quick assessment over him: beat-up ball cap, another plaid flannel, this time green, thick wool-lined vest, stained jeans. Despite his sad choice of attire, that lean, muscled build made him a pleasant specimen to gawk at. If she could block out everything else about him, including the fact that her parents had arranged her *engagement* to him, the day might not be half bad.

"Not so fast, your highness." He gave the rope thingy a tug, and the chainsaw engine gave a sputter. "Your dad said work. That's what you'll be doing."

"Excuse me?" She eyed that beast of a machine Brandon was coaxing to life. Terrifying. She was not going to wield a thing that could cut her hand off—or worse—with one accidental slip.

"Work." Brandon spat. "I know it's likely a foreign idea to you, but eventually you'll catch on. If you don't die first."

Die first? Oh, heck no. She was definitely not the one going down first here. "You said this was dangerous."

"Right." He didn't look at her. "So pay attention."

"You said it was hard." Was she doing herself any favors here?

This time he did look up, mocking brows raised. "But you play tennis, so you'll be fine."

Nothing irked Megan quite like a chauvinistic, sarcastic man. "Look, mister plaid flannel. I can do anything you can do." *Liar, liar, designer jeans on fire!* She needed to put a leash on her mouth, or she was gonna end up in some real danger. Hopefully he wouldn't test her on that.

"You can fell a tree, can you?" He snorted. "I believe I'd like to see that one day, your highness."

Ugh. He was infuriating. The boorish, handsome man. Megan braced her stance and crossed her arms. "If I'm not falling . . . felling . . . " What was the right way to say that anyway? Surely Brandon hadn't said it correctly. She swiped a windblown lock of hair from her face. "Cutting down a tree, what exactly will I be doing?"

"Whatever I tell you to, highness. Start with getting your hair out of your face. Then you can pull the branches I cut off the trunks away from where I'm working and make a pile. Neatly." He fiddled with a squishy button doodad and then some tiny lever thing, then gave that cord another tug. The engine spat and sputtered more than the last time.

A fiery bolt of fear ran through her veins at the snarl of the chainsaw. Megan stubbornly set her chin. "And if I refuse?"

"Your dad asked for a full report." He pulled the cord again, and this time the engine rumbled full. Adjusting his hat, Brandon then applied a pair of clear glasses and picked the chainsaw off the tailgate. He stopped near her and yelled above the rumbling machine. "I don't make a habit of lying, so unless you want your dad to hear otherwise, you're gonna work."

She glared at him, but he seemed unaffected, instead looking over the stand of multiple brown, needleless tree corpses in front of him.

"I'm going to work from front to back, and they're gonna come down fast, that direction." He was still shouting, and now pointing. "Don't get in the way of a falling tree. And pay attention." He revved the engine twice. "Last thing I want is to waste a day taking you to the ER."

And then he strode away. The jerk.

While the engine roared with hungry energy, Brandon stopped at the first dead pine he came to. Looking up, he seemed to be calculating. Maybe gathering courage? Megan certainly needed to. He stood for a long pair of minutes, studying the tree, something in the sky, and his surroundings. Then he looked back over his shoulder at her and held something like a look of warning, or maybe it was concern?

Geez, did he have to be so good looking? Megan jammed her sunglasses back into place and tugged on her gloves, forcing her gaze from the man who already drove her crazy. She knew lots of handsome men. Brandon the mercenary certainly wasn't the first. And she wasn't about to let him know she thought those rich brown eyes could hold her attention for a long while, or that strong, stubborn jawline was attractive.

The buzz of the chainsaw growled louder, and when Megan directed her attention back to where Brandon worked, she found him taking down lifeless branches with shocking speed. One, then another, then the next. He didn't pause between cuts but worked his way around the trunk with focused intensity. When he'd cleared everything that was his height or shorter, he turned back to her.

"Get these out of the way," he shouted.

Attractive? Ha! Brandon was a bully. Not her type.

Picking her way over the uneven and littered forest floor, Megan made her way to where he stood. Scowling.

"Today, your highness." He kicked a newly downed branch out of his way. "I've got a lot to get done."

Delightful. He was a bully *and* her boss.

No sir. She didn't like him at all, no matter how good looking he was.

***

Brandon ran through the fuel in both chainsaws before lunch. He wasn't about to tell Megan, but having someone out there clearing his work area as he went was super helpful. If not for her moving the branches he cut as he went, he'd be about halfway to where he was by then.

And bonus! She couldn't talk while they worked. Securing the second chainsaw onto the end of the truck bed, Brandon smirked. Quite true—if Megan Alexander wasn't allowed to speak, she was perfectly tolerable. He glanced at her standing in front of the truck, where she swigged water from the extra sixty-four-ounce canteen he'd tossed in before they'd left the guest house.

She'd tied her hair back in some kind of glorious messy updo thing and, for the moment, had removed those monstrous glasses. Her coat had been shed somewhere between the first tree he'd felled and the second, and her long-sleeved button-down hinted at her feminine curves. Her well-fitting skinny jeans ran the length of her legs and disappeared into a pair of rubber boots that he was certain she'd purchased for looks, not for workwear.

Man, she was a looker. Especially there in his natural habitat, all unpretentious and covered with earth, sawdust, and dried pine needles.

Brandon shook his head and returned his attention to securing his equipment before they headed back to the guest house for lunch. The loss of time doing that rankled him—he'd have rather brought the cold sandwich he'd packed before his work life was thrust out of order. Then again, Megan's help had propelled the job forward, so maybe the loss of time wasn't that bad. And he could offer to leave her at the house. She'd worked after all, right?

The howling resentment he'd started the day with had settled down to a slight breeze as he shut the tailgate and strode to the front of his truck. This wasn't that bad. He slid behind the wheel, and Megan climbed into the passenger seat, and then he was carefully picking his way back to the road that had led them there. Once off that path, he accelerated toward the creek-side guest house. Megan sat quiet—hallelujah!—and he glanced at her. A telling pink brushed over her nose and on the skin under her eyes.

"You're getting burned." He reached back into the second-row seat of the cab, blindly feeling until he snagged the extra ball cap that was back there somewhere. "Use this. It'll help." He passed it to her.

Megan took the hat between her fingers as if it might be toxic. Holding it away from her body, she examined the thing with a pukey expression. "This thing is revolting."

"Fine." He snatched it back and tossed it over his shoulder. "Fry your face. I don't care."

She sat stiff as a statue with her lips pressed tight. When she thought he wasn't paying attention, she turned her face ever so slightly—enough to catch her reflection in the side mirror—and ran a finger down the length of that pointy little nose. And flinched.

Yeah, your majesty. It's rosy. Bet it's tender too. Really gonna hurt once it reaches the point of blistering.

They reached the house, and he parked. On the front porch, Buck Alexander stood from a patio chair and raised a hand. Good thing Megan had come along.

"Of course he'd check up on me," Megan muttered.

"You must have quite a reputation."

She met his side glance with a death look. "Not at all. I'm actually a daddy's girl. He's called me his best girl ever since I can remember."

Brandon snorted. "Right. So he's just here because he misses you."

"Ugh." She reached for the door handle. "Are you entirely incapable of being nice?"

"Turn for turn, your majesty." A needle of guilt pricked in his chest even as he said that. *Insult for insult* was not the way his parents had raised him, and it certainly wasn't God's way. What was it about this girl that had him so wound up? Couldn't he simply ignore her childishness and act like a better person?

I know your young men are solid people of God. Anna Alexander's penned words came as a blow to his mind. He was doing an excellent job of proving that exactly wrong.

An apology would likely be in order here . . .

Megan popped out of the truck and slammed the door. Yeah, no apology happening right then. After shutting the engine off, Brandon followed Megan as she strode the flagstone path toward her father.

"You're both still alive." Buck grinned.

"Ha-ha, Daddy." Megan stepped up the stairs and stopped in front of her father. She looked up at him, and something silent but meaningful passed between the two. Then Buck raised a tender hand to her shoulder, and she moved to her toes to kiss his cheek.

So she hadn't been lying. Megan and her father did share a tender bond. The intense knot of dislike in Brandon's gut loosened. And a gentle curiosity about that glimpse of softness in the Megan monster sprouted.

"Look at you." Buck spoke to her with a tender pride. "A filthy mess. You must have worked."

"You told me to." Something wounded, though so slight Brandon nearly missed it, lilted in her voice.

Buck nodded, the set of his mouth quietly approving. "There are sandwiches in the cooler. Go wash up."

She stepped away and walked through the front door into what was now Brandon's domain.

Buck turned to him. "I won't make a habit of breaking into your home, I promise."

With a wave, Brandon dismissed it. He didn't own a thing that Buck would want, nor did he have anything to hide.

"I just wanted to check on the two of you," Buck continued. "I wasn't sure either of you would . . . survive."

At that Brandon chuckled. "Once work was underway, we did fine."

Buck turned to look at the house, his gaze directed toward the windows, as if he could see Megan inside. The expression he turned back to Brandon was thoughtful but not readable. And he didn't share. Instead, he nodded with a small grin. "I'll leave you to it, then. Dinner is at seven."

"Yes, sir." Brandon stepped back to let the man pass by.

What had Buck been thinking? Why the small grin? Why the sudden quick escape without so much as a hollered goodbye to his daughter?

This family was a little weird. The letter should have been the telling clue.

Megan appeared at the front door again and stepped onto the porch, a paper bag in each hand. She came near enough to hand one to Brandon and then took a sharp turn that took her to a patio chair. One farthest away from Brandon. That peek of soft Megan closed, leaving only Megan the monster sharing space with him.

"What's with you and your dad?" Brandon made his way to a chair on the opposite end of the porch and sat down. Inside his bag he found a sandwich and an apple.

"I already told you. My dad and I are actually close."

"Hmm." He bit into the whole-grain bread, finding a cold-cut medley complete with bacon and thick mayo. As his taste buds had a celebration, he groaned in approval. Way better than the peanut butter and jelly he usually slapped together for his lunches.

"First taste of real food?"

He met her sassy look. "Are you eating this?"

"Of course I am."

"With bacon and mayo?"

She smirked. "Duh."

"You don't strike me as the bacon and mayo type."

"I don't think you want to know what type you strike me as." She took a large bite of her sandwich, holding a daring look on him.

Brandon stood from the chair and sauntered over to her side of the porch, stopping in front of her. "Fire away, your majesty."

She stood up, wiping crumbs from her lips. After swallowing, she raised her stubborn chin, as if she thought that would make him feel small. He chuckled as he stared down at her. The little shrew.

Jeweled eyes flashed up at him. "You are the most arrogant person I've ever met."

Not likely. Brandon held his unflinching gaze on her. "That so?"

"It's so."

He stepped back and lowered onto the deck railing, still holding her fiery stare.

Her eyes pinched, and she stepped nearer. "That's all?"

Shrugging, he bit into his sandwich.

"You're not going to tell me I'm a brat?"

"Clearly you already know."

Frustration flashed over her features. Brandon might have had a little internal victory party about that—even though he shouldn't have.

"Why don't you think I'd eat bacon and mayo?"

Again he shrugged. "Just thought you'd find such things . . . what was that word you used for my hat? Revolting."

"Do you always assume things about people?"

"Nope. Do you always look down on others?"

She shrank away, her look less feisty and sulkier as her chin slipped downward. Ugh. Of course she was going to pout now. Spoiled child.

"At least you're pretty," he muttered.

Her face whipped back up to his, and he saw that she understood exactly that he meant to insult her. She reached toward him and grabbed something off the railing at his side, and before he remembered the mug he'd left there earlier that morning, a half-cup worth of cold coffee splashed against his face.

What the heck?

He froze, and she did too. Blinking, he slowly wiped the liquid from his eyes and then used his sleeve to dry his cheeks. She'd tossed cold coffee in his face! The little . . . Well, he had been rather low with that comment. Most of them actually. Maybe he'd gone too far. He could go the valiant way and apologize, try to smooth her uppity and now ruffled feathers.

But then . . . He watched her with interest, expecting to see either pouty tears sheen those pretty eyes or bitter scorn turn her lovely features sour. That was not what he witnessed.

Oh, she fought hard, and he saw the battle. She was desperately trying not to *smile*. The amusement fighting to break free served to solidify the pretty in her.

The little monster harbored a corner of good humor. Interesting.

Brandon played a little bit of tug-of-war with the corners of his own mouth. "Brat," he whispered, nearly giving into the urge to laugh.

"Bully," she retorted, mirth making those blue eyes dance.

She turned away on those rubber boots, and Brandon finished off his sandwich. Ten minutes later, they were both in his truck and headed back to the work site. Brandon's revolting hat had somehow found its way onto Megan's pretty head. And she wore the faint evidence of a lingering smile.

Though he wasn't likely to admit it out loud, Brandon felt one too.

CHAPTER NINE

(in which Megan and Brandon would be a disaster together)

HER LEGS, BACK, AND arms ached.

Megan sank into the warm water, frothy, sweet pea–scented bubbles taking her in like a kind friend. As soon as Shay had seen Megan, her face likely contorted with ache and her hands kneading her stiff shoulders, Shay had recommended Epsom salts accompany the bubbles, so they had been added. "It will help," Shay had said, a tempered grin barely kept from splitting wide.

"Are you this sore and tired every day?" Megan had asked the woman who'd been the Alexanders' housekeeper since Megan had been a child.

Shay had laughed and shook her head. "You'll get stronger. Your body will get used to it."

Three days of working alongside that ambitious, plaid-flannel-wearing lumberjack who rarely smiled, and Megan was certain she would never adjust. And did she want to? She'd gone to bed feeling like her body had gone through a wringer and had woken like a stiff mannequin, limbs needing coaxed just to raise and lower. Everything bellowed with pain!

"Tomorrow I get a break," she muttered to the bubbles. Megan relaxed into the glorious warmth of her bath, her thoughts not completely done with Shay, who had gone home for the evening.

She'd never considered how physically demanding Shay's work might be. Nor how strong and steady Shay's husband, Tim, who was their groundskeeper and general handyman, truly must be. Or even Audrey, their daughter, who was three years younger than Megan. The younger woman had helped both her parents in the work on the Alexander estate. How was it that the three of them were always bright and cheerful no matter what time of day Megan would come upon one or the other?

Maybe Megan was truly spoiled. A brat, as Brandon had called her.

Shutting her eyes and lifting her chin to keep her face out of the mass of lovely bubbles, Megan stalled on that. *Brat.* And she chuckled.

Utter shock. That had been Brandon's expression the moment after that cold coffee had hit his face. For a second, Megan had thought he might lose his temper—and what a temper that might be. Brandon was no small man, and from the morning she'd spent with him, she knew he was an intense one. That little impulsive move of grabbing the mug he'd left on the railing and flinging the contents of it in his face might have been a very poor miscalculation. But once he'd wiped the liquid from his eyes, he'd looked down on her with . . .

Shock. And something else.

Not anger.

Wow, those rich brown eyes were intense, in a way that was quite possibly mesmerizing. There was a kindness anchoring that intensity. The kindness she'd glimpsed when she'd first bumped into him, not knowing he was her arranged fiancé. She'd liked him then, before she realized he was the very man she'd already resolved to despise. There in the tub, her memory lingering over the way he'd responded to her audacity with a hint of amusement rather than anger, Megan grinned. Her resolute dislike of Brandon had slipped as she'd been caught in that powerful, but not mean stare, and she had very nearly smiled at him.

He'd very nearly grinned down at her, and when he'd called her a brat, the low tone of his voice wasn't exactly insulting.

What had it been? *Warm . . . and maybe a touch thrilling . . .*

Megan sat up, sloshing the water as she moved, and scooped handfuls to splash her face. Whatever was she doing, lying there thinking of the blue-plaid mercenary with a pool of bursting bubbles growing in her middle? He'd called her a brat! Did it matter what sort of tone he'd used?

Yes. Yes, it absolutely mattered.

The moment replayed again, and her belly tickled again. Ugh. She was a foolish girl.

Megan forced a review of the rest of their time together. Brandon had worked her hard, and she'd forced herself to keep up. Dragging long, dead branches out of his way. Hauling eighteen-inch logs as he'd sectioned downed trees and stacking them. Then restacking them because he'd stopped his buzzing chainsaw to inform her that she was doing the grunt work incorrectly.

The picky beast.

Beyond that, Brandon rarely paused and clearly expected the same out of her—and she wasn't about to give him reason to look down on her with that superior way of his.

I do not like him. I will not like him.

There. Just so she was clear on it. Brandon was an overbearing bully and a workaholic. He was too intense. Too serious. Who wanted a lifetime under the watchful scrutiny of those severe brown eyes?

Ah, but the layer of warm kindness she'd glimpsed in them. A girl could get used to that . . .

Nonsense. She'd have to work day and night just to catch a peek of it. The rest of the time his gaze would be only hard expectations and sharp disapproval. Megan wanted laughter and admiration. She wanted easy and happy. Not hard and stern.

She and Brandon would be a disaster.

Megan had no idea why she needed to remind herself of that. Perhaps because she was so tired? That had to be it. She was exhausted and wasn't thinking—feeling—straight. Good thing she was scheduled at Spruce Acres. She'd get a break tomorrow. From hard manual labor and the man who was taking up too much real estate in her mind.

***

Brandon clenched the phone in his hand, sitting on the edge of the chair on his front porch and staring at the icy surge of spring waters as the river flowed by. Buck Alexander could be a formidable force. No wonder he'd turned his simple invention into a multi-million-dollar business. The man was as determined as . . .

Well, as Brandon was. And apparently—surprisingly—Megan owned her father's tenacity too. Over the last few days, the girl had proven she could be more than a flighty, lazy, pretty face. Because of her, Brandon was well ahead of where he'd expected to be on this clearing job. At this pace, he wouldn't need the full six months to get the job done.

Then again, there was this new wrench in his plans.

"Megan spends a couple days a week at Spruce Acres." Buck had told Brandon this over the phone just a minute ago. "Since you have a connection there too, I'd like you to take her. She goes tomorrow." He made it clear this suggestion was not a suggestion at all.

Even so, Brandon had tried to mount a defense. "Sir, with all due respect, I think that I'm best left to what I know."

The man had chuckled. "What's that?"

"Trees. Chainsaws. Firewood."

"You need to get to know Megan."

"We've spent the past three days together."

"Yes, and I see you haven't killed each other yet. That's progress."

"I don't think Megan will appreciate me imposing on her thing."

"No, she sure won't." Buck's voice still carried humor. And resolve. "Not any more than you appreciated her stepping into your business. That's the thing about marriage. All lines get blown over. You learn to roll with it."

Good grief, why was Buck talking about marriage? *Likely because technically you came here under the awareness that this would be a trial engagement.*

Right.

Man, he'd been a special kind of crazy to agree to this.

While that might be true, at the end of the trial, Brandon had no intention of marrying Megan. Even if she could work. What an absolute catastrophe that would be. How could a man spend the rest of his life tied to a woman who delighted in finding every possible way to get under his skin?

Know what? I'm just gonna find a cozy spot out of your way. Let me know when you're done. Ugh. The only thing more irritating than having a spoiled woman-child thrust into his world would be to have her sitting around watching him work.

She hadn't though. So there was that.

Look, mister plaid flannel. I can do anything you can do. Why did the minx insist on calling him *plaid flannel* or *mercenary* every chance she could? And ha! Like she could do his job. Although, well, he would like to see her wield a chainsaw. For some reason Brandon felt sure that would be quite enjoyable.

This thing is revolting. She'd made a face at his hat, as if it contained the plague. The snot. There was nothing wrong with that hat—just a large, hard-earned sweat stain. What had she expected? It was a work hat.

At that Brandon snorted a small laugh. The Megan monster in his old work hat . . . She had looked pretty cute wearing it later that afternoon.

"From what I hear, you promised Mrs. Knolls another visit anyway, Brandon." Mr. Alexander had saved his final ace to close the deal.

Brandon had done exactly that. His run-on arguments came to a hard stop. Tomorrow he'd be accompanying Megan to Spruce Acres, for better or worse. As he gazed over the peaceful scene of river, pines, rising hills, and the stunning exit of the lowering sun, he resigned to that reality. He'd come here to play her fiancé. This was part of the gig.

Something pulled tight in his chest as he thought of another day spent with the brat. Leaning back, Brandon tipped his head against the side of the house. He named that tug frustration.

And grinned at the lingering image of Megan wearing his cruddy old ball cap.

***

"We are definitely not taking *that* to Spruce Acres." Standing on the top of the flagstone steps in front of the massive mountain home, Megan pointed to Brandon's truck and spat out her proclamation with all the disdain of a girl stepping in dog poop.

Brandon moved up the one riser that had given her a slight height advantage and then crossed his arms, looking down on her. "What is wrong with my truck?"

"It's long past its expiration date. I won't be seen riding around town in it."

"Huh." Brandon fought against the urge to roll his eyes. The spoiled version of Megan Alexander had shown up. Could he truly be surprised?

He appraised her head to toe. Hair curled and tossed to make it seem her beachy look had been effortless. Certainly it had not been. Face made up to magazine perfection, the light dusting of freckles that had made her appear less like a brat and more like an endearing young woman were now entirely smothered. Pink lips glossed. Trendy clothes applied—including holey frayed skinny jeans that likely cost more than the used chainsaw he'd saved for last fall.

The brat was back in full force. Had he actually thought she was cute when his thoughts had lingered on her last night? Brandon snorted.

"What would suit your highness better? Shall we conjure up a pumpkin and test our luck with that?" He made a show of looking around her. "Surely you have a fairy godmother hanging around here, waiting to make your every wish her command."

Megan held a long, unimpressed look on him, then turned on one Sperry-shoed foot to storm back into her house.

Balling his fists, Brandon stifled a low growl as he followed her into the Alexander home. *You agreed to this . . .* Not on these terms, he hadn't. Right then he knew a keen dislike for Anna Alexander. Megan did not need a decent man who would show her there was better out there. She needed a good spanking followed by a few years of real work to shave off her uppity childishness.

Once he'd passed the stone archway and through the full glass double doors, Brandon found Megan slipping into a denim jacket and snagging a set of keys from a glass bowl on a table.

"We'll take my car." She barely looked at him over her shoulder as she grabbed a canvas bag waiting on a hook and walked toward a side hall that would likely lead to the garage behind the house.

"Fine." He could use a nap anyway. The drive into town was at least thirty minutes. Being able to shut his eyes and ignore the fact that he had to spend that time trapped in a vehicle with her would be good.

"Move that ugly thing from the driveway."

He stopped short. "What?"

She turned, chin tilted at the most maddeningly demanding angle. "Move your truck. It can't stay in front of the house."

Man, this girl! Brandon scowled as he held a silent glare on her.

Her confidence faltered for a breath. And then she stiffened her posture, meeting his glare challenge for challenge.

"Say please." He moved toward her.

"What?" Her face wrinkled like she'd never heard of the concept.

Brandon stepped forward again, folding his arms. "Say. Please."

Her eyes pinched. "You're not the boss of me."

"I am not some dog you get to order around. Say please, or the truck is staying put. Right out there in front, where all your uppity friends can see it as they drive their uppity cars by your uppity house."

Her self-assured posture shrank, and she swallowed. "Please," she squeaked.

"Please what, Megan?"

"Please move your truck."

"Brandon."

"What?"

"Please move your truck, *Brandon*. That's my name. Not blue plaid. Not mercenary. Not bully. Brandon."

Megan rolled her eyes, and then she cleared her throat. "Will you please, Brandon, move your ugly, stupid truck? Brandon."

Brandon felt an eyebrow twitch as he continued to hold a long look on her. When a dusting of pink infused her cheeks, a distinct feeling of satisfaction filled his being. *Murphy, one. Monster, zero.* "Yes, Megan. I'll move my truck. Since you said please."

He turned to go do as bid, hearing behind him her mumbled response.

"Bully."

"Brat." He kept striding out the door, unsure if he was amused or irritated.

Definitely irritated.

He parked his truck behind the garage, then slid into the passenger seat of her Rubicon, trying not to be jealous that such a pill got to claim a vehicle he'd have loved to own, and snapped the seat belt firmly. Without a word, Megan backed out of the drive and started toward town. Brandon folded his arms, pressed his head against the backrest, and shut his eyes, fighting to ignore the sweet, warm scent of whatever Megan had doused her skin with and firmly denying that those jeweled eyes had looked particularly lovely that morning.

What did it matter if they did anyway? Beauty was absolutely *not* everything. In Megan's case, it wasn't even a little thing, except for bait on the trap.

Why was he even wasting his nap time thinking about her? Good grief. If he couldn't shut his brain down to snooze, then he could at least spend the time considering something worth the energy.

How was Tyler doing? Had he made it a point to talk to Becca yet? There, the distraction proved fruitful as Brandon thought on the last real interaction he'd had with Tyler's ex-fiancée. Dad had sent Brandon to do the renovations Becca had needed to move forward with her bakery. Brandon had resented Dad's imposition on the issue, and the first few days on the job had been spent in hard silence between he and Becca. Matt, the big brother that he was, had confronted Brandon on it.

"She didn't do anything wrong, Brandon," Matt had said. "And punishing her when her heart has already been broken by Ty isn't dignity. It isn't noble. It isn't anything that you seem to think it is. And it definitely won't help Tyler, if he should ever decide to seek her forgiveness like he should."

Brandon had boiled at Matt's interference and at his know-it-all-ness. But Matt wasn't wrong. Anger had blinded Brandon. Disappointment had powered that anger. And the truth had been, once Brandon forced himself to really think about it, that his frustration with Becca had been conflated with knowing the truth of himself: *he'd* failed Becca and Ty. He'd seen signs of things not being okay with Tyler, and he'd ignored them. Then when everything blew up and Tyler was sent to rehab, he'd blamed Becca for not telling him when he'd known and hadn't been willing to admit it.

It had been his failure too.

Brandon had been mad at Becca because he felt guilty. And he was mad at her because he was mad at Ty. That had been a harsh realization after a long night, and the next morning while working in Becca's transforming kitchen, he'd had to beat down his own pride to attempt to make things right. That had been a feeble thing. But when he'd moved to give Becca a hug, she'd accepted it.

Even so, resurrecting what had been a true friendship between Becca and himself seemed impossible. Why was that?

Man, the path of his thoughts.

If he had to be in this impossible situation with Megan, did he have to swim in the things that needled his hollow places? Brandon opened his eyes, focusing his attention on the scenery outside his window. Layers of green flashed by. Blue greens of spruce. Crisp Christmas green of pine. Bold new green of the opening buds of the aspen. Along the road, dirty piles of melting snow dotted their path.

Changing seasons. For a week or two more, winter and spring would continue to arm wrestle for dominance. Spring would inevitably win, and winter, with all its bluster and chill, would submit and fade away.

The momentum of the vehicle slowed and then swayed left as Megan turned off the highway. She followed that road and then turned left again. Brandon recognized the lot and building as she pulled in. Spruce Acres. Finally. Megan hadn't even said a word, and the drive had still been less than pleasant.

Man, for his maul, axe, a tall stack of unsplit wood, and a few hours by himself. He'd end the day physically exhausted and unable to entertain the torment that seemed determined to run laps in his mind.

"Ground rules." And there went the gift of silence. Megan tapped her freshly manicured fingernails on the steering wheel. When had she done that? No way could those nails have endured the past few days of manual labor.

"Excuse me?" Brandon sat up and unbuckled.

"There are rules for this."

"Whose rules?"

"Mine."

"And here we go." Brandon opened his door and moved to get out, ignoring her highness's proclamation. Showing surprising speed and agility for a girl who, Brandon could imagine, was probably exceptionally sore from her first experience with real physical labor, Megan hopped out of the vehicle and met him in front of it.

"Rules, *Brandon*. Unless you want me to introduce you as the blue-plaid mercenary in there."

Not a threat, as he didn't care. Much.

Maybe he cared a little. Just because that name was ridiculously annoying. "What?"

"These are my people." She adjusted the straps of the large canvas bag of whatever tricks she kept in there. "Don't embarrass me."

"Your people? I'm shocked they even let someone like you in there."

"What's that supposed to mean?"

"You have the personality of a rattlesnake. I wouldn't want you within striking distance of my worst enemy, let alone my grandmother. Do you zombify them for the duration of your visits?"

She tossed her head as a breeze caught the controlled mess of the dark waves of her hair. "They love me here. Don't blow it."

"I can't imagine I could do anything you couldn't do yourself."

"You are in a seriously bad mood today. What'd you do, sleep on a brick?"

Hadn't slept much at all, but he wasn't going to tell her that was because it hadn't gone unnoticed that she'd kept wearing his hat all week, and he'd kept picturing her in it every time he shut his eyes. Which bothered him. "I've spent the past few days with you. It's exhausting."

With a tilt of her head that said clearly *you're a bully*, Megan huffed. "Then today is the day for a break. Agreed?"

"Sounds perfect."

"Don't bother me in there. Don't even look at me."

"Or I'll turn to stone?"

"You're funny. Did you know that? A real comedian, Murphy."

"Usually I leave that for my brother, Jackson, but you seem to bring out all sorts of humor in me."

"Yeah. There's something in you all right." She straightened her spine and stepped in his space. "Just try, with all your brawny might, to leave me alone for the next few hours."

"Me? That shouldn't be a problem. I'd prefer you weren't around anyway. Ignoring you will be a pleasure. You, however, might have an issue." He smirked as that blush he'd summoned from her earlier made an encore appearance. "Don't think I haven't caught you checking me out when you think I'm too busy working to notice."

Those glossy pink lips parted, pretty eyes widened, and then she scowled. "In your dreams, bully."

"I'd get my head examined if you somehow made it into my dreams."

"Ugh!" With one firm palm, she shoved his chest. "You are unbearable."

He swallowed a chuckle.

"Just leave me alone here today," she said. "Got it?"

"Absolutely."

Megan stalked away.

Several moments went by before Brandon realized he'd stood there watching her disappear into the building. He hadn't been checking her out though. Hadn't been thinking about how those carefree waves of hair had looked playful and soft. Not wondering what that warm sweetness that had drifted from her small body to his nose had been. Nor how her delayed nearness had been a little hypnotic.

And he definitely wasn't grinning. Not about her.

That would be stupid. And childish. And utterly impossible.

He didn't like Megan at all. Nothing—particularly something as puny as her smelling pretty—would change that.

CHAPTER TEN

(in which Brandon lights up like a bonfire)

MEGAN LOOKED AT HER list, though she doubted the order of it had changed since she'd left Mrs. Ambrose's apartment five steps ago.

Her eyes moved down the names.

Lila Hinson, nails. She'd chosen a dusty rose and had wanted two layers. Done.

Rita Ambrose, visit. Their chat had quickly slipped into storied memories. Megan had pulled her notebook out of her canvas bag and recorded what she could. She would type it into the Ambrose document later. Done.

Nancy Yang, story. She'd save her for last.

Tilly Knolls, visit.

Stopping in the middle of the hallway, Megan squeezed her eyes shut and sighed. Brandon had gone into Mrs. Knolls's apartment straight after he'd checked in at the front desk—Megan knew because she'd spied him doing so as she'd entered Ms. Hinson's room. To her knowledge, Brandon was still in there.

But maybe he wasn't. It'd been a good hour, after all. He could have made his lame excuses and left. Maybe he was, at that moment, out in Megan's car taking that much-needed nap. One could hope. Goodness, he was a bad-mood beast that morning! What had crawled up his jockey shorts anyway? Just when she'd begun to think there might be a decent, tolerable human being inside that way-too-serious man, he'd turned up the unbearability level to full volume.

Didn't matter. Surely Brandon had made an obligatory ten-minute appearance with Mrs. Knolls and then found something else to do. Why would he hang around just to visit an old woman? That was much too kind a thing to do for an intolerable stoic beast such as Brandon Murphy to even imagine.

Confidence restored, Megan continued on her way. When her tap on the door to apartment 38 was delayed an answer, she felt more certain. Brandon the blue-plaid mercenary was not there. Hallelujah.

Mrs. Knolls peeked around the edge of her door and smiled like a giddy child. "Oh my lucky stars! It's that lovely girl who comes to play cards with me. What is your name again, dear?"

Leaning to kiss the old woman's cheek, Megan laughed. "Megan."

"Yes! That's right." A slender hand, knuckles swollen, patted Megan's cheek. "Come in here and see what I have!"

One never knew what to expect when it came to Tilly Knolls. Megan entered the tiny apartment and lowered her canvas bag onto a chair sitting askew at the small round table. "What do you have, Mrs. Knolls?"

At Christmas it had been a pound cake the woman had somehow exhumed from eons past. The thing had been a puke-brown brick. Valentine's Day had produced dark-chocolate hearts from the eighties, the color and texture having aged to a white powdery substance. Last week it was that lovely arrangement Brandon's mother had apparently sent. Which wouldn't have been strange at all, except reconciling the blue-plaid mercenary with having a kind mother was further than Megan's imagination stretched.

Pushing her walker with childish delight dancing in her eyes, Mrs. Knolls simply grinned with expectation. "Sit down, lovely. You'll see in a minute."

A knowing hole opened in her gut, and Megan braced herself.

"I can't find a leak, M—"

And there he was. Brandon strolled out from whatever dark hole he'd been hiding in. He stopped at the doorframe separating the bedroom from the main room and narrowed a scowl on her. "Couldn't help yourself, could you?"

"Oh, stop it," Megan said.

Oblivious to their flat banter, Mrs. Knolls clapped her hands. "Surprise!"

Megan turned to her, mildly horrified.

The woman beamed. "I found you a man. Oh, and how! Look at that, dearie!" She waved toward the beast loitering in the doorway and then gazed at Brandon as if he were a young Clark Gable waltzing from her bedroom.

Ahem.

Megan tracked the woman's gaze, finding the well-built lumberjack who had been a massive grump and an even bigger pain in her neck standing there scratching his neck like an awkward schoolboy. Brandon's ears were lit up like Christmas lights.

"Don't you just want to stare at him?" Mrs. Knolls swooned.

That fiery red seeped from his ears into his face. Megan grinned with total delight. "Let's do that, shall we, Mrs. Knolls? We could just sit here and gawk while he lights up the room. Have you ever seen such bright-red ears?"

Brandon focused an unimpressed frown on Megan. "Knock it off."

"Oh, but you were right, Brandon. I just can't help myself."

"Brandon! Oh yes, that is his name!" Mrs. Knolls leaned in close to Megan. "How did you know?"

Watching Brandon swimming in discomfort was simply the most fun she'd had all week. Almost made the sore muscles in her legs and back, not to mention the general misery of enduring his personality, worth it. Megan pressed her head close to Mrs. Knolls. "He didn't tell you?"

"No! Tell me what?"

"He's my fiancé."

Brandon's scowl darkened with warning. The red of his skin darkened too. Megan's delight nearly overflowed.

"Oh my stars! What a lucky girl you are." Mrs. Knolls lowered her voice. "I must know. Is he a good kisser?"

Megan snorted a laugh as Brandon's face deepened into the darkest crimson she'd ever seen on human skin. "Hmmm . . . ." She tipped her head.

Mrs. Knolls didn't wait for Megan's answer. "I sure wish I could still draw. Do you know I used to do nudes?"

"I'm gonna go." With five desperate strides, Brandon scurried for the exit.

"So soon?" Megan put sugar in her voice. "But, honey—"

With one quick motion, the door was open, Brandon was in the hall, and the door was shut. Megan sat back against the chair.

That was fun. Let's do it again sometime.

"Well." Mrs. Knolls plopped onto her chair. "Where's the fire?—that's what I want to know."

On Brandon's face.

The playful old woman winked. "He'll come back. This is the second time he's come to see me. Do you know, I don't even remember him from whenever I knew him? He might be a perfect stranger, for all I know. But I sure do enjoy him stopping by, so let's not tell him that." She leaned forward again, employing that conspirator's whisper. "Between you and me, there's not a leak in the bathroom. I just liked watching him look for it. What a view!"

A full laugh rolled from Megan's chest. "Can't blame you for that."

"Are you really gonna marry him?"

Not if he was the last man standing on God's green earth. Megan sobered up. That little stunt might have been a mistake. Mrs. Knolls didn't remember half of anything that was said or done anymore. But guessing which bits she would remember, that was a wildcard.

"He has kind eyes. And a good laugh. Deep and rich. You need a man who can laugh well."

Brandon knew how to laugh? Incredible. She'd yet to witness such a natural wonder.

"And if he's a good kisser . . . "

Doubtful. He'd likely be like a steel post. Cold. Rigid. Metallic. Then again, he was an intense man . . .

This time Megan blushed. She snatched her bag up from the chair, sank onto it, and dug around the bag's contents for her notebook and pen. "How about Mr. Knolls?" She hoped the heat in her face didn't bleed pink, and trained her thoughts away from all notions of kissing Brandon Murphy. *The blue-plaid mercenary.*

"Frank? Oh"—Mrs. Knolls let out a wistful sigh as she dropped back against her chair—"that man could kiss. Make my knees turn to jelly and light me up like a bonfire. I didn't let him kiss me right away though. We went out on five dates before I let him do anything but peck my cheek good night. He was persistent though. Said I looked like Natalie Wood." A distant mist eclipsed her playful expression. "And his laugh . . . "

Megan settled in, her pen gliding between the lines of the page as she recorded Tilly Knolls's memories. From earlier visits, she'd known that Tilly and Frank had had a true love affair, and their fifty-eight-year marriage had been one marked by faithfulness. Tilly adored her Frank, and by the woman's accounts, Frank had cherished his wife.

They'd been happy.

As it did every time Megan listened to such tales of lasting love and happiness, longing brimmed in her heart. Was it too much to hope, to ask, for the same thing?

Is it, Lord?

She pictured Marcus. Remembered the feel of that gorgeous Tiffany's ring on her finger. And then, without warning, she pictured Brandon.

What did his laugh sound like?

It bothered her that she didn't know.

***

"I beg you, find me something to do. Anything."

The middle-aged woman at the front desk stared at Brandon with shock. "I'm not sure I can do that."

"There's got to be something that needs fixed. Or moved. Or replaced."

"You're begging me for work?"

"Exactly."

"Manual labor?"

"The harder the better." That way he couldn't think about Megan calling him her fiancé. Or how panicked and stupid he felt when Mrs. Knolls asked Megan if he was a good kisser.

What if he wasn't? What if he was a really bad kisser?

When it came to Megan Alexander, did it matter? She'd never know either way.

Brandon rubbed his neck, begging heaven to cool down the flames still burning his ears. "I just need something to do for the next few hours while my—" His what? Fiancée. Ugh. Megan was not his fiancée. Well, she was. But he wasn't gonna marry her. "While Megan Alexander does whatever it is she does here."

At her name, the woman smiled. "Ah Meg. She does so well with our residents. It's been a delight to watch her grow into the woman she is now. Such a tender, sweet soul."

Were they talking about the same person? Couldn't be. The girl he was referring to went around in his head by the name *Megan the monster*, breathing fire and bringing misery. Or simply *brat*, because she was one. Neither embodied the qualities of *tender* or *sweet*.

"She's such a blessing to us." Innocent interest rounded the woman's eyes as she continued to look up at Brandon. "How do you know her?"

"Um . . . "

"Oh my gosh!" She smacked the counter with a hand. "You're *him!*"

Him who? Panic ripped in his chest as he braced himself for whatever was coming at him next, certain he wouldn't like it.

"She said she was getting married. Said you were quite a catch. Oh goodness, I should have known right off! I'm sorry. It's just that she hasn't worn the ring in a while, so I thought . . . "

Brandon wanted to rub his hands over his face. This day just kept getting worse. What was he supposed to do with this?

The woman stood up and plowed onward, so maybe he wouldn't have to do or say anything about it. "I feel so silly. But I got the impression you weren't the visiting-old-people sort of guy. Megan made it seem like maybe you were, uh, too busy for this kind of thing." Coming around the desk, she ran an appraising look from his head to his feet. "Wow. She also didn't say what a looker you are." Her lips formed an oval, and then she whistled.

Holy moly, every female in this place was boy crazy.

Brandon tugged on his shirt. "Uh, thanks. But I really just need something to do. With my hands." Yikes, where was that gonna lead? "Working. You know, with . . . stuff."

Amused brows lifted high. "Right." She cleared her throat. Sounded like a stifled laugh.

Good grief. Where was his chainsaw? Put him alone in the forest, for heaven's sake. Out of eyesight and talking range of females.

"Are you opposed to getting dirty?"

Was that a legitimate question? Great. Now he couldn't even take things at face value.

"We've had a leak in the northwest corner of the building." She continued, oblivious to his tumbling thoughts. "My husband drove by the other day and thought the problem might be clogged gutters."

Thank heavens for clogged gutters! "I can check. Know where I'd find a ladder?"

"The maintenance closet." She paused. "But on second thought, that might not be a good idea. I should check with the building manager. Liability and all."

Brandon lunged for a pen and a sheet of paper off her desk. "I'll sign right here. Put down that under no circumstances is Spruce Acres responsible for any physical injury I may encounter while cleaning your gutters."

"What about our liability to you?"

He scribbled on, faster. "Spruce Acres will not hold Brandon Murphy responsible for any damage that may accidentally incur while he cleans the gutters." He whipped out his signature and turned the pen toward her.

She winced. "I don't know. This isn't very official."

"It'll do." He had no idea if that was true.

She hesitated, but he must have been wearing pure desperation. He certainly felt it. After she signed the document that likely wouldn't do anyone any good if something bad did happen, she pointed toward a set of double doors across the large dining room. Brandon nodded, crossed to them, and found the ladder.

Thank goodness. Work, he could do. He understood it. The march of females suddenly imposed on his world?

He had no clue. Didn't think he wanted to get one either.

CHAPTER ELEVEN

(in which the challenge is accepted)

DRIVEN BY A SMIDGE of curiosity and harboring a tiny bit of pride at the fact that Rachel Peddy had gushed about how handsome her fiancé was, Megan strolled out of Spruce Acres' front doors and immediately turned left. She couldn't see Brandon right away, but she could hear the scrubbing that was surely him cleaning the gutters. Her tummy churned and then rumbled as she continued around the corner. Stopping a few feet from the ladder, Megan shielded her eyes from the early afternoon sun and gazed up at the guy who was unaware of her presence.

Not a bad view. Megan stifled a giggle as she imagined what Mrs. Knolls would say, and then she pictured Brandon's bright-eared reaction to it. What if Megan spouted off such audacious things? Seeing the man burn with a blush might be worth it. Then again, he'd get the wrong impression . . .

Obviously, she didn't want that.

Megan anchored her hands on her hips and opted for disapproval over flirting just to make him blush. "You really can't stay clean for more than a half a day, can you?"

Brandon started, bracing with both hands on the roof to steady himself and the ladder. He shot her a glare. "Good grief, woman. Are you trying to kill me?"

"Hmm . . . that might do the trick." The sun too bright in her eyes, she shielded her view with one hand again. Just in time to see that stern frown that seemed to be Brandon's favorite expression aimed dead on her.

"What are you doing out here?" he asked.

"I'm hungry."

He returned to his work, leaning deep right to dig out more debris from the gutter and then tossing it to the ground. The muddy, wet ball of leaves, twigs, and shingle sluff plopped against a square of black plastic he'd spread beneath his work area. "Were you planning to graze?"

"No, smart aleck. Though I might let you do exactly that. You're filthy."

"You've said." Brandon kept moving. "Am I supposed to take you out or something?"

"I always eat in the dining room. They stop serving in twenty minutes."

Finally he paused his work and looked down at her again. That granite expression he was prone to softened into confusion. "Are you inviting me to lunch?"

"If you starve and then fall off this ladder because I didn't feed you, my dad will hold me personally responsible. Unless I can tell him I made the offer. So there's your offer, blue plaid. Lunch in the dining room."

"Brandon," he corrected.

Megan shrugged and started back around the building. After a moment, she heard the rattling of the ladder—Brandon's descent. She tensed as she thought of him striding after her. And sure enough, his looming presence was at her side, making her jittery.

Pathetic. Megan was not the jittery-around-a-guy sort of girl. Specifically, not when that guy was Brandon Murphy, the blue-plaid mercenary.

She tucked a lock of hair away from her face and looked up at him primly. "Amazing. He can be sensible."

Brandon returned her glance and grunted.

No banter? That would not do.

"You'll have to wash up."

"No kidding."

"And Rachel Peddy has basically announced our engagement to the whole residence."

"I don't know who Rachel Peddy is, and I'm pretty sure I don't care what she's announced."

"You do care."

"Why do I care?"

"Because now you have to play the part."

Brandon snorted. "Or?"

"Or nothing. Daddy says that I have to endure this arrangement for six months. If I have to, you do too. So today in that dining room with all the old ladies gawking at you, you'll play the role."

"Of your fiancé?"

"My doting fiancé."

"Let's not get carried away."

Megan stopped just shy of the front door, where no one on the inside could see them, and then pegged him with a warning. "You agreed to this dumb idea." She jabbed him in the chest with a finger. "I don't know why you did that, and I already told you that whatever your reasons were, they can be nothing short of pathetic. But here you are, and I don't really have a choice. So while we're here, or anywhere else public, you adore me. Got it?"

Brandon hovered over her, and as that concrete gaze remained glued on her face, she watched the depth of those brown eyes transform from irritated disapproval to mild humiliation and then to . . . amusement? Shockingly, the corners of his mouth twitched into something that might resemble a grin.

Would he smile full, looking down at her? A million butterflies took flight in her belly.

"You think you can handle that?" he asked.

Goodness, he was close. How had that happened? And why was she suddenly breathless? She blinked, and her hand moved from his shirt to cover her thudding heart. "What?"

"Challenge accepted." Oh, that sly grin grew, and he leaned in closer, lowering his deep voice even more. "Let see how you do, shall we?"

"How I'll do?" She sounded like a mouse. And why did her head swim?

Brandon chuckled. Low and rich. "Your wish is my command, your highness. Just don't go falling in love."

Love! With a sharp inhale, Megan drew back. "With you? Ha! In your dreams."

"We've already discussed that. You bewitch your way into my dreams, and I'll seek an exorcism. Preferably with pigs and a steep cliff nearby. Now." He turned and offered her his arm. "Let the theatrics begin."

She shouldn't laugh at that—it was insulting. Possibly sacrilegious. Not funny. Pinning her lips together, Megan hesitated, and in that breath, a tendril of warning seeped into her mind. This could be worse than working with him in the woods.

No way. There was no reason to worry about that. If she could endure day after day of manual labor with a beast, she could pretend to like him in front of old women. Megan slipped her hand through his arm and walked on.

Later it hit her. At home, while she lounged in another warm bubble bath, replaying the afternoon with more than a little satisfaction, Megan realized exactly why she should be worried.

Brandon had laughed. And she'd liked the sound of it.

***

He'd been charming, just like his dad had modeled and instructed him to be. A gentleman. That was all. No reason to be treading in the uncomfortable depths of guilt. After all, Megan had it coming, demanding that he play her *doting fiancé* as if he were a hired actor sent to ensure her picture-perfect image.

Was that what he was? Brandon smacked the closet door shut, clean towel in hand, and stalked toward the bathroom. He really needed a hot shower. A long, steaming shower to wash away the mud packed under his fingernails, and hopefully, while he was at it, this slimy garbage plaguing his conscience.

With a hard flick of his wrist, he turned on the water, pushing the lever all the way to hot. The steam rolled over the top of the glass door before he stripped and stepped inside. Let the washing bring relief . . .

That charm . . . he'd laid it on thick. After scrubbing his hands clean in the public restroom, he'd found Megan waiting beside the front desk, talking to who he assumed was Rachel Peddy, the worker who had sent him to the gutters. Without hesitation, he'd sidled next to Megan's side, dropping a possessive arm around her, grinning down at her with every scrap of forced innocence he could muster when she looked up at him with warning.

"You going to feed me?" Hand on her hip, he squeezed her against his side.

"Ah, you make the most striking couple," Rachel Peddy gushed.

"Hear that, honey?" He winked. "We're striking together."

"Yeah. Striking." She extricated herself from his hold and moved toward the dining room.

Brandon snagged her hand before she was out of reach and matched her stride. Leaning down, he whispered, "I'm winning this game already. Try to catch up."

Fire shot from her eyes, but she smiled as they stopped beside a table. With the hand not gripping his fingers as if she thought she could hurt him, she reached up to pick something off his shirt. "You are a mess, babe." She pinched his shirt, snagging a bit of his skin beneath it, and then tugged. Again. And yet again. "Look at all these bits of leaves and twigs."

The savage little thing. Brandon clenched his jaw, forced a smile, and then covered the hand she'd turned into an annoying weapon with his. "Didn't you say you were hungry?"

"I did."

He turned and pulled out a chair. When she moved to sit in it, he had to fight the urge to tug it backward and watch her fall.

"Babe?" She fluttered her lashes at him. "I sure would like some sweet tea."

Off he went to fetch her highness some sweet tea. He thought to dump it over her head, but instead he set it on the table in front of her. Taking advantage of his position right behind her, he bent, wrapped an arm around her shoulder, and nuzzled her neck.

"I thought we weren't getting carried away," she hissed.

He chuckled. "You said you could handle it. Honey."

"Act like a grown-up, not a hormone-charged teenage boy."

He lay his cheek against hers. "You keep changing the rules on me. It's like you don't know what you want."

"Stop touching me."

He might have overplayed that. Especially since that warm sweet scent of hers was intoxicating, and the soft skin of her neck, mere inches from his lips, was awfully tempting. It'd taken a heartbeat to stop the heady spinning and make himself move away.

Standing under the warm stream of water hours later, Brandon replayed the whole scene again. He didn't feel good about it.

Yeah. He'd been charming. His father had certainly not taught him to be deceitful and intentionally irritating. Shoulders sagging, Brandon braced a hand against the wall and paused all motion while the shower massaged his neck.

Lord, help me get my head on straight.

As he remained still, forcing his whirling emotions to settle, his thoughts became clearer, which felt much more like himself. Logical, not simply emotionally driven. That was so much safer.

Why was he there in the first place? Because he'd sensed that God had wanted him to do this. Even though it seemed crazy. There had been a soul-deep prompting to answer Mrs. Alexander's audacious request.

God, had that been my imagination?

No revelation. Other than to know for sure that whether this was a mission sent by God or a fool-headed misunderstanding, Brandon was there now, and he was not doing well with the situation.

Clothe yourselves with compassion, kindness, humility, gentleness and patience.

Where was that verse again? What was the context? Brandon wasn't nearly as skilled as his dad was at recalling Scripture chapter and verse. He'd assumed Dad's abilities were natural. But maybe they'd been acquired? Practiced. Brandon could definitely use more practice.

With a redirected purpose—and emotions not entirely inflamed by the frustrating girl he was supposed to be engaged to—Brandon finished his shower and searched out his Bible. A tug of shame yanked on his conscious as he realized that piece of vital equipment was still tucked in the bag he'd packed before he'd left home. Hadn't touched it since he'd arrived. An echo from his childhood surfaced—something his dad had said long ago. *Seven days without God makes one weak.*

Brandon had only been six or seven when he'd heard that phrase, and he didn't get it. *Seven days made a week.* Why would Dad say something obvious as if it was important? He hadn't wanted to ask his dad though, so he'd slipped his question into conversation with his older brother, Connor, who seemed to know everything about God and the Bible back then.

"It's a play on words, buddy," a teenage Connor had responded. *"Week* and *weak* are homophones. Sound the same, spelled different. And don't mean the same thing."

Ah! Brandon had got it then.

The memory summoned a faint smile.

It'd been more than double that seven-day warning. He'd better get to nourishment.

Gripping his leather-bound Bible, Brandon dropped onto a comfy chair next to a window that faced west. Outside, the sky was darkening, reminding him that he would be expected down at the big house for dinner soon. But for now, sustenance. The kind he needed most.

Employing a quick internet search first, he found where that Scripture was found and then flipped through the pages of his Bible to Colossians 3.

Quiet held him gently as he read through the chapter twice, tallying the worldly, sinful things he was supposed to put off and highlighting the godly things he was supposed to be putting on. Then, *Let the peace of Christ rule in your hearts . . .*

Though the list-making made his head swim, this one statement nailed him into place. The peace of Christ had certainly *not* been what was ruling his heart these past weeks with Megan. Directing Brandon's thoughts and actions when it came to her had been irritation, resentment, pure dislike. And digging into some blunt truth even if he didn't like it, physical attraction.

He'd resented her for that maybe more than anything else. Or maybe he'd offended himself with that? Why would he have to battle attraction to a girl who drove him nuts?

Either way it didn't matter. He'd acted poorly. Took delight in making her mad. Hadn't even bothered to get to know her true self because he'd immediately disliked her.

No, Christ was not ruling in Brandon's heart when it came to Megan Alexander. Chaos was on the throne there.

That should not be. Sincerely, Brandon wanted to do better.

Shifting to knees pressed to the floor, he started with the humility to confess. And to ask for the grace to do better.

***

Megan's mind came to a hard stop as she stared up at the clean version of the mercenary. She blinked under his intense gaze.

"Megan?" Brandon stepped nearer but made no move to touch her as he had at Spruce Acres—all possessive and showy and perfectly annoying. Had he really just . . .

"Please? Forgive me. I shouldn't have behaved that way." There was absolute sincerity in those deep-brown eyes. And was that . . . humility too?

The bully was apologizing?

Who was this man? Was it possible he had a split personality?

He waited another beat, then pressing his lips together, he rubbed his neck and moved back. The nod of his head was surrender. As if he accepted that she was angry with him and was going to stay that way.

Was she truly angry with him? He'd been over-the-top, ridiculously showy. But then again, she'd asked for it, hadn't she? *You'll be my doting fiancé.* That was her command. Spouted off all high and mighty while he'd stood there with grime up to his elbows because he was doing a job no one else had seen to. A dirty job for which he wouldn't even be paid.

Full conviction dumped on her. He wasn't the only one who had been acting like a beast.

"Brandon."

Half turned away from her and ready to go into the dining room, where her parents waited, Brandon looked at her again. He looked tired. Maybe resigned?

To her? To this engagement? To a fate he clearly thought was worse than bachelorhood?

A guy that good looking should not have to *resign* himself to a relationship. Not any more than she should have to do so just because her father was wealthy.

Megan swept away the thoughts that would surely prick her ire. Instead, she focused on what he'd just shocked her speechless with. *I'm sorry for today, Megan.*

Words she'd never expected from a bully.

She crossed the space of wood floor separating them and laid a hand on his arm. "Thank you . . . for the work you did at Spruce Acres. I know they appreciate it."

His brows folded inward. After a heartbeat, he swallowed, then nodded.

Megan's tummy tightened, and she pulled her touch from Brandon's muscled arm. She should follow his lead and apologize too. She hadn't treated him very well, and not just while they were at the retirement home. In fact, she'd acted every inch the spoiled brat he'd proclaimed her to be.

But she said nothing to that.

Brandon spoke into the awkward lull. "If you could call ahead the next time we go, and find out what needs done, I'd appreciate it."

Now was her turn at confusion. "What needs done?"

"I need something to do when we go there. Work." He looked at his half-raised hands and then back at her. "I can't just follow you around pretending you and I are real. I need something productive to do."

A twinge pierced her heart in the middle of that, though Megan wasn't sure why. Ignoring the sting, she nodded. "I'll call and ask then."

"Good."

"Good."

He remained unmoving. Was there uncertainty in his expression? Megan definitely felt it. In the space of that uncertainty, she also sensed a sprout of longing. What would it be like for this gentle version of the handsome Brandon Murphy to take her hand? To rest his fingers on her back and guide her into dinner, as if he actually liked her and wanted to be at her side, not to mock her high handedness and to be annoying?

That would be . . .

Impossible. He didn't like her. And she didn't like him.

CHAPTER TWELVE

(in which Brandon meets Megan's friends)

BRANDON HAD DEBATED HARD whether it'd be foolish to join the Alexanders for services at their church. He wasn't sure either he or Megan were ready to face the inquisitions that would surely come with his appearance. But two things had outweighed his hesitancy: one, Buck had asked him specifically to go, and two, after several weeks without attending church, Brandon knew he needed spiritual nourishment.

Standing in a grand, showy foyer, muscles bunched as if an imminent threat stared at him, rather than a circle of three well-dressed, perfectly made-up young women, he regretted this decision.

"What have we here, Megan?" The runway-perfect girl with sharp blue eyes took him in with something very much like hunger.

Brandon battled against the heat threatening to storm up the back of his neck. He could have listened to a sermon online. If he still felt the need for more depth—for a connection and fellowship—he could have called one of his brothers. He had six of them, for heaven's sake.

No, he'd taken the bolder route. As usual. How had he not yet learned in this life, during most of which he'd been tagged *Brandon the bold*, that harder didn't always mean wiser?

As Megan shifted at his side, tension radiating off her posture, Brandon was quite sure she was regretting his decision as well.

Strain pulling on the headache already sprouting, Brandon glanced down at Megan, standing to his right. She swallowed and peeked up at him. Whoa. Gone was the high-browed sass who was ever ready to issue him a command. In her place stood a girl dressed up like a confident woman, secretly unsteady and unintentionally giving him a glimpse of her vulnerability. Because of him, or because of the society they were facing at the moment?

Brandon turned his attention back to the socialites who were openly appraising them. To the one in the middle, a petite blond bombshell with the sharp blue eyes who had asked who he was, he offered his hand.

"Brandon Murphy," he said, putting out pure confidence to fend off whatever was fueling this girl's arrogance.

The bombshell produced a sly grin. Looking him up and then down as if he were an item in a store, she then looked at Megan with a foxlike glint. "You traded the Tiffany's diamond for this?" Looking back at him, her tongue ran along the edge of her teeth. "Might be a good deal." One heavily painted lash dropped over a twinkling blue eye.

Brandon pulled back. Good grief, they were standing in church, and clearly he'd come with Megan. What was wrong with this girl? He glanced at Megan and found a hint of apology in the look she gave him. Then she cozied up to his side, one hand slipping through his arm.

How was he gonna play this?

He could go stiff, be the chilled distant sort of man, which might put off the bombshell's obvious intent to flirt but would also make Megan look bad and ignite her anger. Or he could act her doting fiancé—though not the way he'd done so at Spruce Acres. Not in a way that Megan would find completely irritating. He could be truly a gentleman, the kind his dad had taught him to be.

Brandon covered the hand Megan had settled on his bicep.

"How did you meet?" one of the other painted barbies asked.

Megan gently squeezed his arm. "Our parents are old friends."

Was that a thank-you for playing along, or a prompt for him to do more? Brandon had no practice in this charade. Well, except that one time when his aim had been Megan's exasperation, not her protection. He cleared his throat. "My mom has a friend at Spruce Acres, and she sent me with a bouquet to visit her. Megan happened to be there the same day."

"Aw!" the bombshell gushed. "Look, Meg! Your sweet little community-service project finally paid off. And we all thought it was a waste of time." The vixen stepped nearer and . . . *Holy flirt buckets!* She dared to run a finger down Brandon's free arm. Who on earth did this cat think she was? "Maybe I ought to try a little community service, hmmm?"

Maybe she ought to try some humility. Sheesh. Brandon scowled and glanced to gauge Megan's reaction. The young woman at his side swallowed and ignored his attention. In a move that was meant mostly to replace some distance from the blonde, Brandon moved closer to Megan, slipping his arm around her.

"It must have been quite a connection," the other brunette, who hadn't spoken yet, said. Her eyebrow slid upward, as if doubting Megan and Brandon's tale.

Megan went rigid. In the next breath, she leaned her head against his shoulder. "Sparks flew the moment we met."

That was true. There had definitely been sparks.

"So he's the reason you and Marcus . . . "

"No." The bombshell cut off the brunette with a sugary tone that was obviously meant to be anything but sweet. "Marcus told me *he* called it off. Isn't that so, Meg?"

Brandon could feel the woman under his arm wilting. And he felt bad for her. "What man in his right mind would walk away from this?" He reached to tuck a lock of wavy hair behind Megan's ear.

Gratitude filled her expression as she locked gazes with him. Hopefully, to their shallow audience, it looked like adoration. To secure the illusion, Brandon leaned down and pressed a soft kiss between her brows. Her hold on his waist tightened, but he had no notion if that was a warning grip or silent gratitude.

Either way, the move seemed to have done the trick. With a glint of haughty challenge, the bombshell turned and swayed her way through the foyer, her entourage following in unquestioning obedience.

Bizarre. And utterly absurd. Were all girls in this world of spoiled prestige like that? If so, at what age did they grow out of such nonsense? Did Megan normally act as such too? His stomach twisted imagining it, and it hardened at the realization that picturing the woman on his arm with that group of snobs wasn't too difficult.

He didn't like it one bit.

Megan didn't have to be like that. Though he'd witnessed her act the brat toward him, he'd also seen her be a better person. Something powerful within him revolted at the thought that she would act less than who she was to fit in with that flimsy bunch of cardboard beauties.

"Who was that?" Brandon continued to stare after the beautiful-but-really-not-attractive flounce sauntering into the worship center.

Megan remained under his arm, her response leaning toward melancholy. "Livy Isaacson."

"Livy Isaacson." Brandon turned to face Megan, dropping his touch and wondering at the feeling of regret stirred by doing so. He studied her drawn features. Was that a wince? And why did this fiery young woman who was more than capable of standing her ground look down, as if she was weak and bruised? As she moved toward the worship center, he gripped her fingers before she could pull away. "Is this Livy Isaacson someone we should care about?"

"She's an Isaacson."

"So?"

"They're one of the . . . " Her voice trailed off, and she turned her chin away from him.

"The wealthiest families here?"

Megan shrugged. "That. And most influential."

"Do you really think those things matter much?"

"You clearly don't understand this world." Raising her chin, some of her strength rebounded. "She's also a friend."

That was someone Megan considered a friend? Why?

This girl was a walking contradiction. She acted flimsy, spoiled, and superficial. And she could fire verbal shots like an Olympic marksman. But she was also entirely capable of work, and did, in fact, own a depth of kindness and compassion—things he'd witnessed while they'd worked together over the past weeks and while he'd accompanied her to Spruce Acres.

Did Megan Alexander even know who she was?

Brandon held her gaze steady, raising his brow. "Maybe you need to broaden your view."

Megan scowled, tugging her hand from his. "Maybe you shouldn't offer a commentary on things you know nothing about. There is history. Livy has been kind, and whether you like it or not, her opinion matters to me."

"Perhaps her opinion would matter less if you stopped living a shallow life, wasting the talents and opportunities you have—things that are profound and useful."

Anger darkened her eyes. "You have impossible standards—you know that, right? Does anyone gain your approval?" With that she turned and strode away.

That hook had barbs, and they sank in deep.

Ignoring the fresh sting, Brandon followed her into the large worship center, staying on her heels and sitting beside her when she found a semi-secluded spot in the left wing. She thought she could simply shut out what she didn't want to deal with.

Brandon wasn't the type. Although he did spend a significant amount of time alone out in the woods. Avoiding things he didn't want to deal with. In any case, they weren't addressing *his stuff* now.

He leaned into her, taking advantage of the fact that if she got up and walked away, she would draw the sort of attention she didn't want. "What does your dad think of your friendship with Livy?"

"I'm a full-grown woman."

"Maybe you are in body. As to the rest, that seems questionable." Brandon knew better than to believe the implication that what her dad thought didn't matter. He wouldn't be stuck in this arranged engagement if that was true. Not to mention, she'd said she was a daddy's girl. Also, his evaluation of Buck went up a few notches knowing that he didn't approve of Livy Isaacson's influence on his daughter.

"I don't like what you're insinuating." Megan stared forward as she hissed. "I'm not a child."

"Then don't act like one."

"It isn't childishness to admit that friendships matter."

"No. That's not childish. Good friendships should matter. What is childish is that you can't seem to distinguish between what is shallow and what has depth. I doubt you know what a good friend really is." Audrey, for example. Brandon had chatted with Tom and Shay Smiths' teenage daughter a few times at the Alexanders'. Why didn't Megan put as much weight into what Audrey thought? The girl was sweet, smart, and didn't treat Brandon like a hunk of meat for hire. The fact that Megan had basically ignored Audrey the moment they'd all arrived at church hadn't slipped Brandon's attention—and he wasn't impressed.

Megan pressed her lips together.

A better person resided within Megan. Maybe it was time someone told her so. "Livy, for example, all painted up and parading around like the queen who must be obeyed, she's nothing but a peacock with money. Her opinion about you and Marcus, or you and me, or you and anything else should not have the power to make you wilt."

Megan turned a glare on him. "You don't even know her. And in any case, I very much doubt anyone on the planet could meet your extraordinary expectations. What does that make you, Mr. Judgey?"

Refusing to back down, Brandon ignored that slap of truth and held her blazing gaze.

"I'll tell you what it makes you," Megan continued, chin raised. "It makes you too hard. Too severe."

Several heartbeats throbbed by, and then the flare in her eyes died, replaced by that trace of vulnerability he'd glimpsed moments before. A trickle of compassion filled his chest. He still couldn't understand her—this young woman who could stand on her own, spar verbally with the best of them and win, and also do good things—admirable things. Either she didn't realize she owned that strength, or had decided it was too much effort to employ.

She frustrated him. Again. And yet he wrestled with the urge to trace that stubborn lock of hair that drifted over her cheek.

Brandon had spent time in prayer over this volatile relationship he'd stepped into, and then over Megan herself. Strange, how one couldn't pray honestly for the welfare of another without having their heart soften for that person.

Was prayer God's chosen instrument for heart surgery?

A question it seemed that Connor or Jackson, or even Tyler, would be more likely able to answer than Brandon. Thoughts of his brothers, who had grown in godliness in ways that made Brandon feel small and feeble, needled him and further irritated the barbed hook Megan had only moments before embedded. Though at different points, Brandon had been disappointed in each one of his brothers, their stories had tugged on the desire to be a better man—a more godly man. One who wouldn't hold on to disappointments with such a death grip.

One who wouldn't be too hard any longer. Too severe.

So far, with Megan, he'd been failing spectacularly at that.

Moved by a steady stream that had warmed his heart—though it didn't make a lot of sense—and a renewal of the desire to be better, Brandon eased his rigid posture and reached to tuck that wayward lock of soft dark hair behind her ear, drawing her attention again. Megan's eyes widened at his gentle touch, and Brandon was nearly certain she held her breath.

So much potential... The thought caught him off guard, and for a moment he stared at her.

"Maybe I am judgey." An accusation he might have to examine later, even if it did sting. Hadn't he agreed to do this with the hope that he would grow? He lowered his hand to his lap. "But I don't think you're the wilting kind, Megan. Any girl who can work the way you have and who visits the elderly because she is kind and sees value in spending time with those who can give her wisdom, has nothing to feel inferior about."

Megan's lips parted, and she turned her attention back to the front. Even so, he caught the glitter of liquid glazing those jeweled eyes.

There was something there, and Brandon wanted to know what it was.

CHAPTER THIRTEEN

(in which something strange is happening)

HOW COULD ONE SMALL touch move her so profoundly? Especially when it had been Brandon Murphy's rough fingers sliding through her hair?

Did she care what he thought? Did it matter how he seemed to examine the depths of her heart when he looked at her with those intense brown eyes?

Did it matter what he found when he did so?

No!

Megan fought to hold on to that answer. But the struggle itself proved the reality otherwise. Something within her heart had flipped when Brandon had apologized for his behavior at Spruce Acres. She hadn't been able to ignore it since. Where she should have felt vindicated and a solidifying of dislike for the arrogant man, instead he'd nestled against her heart.

Against her plans and resolve, he was nestling deeper still.

It hadn't been just the tender way he'd smoothed that lock of hair away from her face. It'd been the words he'd spoken. Said softly, deeply, heartfelt. *I don't think you're the wilting kind.* A sincere compliment, one that Megan had no doubt was much higher praise than *you're pretty* or *you're popular* coming from a man like Brandon Murphy.

He saw strength in her. And he valued it. More, it mattered to her that it mattered to him.

What was this strange thing going on with her?

Having changed into comfortable jeans and an oversized sweatshirt after church, Megan finger combed her perfectly beach-wave-styled hair and gathered the dark mass of it into a ball at the back of her head. She left her room while still in process of securing the elastic that would hold it out of her face and wandered through the hall that contained two guest rooms. When she came to the curving staircase, she stepped down the distance. At the bottom, she paused, taking in the view through the window near the front doors. The sun summoned her out, the green grass echoing the invitation. But something inside her resisted. A melancholy that had latched on to her heart at some point over the past few days. Though she didn't want to admit it, there was a clear notion in her mind that it had something to do with Brandon.

I don't care what he thinks.

Goodness, she really felt the need to repeat that. Even so, as she turned from the scene outside and wandered toward the kitchen, where she was sure to find Shay and maybe Audrey, Megan began a fresh list of all the reasons why she didn't care what Brandon Murphy thought of her.

He has no idea what growing up was like. Poor Megan had to suffer in a gated community of millionaires in a beautiful, rural area. Such hardships!

He doesn't understand how hard it was to come in as the turkey girl. How everyone looked down on me because of how my dad made his fortune. How rough was that? Her father stumbled onto a fortune doing something he loved, changing her financial future. That was so sad.

Who the heck is Brandon Murphy anyway? What kind of man would pack up his ugly truck and leave his home to become engaged to a stranger who doesn't want to marry him? What kind of a girl would need her mom to write to a stranger and ask him to come and marry her daughter before she threw her life away?

He didn't even finish college. And wood splitting? Is that a real job? Point of fact, she hadn't even gone to college. She'd taken a few classes here and there but couldn't decide what she wanted to study, and as life was perfectly comfortable at home, she saw no reason to go. She didn't even have a job, nor was she on a path to getting one.

Anyway, above all, he's a bully. Harsh and severe. An infuriating man who gets under my skin on purpose. Only because she started it.

With every mental bullet point, a counterpoint fired fast and hard, each one hitting its mark. Suddenly she knew exactly why Brandon's statement at church had bothered her so much. It was because it *had* been a compliment. And because his saying so meant he'd been watching her. It was unnerving to think that serious man with those deep, intense eyes was watching her. Examining her, looking well past the surface.

He'd been peeking into her heart, and that was terribly alarming. Was there anything worth searching for in there?

Clarity hit right before she passed into the kitchen, where she could hear both Shay and Audrey. Sucking in a breath, Megan had to stop. She pressed her back against the cool wall and shut her eyes against the stabbing realization.

Megan wasn't sure she had anything Brandon would consider worth finding.

For a girl who had spent most of her life praying she'd be popular so she would be happy, that thought didn't feel very nice. And once formed, it held like a grappling hook—sharp and securely unmoving.

"Meg?"

Audrey's cheerful voice distracted her from the sudden ache. Pushing away from the wall, Megan painted up a smile and entered the kitchen. "Hi, Audrey. How was school this week?"

Audrey's light-brown gaze gleamed with the usual admiration. "I finished that paper for history. Thank you for taking me to see Mrs. Hadley. Her stories from her time in East Berlin helped so much. I think I'll get a good grade."

Megan squeezed her shoulders. "I'm glad."

At seventeen, Audrey was a lovely, sweet girl. She and Megan had basically grown up together, as Audrey's mom and dad—Shay and Tim Smith—had come to work for the Alexanders within six months of their moving into the luxury home. The little family of three lived in a cottage on the edge of the Alexander property, up the creek from the newer guest cottage now occupied by Brandon.

Audrey had often accompanied her parents when they came to work, especially during school breaks, and she and Megan had gotten along wonderfully. Audrey had become almost a little sister to Megan. It had been nice to have someone around with whom Megan didn't have to try to be special. Audrey was quiet, a little shy, easygoing, and likable. She also had admired Megan from the start and didn't seem to be outgrowing that.

Selfishly, Megan rather liked that. Surely something that would make Brandon frown in that disapproving way he had. *Mr. Judgey.*

Megan pushed aside all thoughts of Brandon. It was their day off, after all. They didn't have to endure each other for the rest of the afternoon. Such a relief.

Wasn't it?

She refocused on Audrey and Shay. "What are we making in here?" Inhaling a long breath, she took in the warm aroma of white chocolate and sweet raspberries.

"Cheesecakes." Shay shot a smile from the other side of the massive white marble island. "For the spring gala."

Ahh. Megan's favorite. "That's why it smells divine. But why are you doing this on your day off?"

"This is one of my side hustles, sweetie. Your mom let me use her big kitchen for it." Shay winked and put another springform pan in the oven.

"Ah." Shay often took on extra work. Every member of the Smith family, it seemed, was always doing some kind of hustle. And there was Megan, doing a whole lot of not much with her life.

Of the two types, Megan knew exactly which Brandon would approve of, and it wasn't her.

"Are you okay?" Audrey nudged Megan's shoulder.

"I'm fine. Can I help in here?"

"I always need a taste tester or two." Shay slid a mini-cheesecake across the counter, along with two forks.

"My favorite job." Dropping onto a stool at the island, Megan picked up a fork.

Audrey sat on the stool to Megan's left. "Mine too." She raised her fork, and Megan clanked hers against it.

Grinning, Shay set to combining ingredients. "After your approval, and the two cakes I've got cooling are completely rested, you girls can wrap them for the freezer. Then I think the garden is calling. You should both go out and get some vitamin D."

Megan slowly scraped the white chocolate raspberry bit of heaven off her fork and groaned. "Perfection, as always."

Shay nodded. "Good."

Loading another forkful, Megan asked, "Would Tim mind if I cut a couple dozen ranunculus? They're a favorite with the ladies at Spruce Acres." That was something, at least. Wasn't it? Did Brandon think well on Megan's spending time with her ladies? Her other friends thought it was a ridiculous waste of her time. Even Marcus had insinuated that it was beneath her.

Laughing, Shay looked at her. "They're your flowers. I'm sure you can do whatever you want, as long as your mom doesn't mind."

"Tim works so hard with the garden." Megan slid another bite in before she continued. "I'd hate to ruin it."

"If the ladies appreciate the flowers, then I'm sure Daddy will be thrilled." Audrey leaned to drop her fork into the sink, leaving the last bite of mini-cheesecake for Megan. "I'll help you cut them, if you want?"

So Audrey. Pleasant. Helpful. Not a trace of ulterior motives in her simple offer. Oh, if everyone could be such a person.

The type of girl Brandon would approve of.

Megan's stomach constricted, and she found she couldn't finish that last bite of deliciousness Audrey had left for her. Instead, she also deposited her fork and summoned a smile that felt shaky. "Let's go do it then." She rounded the island, opened a drawer on the far side, and plucked two pairs of sharp scissors from it.

The girls left the kitchen and wound their way to the back of the house, where a sunroom opened onto an expansive flagstone patio. It curved gracefully around the water feature, containing native boulders and shrub beds, most of which were budding out on that midspring day.

Everything wonderful about summer lay poised to erupt. So much possibility! Simple, stunning beauty.

Much like Audrey. Megan glanced at the younger woman. Bright copper hair, tightly coiled with natural curl, was kept off her face with a simple white kerchief. Audrey wore little to no makeup, leaving her bronze freckles exposed to the world. She owned soft brown eyes and was an understated beauty. She was also wholesome and shy. And though she appeared delicate with a small frame and a tendency to remain quietly at the side of things, Megan knew Audrey to be a stout worker. And a faithful friend.

All things that Brandon would indeed approve of.

Her tummy twisted again, and an ugly feeling wrung out. Jealousy, and Megan knew it instantly. Why she would feel that way about a man she cared nothing about and a girl she adored, Megan couldn't define. So she ignored it as they continued through the sculpted backyard.

They followed the path that wound around the water that flowed over stones, recently set back in motion after a long winter's rest, and descended three flagstone steps leading to a wide arch flanked by evergreen boxwoods and in early summer would display the heavenly fragranced sweet pea vines that mingled with the later-flowering honeysuckle.

The flagstone path continued around a groomed bright-green stretch of grass and brought them to another berm, this one long and wide, the whole of which was currently flooded with ruffly, cup-shaped blooms in shades of pinks. Some blossoms were open, their soft petals fluttering happily in the breeze. Others were still closed, though color cracked through the green protection of the bud.

Ah, the beauty. Megan stopped to take in the symphony of delight before her. How could one not love them?

"Two dozen?" Audrey asked, reaching for a pair of scissors from Megan's hand.

Megan glanced at her companion, and again she was struck by how pretty Audrey was. Not just in appearance.

Audrey lived in a small cottage her family didn't even own. She rarely wore designer clothes unless they'd been handed off to her by Megan. Audrey's social circle was small and unremarkable. Actually, she spent most of her free time with her parents or with Megan and seemed perfectly content to do so. She attended the public school and rode the bus to get there. Everything in Audrey's life seemed beneath Megan's when it came to material things, and yet the girl was always soft and kind.

Always, it seemed, happy.

The pain gripped Megan's stomach again, and this time the envy had nothing to do with Brandon. Audrey was happy in her simple life.

Was Megan truly happy in hers?

She should be. How could she not be? She absolutely shouldn't be anything less. After all, she had everything. All comfort and beauty and ease surrounded her. And yet as Megan considered it, and traced the past decade or so, she saw an ever-growing struggle to chase happiness. That had been the whole reason she'd said yes to Marcus Kensington. He was her next step to the elusive *happy* Megan desired more than anything.

Something was wrong with her.

"Meg?" Audrey stood from snipping a third stem from the wave of pink flowers. "Everything okay?"

"Yes." Megan swallowed and quickly smiled. "Of course."

"You seem off today."

Bending at a color-cracked stem that would likely open into a dark fuchsia, Megan busied herself with gathering flowers. "My mind is scattered, I guess."

"Because of Brandon?"

Megan glanced at her. "What do you think of him?"

With a thoughtful look, Audrey tipped her head. "He's a little on the serious side." Then she grinned wide, pink dusting her cheeks. "But he's handsome."

Megan sighed. "He is."

"But?"

"He's arrogant. And a bully. And definitely way too serious."

An immediate frown pulled Audrey's expression. "Does your dad know he's a bully? Maybe he'd change his mind if he knew—"

"I'll call him right now." Megan's father's voice cut off whatever Audrey was going to say. "I'm sure he'll come over, and we can discuss it."

Both girls turned. Daddy came around the side of the house with Tim Smith striding beside him.

"Hello, girls." Daddy grinned. "Stealing Tim's hard work, are we?"

Heat crept up Megan's neck as she held a bundle of five ranunculus in one hand and the scissors in the other. She felt like a child caught shoplifting. "Shay said she thought it'd be okay."

Tim laughed. "They're not mine."

Daddy smacked his back. "You grow them. How do you summon such things from the ground? Back at Sugar Creek, I tried to grow things. I'm telling you, I could wilt a dandelion with one look."

Though he glanced toward his feet, Megan caught Tim's humble pleasure. "Neither he who plants nor he who waters is anything. It is God who makes things grow." He looked up and settled his gentle gaze on his daughter, standing near Megan, and winked. "We simply get to tend the garden."

"You tend it well," Daddy said. "Even if my daughter has a penchant for looting it."

"For the ladies," Megan defended herself.

Approval in his eyes, Tim nodded. "In that case, loot away."

Daddy pointed toward an iron table centered on the flagstone patio, and both men stepped toward it.

"Let me call him," Daddy said.

Call who? Turning back to gathering flowers, Megan sensed even before the question formed in her mind who would be summoned.

After a brief pause, Dad spoke into his phone. "Brandon. What are you up to this afternoon?"

That had been exactly whom she'd guessed. Megan nearly groaned as she glanced Audrey's direction. "The beast has been summoned."

"Will he come?" Audrey whispered back.

"He moved here at Mom's request." She peaked her brows. "The mercenary moves as told."

Audrey cast a sweetly suspicious glance toward their fathers.

"Don't let him bulldoze you, Audrey. He's only here for six months." Megan stood, nearly a full dozen stems in her hand. "Actually, just a bit over five now. Thank heavens."

"I have no doubt you'll come out victorious, Meg. No one can roll over you."

Though Megan tipped her chin with a smirk and a nod, inside she stumbled over that declaration. Not unlike what Brandon had said of her earlier—that she wasn't the wilting kind. Both had meant the statement as a compliment, and maybe it truly would be, if it were true.

But it wasn't.

Megan was a flimsy girl, driven by the whims of people with wealth and social standing, and unable to grasp happiness the way Audrey had done effortlessly. She didn't like that about herself. And she really didn't like that Brandon's forced presence in her life had dawned such a revelation. It made her feel shaky, lost, and wanting. None of those were anything like happy.

Unfortunately, Megan had a nagging sense that even once rid of the stern and intense Brandon Murphy, she'd be left with the hollow knowledge he'd revealed about herself.

What would she do then?

CHAPTER FOURTEEN

(in which a tricky job is ahead)

BRANDON GATHERED HIS FISHING gear from the patch of creek-side grass and sighed. So much for an afternoon alone, one during which he'd hoped to regather his bearings, redefine his purpose in this assignment. And to pray. That most of all, because Brandon knew he needed it.

"What am I doing?" As he closed his tackle box and secured a fly onto the patch of his vest designated for such, Brandon spoke into the gentle sound of moving water and birds calling high in the trees.

The grand plan was not revealed to him in that solitary moment. Instead, he had the next thing: go to the big house and meet with Buck Alexander and his groundskeeper/handyman/lifelong friend, Tim Smith. Go, because he'd been asked to. Go, because his life had now come under the direction of the Alexanders. Resentment rose. *You agreed to this voluntarily. No one made you do it.* True, except it didn't feel so. He'd felt compelled.

Brandon set his tack in the passenger side of his truck, then removed his ball cap and mussed his hair. "Is this what You wanted?" He glanced skyward, as if he expected heaven's reply to come down. Only the chatter of birds drifted to him from above.

Replacing his hat, he shut the door and rounded the front of the truck. Having only the facts of the present to function on—that he was there, that he'd agreed to this outlandish idea, and that Buck would like to talk with him about something that afternoon—Brandon left the solace of the river and made his way to the big house. As he bounced his way over the dirt trail until his tires met the smoother surface of the road, he wondered if he'd have to endure Megan's glares when he arrived.

Into the flare of resentment that thought provoked came a brief but distinctive intrusion. After he'd apologized to her, Megan's touch on his arm outside the dining room had been gentle, sincere, and unexpectedly moving. Perhaps because the look in her eyes when she'd glanced up to him had been unmasked humility and honest gratitude. She'd been truly pretty. Not just in face, but for a moment, he'd glimpsed a girl he could actually like.

If he was being honest, though that might be difficult in this matter, Brandon would have to admit he'd like to see that girl again. Had even breathlessly hoped for it at church earlier that day.

Instead, she'd called him too severe. Likely because he was, particularly with her. But it drove him mad to know she was capable of more than she was being. He sighed as these musings continued to tie him in knots. This would have been so much easier if Buck had left them alone—not required that they spend every day together and now, on his one break for the week, summoned him away from his solace.

Pulling into the drive in front of the big house, Brandon remembered Megan's demand that he park in back so the snooty neighborhood wouldn't see his ugly truck. Immediately all imaginings of a softer version of Megan Alexander vanished. Who cared what his truck looked like? More, what neighbors were going to see it? The Alexanders' property backed up to federal land, and hardly anyone passed this way.

Megan was not that gentle, humble girl he'd been longing for another glimpse of—that had simply been a moment of . . . something. Not anything real or lasting. She was a snooty brat and that was all. Brandon was not going to spend his life trying to appease a snooty brat.

He parked in front of the house and shut the engine off. Let her highness come and sulk about it.

Smacking the door shut, Brandon strode toward the steps that would guide him to the front door.

"Brandon." Buck intercepted him on the path that led to the back of the house. "We're on the patio. Come on back."

Nodding, Brandon adjusted his direction, and as soon as he was near enough, Buck smacked his shoulder. "Sorry to interrupt your fishing. We could have come to you."

"No problem. Nothing was biting anyway."

"Tim asked to meet with you. He and I often spend Sunday afternoons together."

Buck spent his afternoon off with his hired man. Brandon tried to imagine Megan lowering herself to such a thing. Impossible. How on earth was the father so opposite the daughter?

"He mentioned a concern with a tree near their place," Buck continued. "Just seemed like good timing, since none of us are about our business today."

"Of course." The tension pulling at the back of Brandon's neck loosened. Spending time with Buck wouldn't be a strain. Not the way it was with Megan. And he was being paid to deal with tree issues on the property, so that made sense.

The path opened onto the wide flagstone patio. At the round iron table in the middle, Tim sat with a tall glass of ice water. When he looked at Brandon, he stood. "Brandon. It's good to see you again. Sorry to pester you on your day off."

Brandon met his outstretched hand. "No bother."

"Shay's making cheesecake. Can I offer you some as appeasement?" Tim gestured toward a plate on the table.

"Not gonna turn that down." Brandon patted his belly. "I've enjoyed your wife's talent in the kitchen."

Pride shone in Tim's eyes. "She has that." He turned toward the yard, and Brandon followed his look toward a bank of vivid pink blossoms. "Audrey, come and say hello to Brandon."

Two forms peeked up from behind the berm flowerbed, hands loaded with unopened stems of flowers. Dark hair tied loosely back, dressed in a worn sweatshirt and jeans, and a load of ready-to-burst flowers tucked into the crook of one arm, Megan looked like she could be in a feature spread of one of his mom's flower magazines.

Both young women rounded the flowerbed and made their way up the flagstone steps. Brandon moved his focus from Megan to Audrey. She was young—probably a couple years younger than his younger brother Brayden, which would likely put her in high school. Her copper hair was tied back in a similar fashion to Megan's, and if she wore make up, Brandon couldn't tell.

Tim tucked the shorter, younger girl under his arm. "Aren't these two a pair?"

A brush of faint pink dusted Audrey's cheeks. "Like sisters." She looked at Megan, and in that glance Brandon saw the clear evidence of hero adoration. He knew, because he'd been that way once too, with Tyler. Audrey's expression clearly declared that in her eyes, Megan was everything Audrey hoped to be.

Poor sweet lamb.

Looking back at Megan, Brandon expected to find the heiress divine with her nose stuck in the air. Instead, he found a girl with dirt in her fingernails, winking at Audrey with a shared mischievous gleam. Along with another strange heart lurch, curiosity billowed in Brandon. The girls were a pair at the Alexander place. He'd witnessed it a few other times. Just not in public.

But not when they were around Megan's other friends. Why? And was Audrey really okay with that? She shouldn't be. Brandon wasn't.

The object of his frustration turned her gaze to him. One challenging brow slipped subtly upward, but not in a snooty way. In a . . . fiery, attractive, teasing way.

"Look at you, with dirt on your hands," he said.

"Didn't think I could do it, did you?"

"Of your own volition?" He shook his head, the corners of his mouth twitching to be set free. "No."

"He *is* a bully, Meg." Audrey laughed outright. "How are you ever going to survive?"

Brandon froze, suddenly caught in something that was either amusing or insulting. Which was it? He looked at Audrey, believing he could decipher their banter better from the more innocent of the pair. Except the girl gave him a sly smile and then turned away. A mini-Megan? Heaven help them all.

"What are you doing?" Brandon spit the question out a bit harshly and without considering they had an audience.

A quizzical look creased Megan's brow. "What do you mean, what am I doing?"

With that innocent girl who clearly adored her, that was what he'd meant. But now remembering both Buck and Tim being there, he wasn't about to toss that out in public. "With the flowers?"

The smile that lit Megan's face was a wonder. All joy. No calculative snipe. Brandon's breath caught. *There she is again . . .* That softer, truly pretty version of Megan that Brandon had convinced himself had been an illusion. No illusion. She stood there in the flesh, drawing Brandon's intrigue with a strength a small girl such as herself shouldn't possess.

"We're taking them in to the house." She lifted her chin with a sassy challenge that wasn't off-putting. At all. "Then on Tuesday you can help me deliver them to the ladies. You did say you needed something to do at Spruce Acres."

Brandon swallowed a chuckle. "As you wish, your highness."

Stepping toward the house, the way Audrey had gone, Megan slid him a glance that was ornery and attractive all at once. What had just happened?

Brandon had lost another piece of his mind, that was what.

"I see we're no longer giving each other the cold shoulder." Buck brought Brandon out of his head.

"What?"

Humor glinted in Buck's gaze as he lowered onto a chair. "After church, things were a bit chilly, don't you think?"

Buck was watching them closer than Brandon had suspected. Unease moved in his gut.

What would Buck think if he'd witnessed the way Brandon had handled that first visit to Spruce Acres? He wouldn't be sitting there amused. Nor would he hold Brandon in as high esteem as he did now. And what was with that anyway? Buck really didn't even know Brandon. Why did he trust him as he did?

Dad. That was why. Buck thought the world of Dad. If Brandon didn't want to ruin that—and to be sure, he did not—he'd better get his head on straight.

Brandon cleared his throat and sat on a chair facing both Buck and Tim. "It's been a long week. Just needed a break."

"Megan has a way of driving one crazy when she has a mind to."

Stone cold fact. Brandon probably shouldn't agree with it though.

Buck continued. "Is she working with you okay?"

"We're ahead of where I thought we'd be." She was a surprisingly good worker. And they'd found a rhythm between them. Should he tell her father that?

"Excellent. I think there will be a few days in the next week or two when she will want to help Shay as they prepare for the spring gala. And then there's Spruce Acres. But other than that, plan on having her help."

Megan would help Shay?

Megan was friends with Audrey. Was easy with both Shay and Tim. Did as her father asked, though sometimes begrudgingly. She could and would work. And she loved those old ladies at the retirement home with dignity and respect. None of which were marks of a true brat.

Who was this woman he'd entangled himself with?

She was a contradiction. A mystery. Before he could stop it, the hook of fascination sank in deeper, and Brandon was mildly aware that there might be trouble. For some undefined reason, however, he didn't want to admit it.

He turned to Tim. "Tell me about the tree issue."

Nodding, the men complied with the change in subject, and before ten minutes passed, and before Megan could make a reappearance, all three men loaded into Brandon's ugly truck to see the issue in person.

Brandon assessed the problem quickly.

The lodge pole pine soared proudly toward the sky. One of the oldest and tallest in the space. And now, dead. A precarious issue, as the hill on which it had sunk in roots sloped toward the Smiths' home. A surge of strong wind rolling off the rise could push the trunk down, and the trajectory of the fall could be disastrous. Especially with where the power lines to the cabin ran.

"It definitely needs to come out." Arms crossed, Brandon tipped his gaze skyward and then examined the lay of the land. "It'll be a bit tricky though."

"I thought so too," Tim said. "Or I'd have done it myself."

Brandon glanced at him. "I might need your help."

"Name the day." Tim glanced at Buck, who nodded approval.

Brandon adjusted his hat. "I'll need another week or so to finish up the area I started. Next week?"

"That'll work."

Another check over the precarious job and Brandon dipped a nod, ignoring the pit that yawned in his gut. It was a tricky job—most of his work was done in undeveloped forest areas. While he was always careful not to damage healthy trees, that was a little different than needing to make certain not to damage a man's home. Adding in the tilt of the old tree, the angle of the slope, and the added obstacle of the power lines, everything together was a puzzle that would require precision planning.

He could do it though. With Tim's help, he was certain. Not to mention Megan's. She'd proven herself able, even if she did act like a brat sometimes.

They'd get it done.

CHAPTER FIFTEEN

(in which it's not Brandon's fault)

"NO ESCORT TODAY?" BRANDON pushed through the screen door and stepped onto the front porch. For the past weeks, Buck had been dropping Megan off. Today, her Rubicon was parked in the drive.

Megan lifted her chin, tipping her face so that he could see her smirk from beneath the bill of her hat as she climbed the steps. "I told you I'm not a child."

The screen door slapped shut behind him, and Brandon sipped his coffee. Megan crossed her arms and leaned against the rock piling post. Dressed in what he assumed had now become her work boots, a pair of worn skinny jeans, and a long-sleeved T-shirt, and hair tucked into the nasty old ball cap she'd not returned to him, she looked ready to work.

And really good.

Man, where was his head? This woman was a pain in his neck. Who cared if she wore work clothes well?

"Are you slacking off this morning?" A dimple poked into one cheek as she tilted her head and met him with sass in those jeweled eyes.

Brandon couldn't stop a soft chuckle. "Just finishing my coffee."

"Just leave it here." Patting the railing beside her, Megan's smile bloomed full. "Might come in handy later."

Now he laughed out loud. "Not a chance." He drank another swallow and then walked toward the railing, where he flung the remaining liquid onto the lilacs below. "You're bright and cheerful this morning. Did you get rid of the pea under your mattress?"

After momentary confusion scrunched her face, Megan rolled her eyes. "You're almost clever. One or two more fairy tales in your education, and you could have been something." She pushed off the post and followed him into the house. "Tell me, which princess story was your favorite?"

Ugh. He'd walked into that, hadn't he? Striding into the kitchen, he set the empty mug on the counter and snatched his hat off a hook near the back door.

Megan continued on his trail, suddenly clapping her hands. "Oh! Even better, tell me your Disney princess crush!"

Pulling the hat on low, he pinned a glare on her, though another laugh threatened to break his scowl. "You're ridiculous."

"Aww, little Brandon had a crush!" She folded her hands and tucked them under her chin, leaning into his shoulder and looking up at him with batting lashes. "Should I guess?"

"No."

"Couldn't have been a princess. Brandon Murphy does not like pretty damsels who cannot fix their own problems."

"Yet here I am." He placed a hand on her back and nudged her forward.

Megan laughed, filling the house with a confident, joyous sound that caught Brandon so that he nearly stopped midstride. A sudden need to hear it again snared his purpose. Megan paused beside him and met his study with honest humor.

A moment passed. Or maybe five?

Megan blinked and looked toward the front door. Was that a blush coloring her cheeks? Warmth creeped into Brandon's chest, and he had the most peculiar urge to touch her.

Weird. Why did that keep happening?

Brandon cleared his throat. "I have an idea."

"Is that rare for you?"

"Cute."

A full smile lifted her mouth as she looked back at him. "I thought you didn't think so."

"You're allowed three real questions a day." He began moving again, taking her elbow as he strode toward the door. "Don't waste them."

"Real questions about what?"

"Me."

"Ah! The privilege I have gained!" Dramatic flair was clearly in Megan's toolbox, and she employed it steadily as they walked to his truck. "I get to pry into the mysterious world of an isolated woodsman. Perhaps I'll uncover the strange motivations of a mercenary? Maybe discover what is with his unnatural fascination with plaid flannel? The possibilities! How did I ever get so lucky?"

"Your mother intervened on your wayward path." Brandon kept his tone dry as he opened the passenger door for her. "That's one. You have two left for the day."

Her mirth immediately died as she settled on the seat. "No way. That wasn't about you at all."

"My game. My rules." Shutting her door, he rounded the front of the vehicle and climbed in.

She waited only until the engine rumbled and they were pulling out of the drive. "It wasn't a real question."

The corner of his mouth threatened to poke up. "I told you not to waste them."

"Huh. You *are* a bully."

"So you've said."

"Fine then. But you only get a daily allowance of three real questions about me."

"What makes you think I want to know about you?"

"You came here to marry me."

He turned off the main road and onto the small trail to their work area. "Think that's gonna happen?"

"We already agreed. Not a chance."

"Then why would I bother?"

"You're stuck with me for the next six months."

Brandon snorted. "Five months."

"In that case, why would I want to know about you?"

"I don't know." Was bantering with a girl always this fun? Brandon hadn't done much of it, but he'd watched his younger brother, Brayden, tease his longtime girlfriend, Leah. He hadn't understood why the pair had so often volleyed. Clarity was dawning. "Why'd you blush back there?"

"I did not blush."

He chuckled.

"I didn't!" By the pitch of Megan's voice, she knew she had.

They came to the spot where they'd started working last week, and Brandon backed up to the eight-foot-long pile of eighteen-inch-long logs that had been stacked neatly. This pile had been a couple of trees that had been dead for well over a year. Should be dry enough. At the end of the day, they'd load the full cord into the back of his truck, and he could work on splitting logs in the evenings. He shut the engine off and set his gaze on Megan, smirking.

Those lovely eyes met his and widened. And then . . .

He grinned wider. "You're blushing."

She pressed fingers to cheeks. "I'm not." Her protest was a flimsy whisper.

Acting on an impulse that had never once pressed him before, Brandon leaned close until his mouth hovered near her ear. Her warm sweet scent made him heady, and the wisps of wayward hair escaping her hat tickled his face. "How about now?"

"How about now what?" she whispered back.

"Are you blushing?"

She angled her face so that her breathy response fanned across his cheek. "Are you?"

Delicious warmth bloomed in his chest and flared up his neck. Surely the honest answer was yes. "Is that one of your official questions?"

"No. Is it one of yours?"

He pulled away, hoping the dark whiskers of his shadowed stubble hid the heat still in his face. "Yes. Why'd you blush in the kitchen?"

Megan visibly swallowed. Then set her chin at that arrogant angle. "Because you stared at me. Why were you staring?"

"Is that an official question?"

"Yes. Which means you have to answer."

Though he couldn't understand himself, Brandon nodded. "You laughed."

"I laughed?"

"Yes, and not in a snooty way. I liked the sound of it."

All challenge drained from her expression, quickly replaced with something soft. And lovely.

What in the blazes was going on with him? *Flirting!* He was flirting. With the Megan monster. Brandon had never been the flirting type. That was Matt and Jackson. And Brayden—him more than them all. Not Brandon. He'd better get his personality figured out—and his pulse under control. Hadn't Mom always said she never needed to worry about Brandon carelessly breaking a girl's heart? He was too responsible. Too serious to be that idiotic.

He forced his stare from her entirely too endearing face. "It startled me that something so sweet could come from a brat." There. Back to normal.

Was *jerk* normal for him?

Swallowing a growl, Brandon turned and let himself out of the truck. He had work to do. They had work to do. Too, he was determined to keep the facts straight. They were as follows: he was never going to marry a brat, and he had a whole lot of dead wood to clear before he could leave her behind.

And he certainly wasn't going to flirt with her. He wasn't the type.

***

Megan rolled her shoulders back, noting that she wasn't nearly as sore midway through the day as she had been the first week of this nonsense. A sense of accomplishment filled her. She was getting stronger. And surprisingly, she didn't loathe the work.

In fact, when she'd awakened that morning, she almost looked forward to it. There was something empowering about discovering that she could keep up with Brandon, and even contribute to what he was doing. He'd said the end of last week that they were farther along than he'd expected. That was pretty close to a compliment. As had been that line he'd rumbled at church.

She wasn't the wilting type.

Megan embraced that with a quiet smile. She'd never thought such a thing about herself before. Having it dance through her mind was simple joy. What a beautiful day! There was the benefit of fresh, cool air, piney goodness, and the unending sounds of forest life. And an emerging strength Megan never knew she could own.

And maybe Brandon wasn't so bad either. At least, for a few moments at the start of the day he'd shown a hint that he could be something other than dour faced and taciturn. For a sweet second, he'd even been . . . a little breathtaking. Unbidden, the impression of his breath moving the hair near her ear summoned another round of gooseflesh at the back of her neck. Why had he done that?

Would he ever do it again?

The rush of warm adrenaline provoked by simply the memory of it told her plainly that she hoped for it. What on earth was with that? She'd never been so . . . ignited by the simple nearness of a man.

Before she was forced to ponder that reality, Brandon appeared. He set down the metal canteen he'd carried and fixed his attention on a towering pine.

He pointed. "That one will need to come down."

Following the direction of his finger, Megan took in the tree Brandon planned to put his chainsaw into next. Tall and regal, and still mostly green, Megan cringed. "It's not all the way dead. Can't you treat it or something?"

He shook his head. "See the top third? All the branches are dead. Beetles kill from the top down. And look." Starting toward the tree, he waved her to follow, which she did. "These holes, with sawdust and pitch? All of them are entry holes. This big guy is infested, and the gray streaking you saw in the other trees we've cut up? That's from a fungus the beetles inject into the wood. It blocks the sap, and if the sap can't run, the tree won't live. This pine is already dead—he just doesn't know it yet."

Megan looked skyward and then ran her gaze along the trunk. There were indeed many holes with sawdust and pitch. She expanded her view to the other trees. "How many more will need to come down?"

With a sigh, Brandon stepped back, turned slowly, studying the area. "After this we're about done here. Unfortunately, we're late in the season to do much in the way of prevention. The larvae have already hatched, left their dead host, and have found a live one. I likely need to come back in the winter, when they're not active, and take out whatever they infect this season. If your dad wants to prevent more damage." Hands on his waist, he turned back to her. "In the meantime, we'll chip the small dead branches, burn the infected bark, and chop the good-and-dead stuff for firewood."

That was more words than she'd heard the man utter at once since he'd arrived. And all intelligent. If only that stern face would break. What would it take to find that man she'd bantered with this morning?

Megan followed him as he pivoted away. "Where did you learn all this?"

Shrugging, Brandon moved back toward the truck. "Some in college. Not a lot though."

"I thought you didn't go to college."

"I started. Didn't finish."

"And?"

"And I read a lot of material and watch a lot of videos put out by the extension office, and I've spent some time with the arbor specialist at my local office. Colleges aren't the sole possessors of a useful education."

Megan met him at the tailgate of the truck, where he tugged on his leather work gloves. She chuckled quietly. "Daddy says there are a lot of highly educated idiots in our world."

Brandon grunted. Likely that was an agreement.

Perhaps there was a commonality between her father and Brandon Murphy that had lent an easy bond between the two men so quickly. If so, that was interesting. On the whole, Megan adored her father, though he'd acted high handed with her lately. Daddy was a good man, a determined man, a fiercely protective man. Not a perfect man, but one of character and strength.

What if she discovered Brandon Murphy possessed all those traits? Could that erase the fact that he'd been summoned into a place in her world that she resented?

Dare she even entertain such thoughts?

"Why aren't you at school?" His cool tone sounded almost condescending. How on earth did that make sense?

Megan stiffened her spine and lifted her chin. "I took a gap year."

"Just one?"

She crossed her arms. "More than one."

"How'd that go over with your parents?"

"Daddy approved."

Brandon nodded, expression concealing all thoughts. Was he judging her? Seemed like the mercenary she knew—all superior and judgey. And now a hypocrite. "I didn't want to waste Daddy's money when I didn't know what to study."

He messed with one of the dumb chainsaws, barely listening.

The need to defend herself made her edgy. "Daddy said that was smart. Said as long as I didn't sit around and waste my life, there was no reason to run after something I couldn't even define."

A grunt. That was all he managed. The infuriating man.

"I go to Spruce Acres and spend quite a bit of time there," Megan continued in a rush. Why did she feel it necessary to defend herself to this man?

Finally, he looked up. She expected to find censure in his intense gaze. Instead, there was something else entirely. It made her pulse surge and pleasant warmth flood her belly.

Smile at me!

Where had that weed of a thought sprouted from?

Brandon didn't smile. But he held her with a look that wasn't entirely unpleasant. "You've been volunteering at Spruce Acres for two years?"

"No. For eight years. My mother took me when I was twelve—and since I know you're going to ask, I wasn't a willing participant back then. Things change, and I started to enjoy visiting with the ladies. The last two years have allowed me to go more often and to spend more time with them."

The tight corners of his mouth softened, and Megan's heart skipped at the idea that Brandon would look at her with full approval. Maybe even admiration?

He focused on his equipment. Megan exhaled disappointment. Which was dumb. She regathered her sanity. "That's two for you today."

Barely a nod over his shoulder. Then, "Break time is over." Brandon lifted the larger of his two chainsaws and then shouldered a coiled rope. "This one will be tricky. I don't want to damage the healthy trees around it —that will only worsen the beetle problem. There's an alley right here." He drew a line from the tree he was going to cut and through the forest. "I'll need your help to make sure it falls exactly right."

She almost puffed up hearing him say he needed her help. Goodness but she was on quite a ride when it came to her reactions to Brandon. "Okay. What do I do?"

He nudged his chin to the rope. "I'll rig this. And I'll get the initial cuts so that it should fall where I want it to go. But I'll need you holding the end of the rope to help guide it, just in case it decides not to cooperate."

"In case you miss?"

A wry grin moved his mouth. "Exactly."

Megan looked away, not allowing herself to enjoy the subtly boyish way his eyes danced, and yet unable to miss it. What a paradox Brandon was turning out to be. This stern man whose intense eyes could straighten the posture of a nun and make her think she must have something to confess. He'd teased her in the most flirtatious way that day. And had even admitted to the possibility of making a mistake.

Was it possible this iron-armored man was human? Not a cold-blooded mercenary who enjoyed making her miserable?

Megan tallied the little insights she'd gleaned so far. Brandon owned a deep, quiet laugh, though it was perhaps a little bit of work to rouse. He was a man whose hard-earned smile transformed such a stern, serious countenance into something warm and inviting.

Megan wished he would smile at her again. She didn't even bother denying it.

Brandon climbed partway up the large tree, a task that made him seem younger than he had before, and also looked precarious. He then looped his rope, tied some sort of fancy knot that would have likely taken Megan hours to figure out, and then scrambled back down the bark until he landed with a thud on the forest floor. With calculated purpose, he strode to another large pine, threaded the rope between two thick branches and around the trunk, and then walked to where Megan stood.

"Stay here, out of the way. Listen to what I tell you. If I say pull, use every one of your ninety-five pounds."

Pshh. Ninety-five pounds. Megan looked to the ground, hiding an eye roll. She weighed significantly more than ninety-five pounds.

"Pay attention, Meg."

She glanced back up at him.

"It's dangerous work. You have to pay attention."

With a mocking solute, she stood at attention. "Got it."

No smile.

Brandon turned from her, paused one more time to check his setup, and then strode back to where he'd set down his chainsaw. A couple of pulls, and the quiet forest was filled with the buzz of the machine. He cut the initial wedge, checking his chainsaw and then the space where he wanted the tree to fall. From an earlier lesson on tree felling, during which Megan had pretended boredom, she knew he was verifying his line.

Wedge cut, he kicked the free wood away from the trunk and began to score a line into the bark for his back cut, leaving a couple inches on either side near the wedge for the hinge. Again, Brandon looked at the space he'd wanted the tall pine to land. His deep breath was visible.

As soon as he moved to begin the back cut, Megan's heart hammered, and the hot flow of blood made her tremble. She looked up to the top of the tree, the dead needles seeming to brush the blue of the sky. Goodness, this pine was tall. One wrong move, one slight miscalculation . . .

Lord, please help him do this right.

This could end badly.

He knows what he's doing, right?

Perhaps. But she didn't. Megan looked to the rope in her hands and then gripped. The loud buzz of the chain sawing through wood softened to a consistent rumble of an idling engine.

"Give it a tug, Meg. Nice and easy."

She glanced at him in time to see him press a shoulder against the trunk. The tree creaked and then swayed, but it went left of the direction Brandon had ordained.

"Pull, Meg!"

With a hard grip, Megan did as told, digging her heels into the dirt and trying to act as a counterweight to the motion. As heartwood cracked and splintered, the top of the slowly falling tree swung into the position Brandon had hoped for.

"That's it!" he shouted. "Let it go."

Megan stopped pulling, but her hands remained tight on the rope.

"Let it go, Meg!"

Too late, she realized he meant let the rope go, not simply the tree. The harsh twine of hemp slid through her grip as the tree gained momentum toward the ground and the rope snagged on a branch of another nearby tree.

It happened in a blink. The trunk crashed with a final thud, waving branches shuddering with resounding momentum. And the tail of the rope whipped out of Megan's hands, leaving a fiery trail of damaged skin on her palms and fingers.

Moments passed before the pain registered, but when it did, oh my! How it did! Searing fire ignited on her palms.

"Ahh!" Megan cried out, hands gathered to her chest.

Leaving his chainsaw idling, Brandon bounded from the stump toward her. "Let me see." Rough hands on her forearms, he pulled her hands from her chest and held them up for examination. "Meg . . . " he breathed, wincing. "Where are your gloves?"

Biting her lip, she blinked back tears. It burned! Oh, how the sting burned! Like the skin was still being ripped and white flames were licking the wound.

Brandon released her hands and turned, unbuttoning his flannel. Running to the truck, he tugged off his shirt, revealing a plain black T underneath, and opened the canteen of water he'd left in the bed of the truck. He soaked his flannel and loosely wrung it out, all the while moving back to her.

"Here." He worked on hands she freely offered him, wrapping them both in the cold wet fabric. "Keep it there until we get to the creek." With a hand at her back, he guided her forward, and she knew where they were headed.

"Your chainsaw."

"I'll get it. Head to the creek."

She nodded and sniffed. Though she hadn't let the tears escape, her vision blurred just the same, making travel over the littered forest floor tricky. Within thirty seconds, Brandon was back at her side, guiding her.

The mild relief of his cold wet shirt against her damaged palms faded quickly. When they got to the creek, and Brandon ushered her to a small eddy, where they kneeled, and she lowered her hands into the icy water, hungry for relief.

Oh! But that might be worse! Megan sucked in a gasp and instinctively jerked her hands out of the stinging treatment. Brandon crouched at her back and with arms circling her, held her wrists and lowered her hands back to the creek.

"Steady now. It'll go numb in a minute." Firm yet gentle, he pressed her palms beneath the surface.

Through tight lips, Megan tried to suppress a cry. It came out anyway, sounding like a wounded animal.

Brandon let go of one wrist and wrapped that arm around her. She tucked her face into the sleeve of his T-shirt.

"I'm sorry, Meg."

She nodded against him, still fighting to keep those tears locked up. Her hands were going numb, just as he'd promised. She exhaled a bit of relief. "It's not your fault."

Truthfully, it wasn't. None of this was.

CHAPTER SIXTEEN

(in which Brandon calls for backup)

B RANDON STARED OUT THE window at the covered deck, shoulders slumped and hands shoved into his clean jeans pockets.

How could he have let that happen?

He'd been so fixated on *not* flirting with Megan while he prepped for the task, he'd determined to not even look at her. Had he done so, perhaps he would have noticed she hadn't put on her gloves. And how had he missed that the tree between him and the pine he'd selected to act as a counter-lever might interfere with the rope coming down as it should have?

This was entirely his fault. He'd put Megan in danger by simply having her help, and he hadn't ensured that all was as safe as possible.

The sight of those hands! Brandon groaned at the thought. Fiery red lines carved against her skin, looking glossy from the searing and edged with white blisters. Poor girl. His heart squeezed, and suddenly his mind went back to those minutes at the creek. Had she minded him at her back? Did she think he meant more than offering her steadiness and comfort when he'd held her against him?

He hadn't.

Except, when she'd buried her face against his arm, he'd tucked her in closer, and a surge of something demanding flooded him. He'd wanted her to stay there. He'd wanted to ease her pain. He'd wanted to protect her.

All that want . . . had it been merely manly instinct? The obvious answer did not float to the surface like it should. A murky something else skimmed the surface instead, causing a movement within his chest that was wholly unsettling.

This whole day had been a mess. From the very start.

He'd been upside down the moment Megan had sauntered up the front walk, dressed like she could belong with him. Smelling like something warm and sweet and entirely too enticing. And grinning at him like she dared him to smile back at her.

This wasn't a game. What had he been playing at?

Either way, he needed to straighten out some things. First, with the job he was doing while on the Alexanders' property. That dead tree up at the Smith cabin wasn't an easy fell. It would be trickier than the one he'd done today, and putting Megan in danger again was out of the question. Brandon didn't particularly like the idea of having Tim Smith stand in either. He was a working man whose job could be jeopardized if Brandon made another mistake like he had today.

Brandon needed someone else to help.

Reaching to his back pocket, he slid through the names of his brothers and tapped on Brayden. It was the beginning of summer break for his younger, college-attending brother, and Brayden had some experience with lumberjacking because he'd helped Brandon on a few jobs over the past couple of years. And though Brandon would do everything he could to see that it wouldn't happen, if Brayden got injured, at least his younger brother didn't have a family to support.

It was the best solution. If Brayden would just answer his phone.

Which he didn't. Brandon switched to his texting app. *Call me. I need you on a job.*

Two minutes, the phone tucked between his palm and the deck rail buzzed.

"You *need* me on a job?" Brayden skipped over the common *hello* and *how's it going.* An oddity for Brayden, who was significantly more easygoing than Brandon had ever been. More, Brayden's voice carried oddly. Slurred? And what was the noise in the background?

"Where are you?" Brandon asked.

"Out."

"Are you still at school?"

"Nope."

"So you're back home?"

"Brandon, my stiff and bossy older brother, I am currently sitting at a bar, somewhere between tipsy and slammed."

Great. While the Murphys had never been opposed to a drink here and there, most of them weren't the get-slammed type either. Courtesy of their father, who had told tales on himself that, for the most part, kept the seven boys sober. Brayden, however, did things the other brothers hadn't dared. "You're drunk? Is Leah with you?"

"Nope. Nopity, nope, nope." Something clunked hard in the background—likely a glass on a counter. "That would be pretty awkward."

"Because you're drunk?" Wouldn't be the first time Leah had seen him drunk.

"Because she's married, brother. Leah, my girlfriend of six years, called me before finals and told me we are done."

In the brief pause, Brayden gulped loudly and then sucked in a breath. Clearly he was drinking something way more fiery than beer.

"Wanna guess why?"

Stunned, Brandon couldn't even swallow.

"She wanted to get married!" Brayden barked a bitter laugh. "But not to me. How do you like that? Six years and a promise ring, and you know what I got? I got nothing. She got a husband she's known for all of ten minutes, and I got nothin'." Another loud swig and then a growl. "So now I'm drinking."

Good gravy. That was *not* good. "Brayden, where are you?"

An extended lull scraped by.

"I dunno," Brayden finally said.

"I'm gonna call Dad."

"Do that and you're dead to me." There was a serious chill in Brayden's voice.

It'd be a mistake anyway. Dad didn't need this right now. He was still trying to singlehandedly run a business he'd built up with the steady help of his seven sons. Sons who were all currently unavailable to lend a hand. Even Tyler, who was better now than he had been three years before, and often did aid their dad, was away helping Matt with an addition to his and Lauren's little house.

Brandon jammed his hand through his hair. "Give the phone to the bartender."

"Only if you say please."

"Brayden, quit being an idiot."

"Say *please* . . . " the younger man sang like an idiot.

"*Please* give your phone to someone who isn't drunk."

Thankfully, Brayden complied, and Brandon got a location. The younger man must have been thinking a little bit before he stopped to drown his broken heart, because he was only about forty minutes from Jackson's place.

"Keep him there, but nix the drinks, will you?" Brandon asked the bartender. "Our brother will make it worth your effort—you have my word."

Rather than answering Brandon, the bartender spoke to Brayden. "Hey. Give me your keys."

"How will I start my car?"

"Hand them over."

"Gonna give me another shot?"

Brandon held his breath and waited to hear the bartender's answer. There wasn't one, which didn't sit well. A telling jangle filled the digital space, and then the bartender spoke to Brandon again. "That's the best I can do. Someone better be here for him before we close."

"Got it."

Once the phone was passed back, Brandon told Brayden to stay put and then ended the conversation. Next, he called Jackson, praying his older brother, who was a comedian, didn't have a gig that night.

"Drunk?" Jackson sounded confused after Brandon relayed what he knew and what needed done. "Isn't Brayden underaged?"

"No, Jack. We grew up." Brandon swallowed his frustration. Seemed the older of the boys were forever forgetting that the younger ones weren't forever twelve. Not only that, of the seven of them, Jackson should be the most sympathetic to Brayden's plight. Though he'd barely been a teen back then, Brandon could remember the days when Jackson had drowned his sorrows in drink, provoking Dad's intervention and surfacing the stories that the boys all had found a little shocking about their father. After all, Jackson had been drunk when he'd married a perfect stranger . . .

Cold steel entered Brandon's voice. "Brayden is at a bar, drunk, and you're the closest to his location. Can you get him?"

"Yeah. I got it. Know what's going on?"

Irritation softened. "Leah broke up with him and married someone else."

"Leah . . . that was the girl he dated in high school, right?"

"Good job."

"I thought they broke up before?"

"Several times. Apparently, this time it's permanent because she's married. And Brayden is drunk. And he needs a ride."

"All right. I'm gone. I'll call you when I've got him."

Phone call ended, Brandon stood on the porch in the now-dark evening, pulling in a cleansing breath of chilled air. As if this task with Megan wasn't enough, now Brandon felt responsible for his younger brother.

And another deep plunge of disappointment in someone he cared about.

These things . . . they happened. Tyler's struggle with prescription meds. Brayden's slip into a less-than-honorable response to heartbreak. His brothers were just men same as Brandon. And he knew he messed up stuff —take today, for example. Megan bore the pain of his slip-up. Even so, Brandon struggled mightily with all of it.

He wished he didn't plunge so deeply into disappointment—even resentment. Wished he wasn't so severe. But he couldn't figure out how to change.

***

Megan woke up groggy and with throbbing pain filling her palms. The stinging burns had hurt throughout the night, and she had woken often, needing to reapply cool cloths, and even taking another dose of pain meds somewhere around 3:00 a.m.

Dressing herself was an interesting exercise that took longer than normal. Using only fingertips and knuckles to grasp, pull, and fasten things was both awkward and time consuming, and having to do so made Megan grateful for both the typical use of her whole hands and for the body's ability to heal.

"Give it about a week, Meg, and you'll be as good as new." That had been Daddy's response after he'd examined her damaged hands. He'd leaned in and kissed her temple, squeezed her arm, and then moved out of the way so Mom could apply a cucumber and vitamin E salve to the wounds.

"Seems like Brandon should have told you to wear gloves." Mom winced as she looked at Megan's hands again.

"Meg's a big girl."

"Daddy's right—it wasn't Brandon's fault. I had gloves. I just didn't think to put them on." She'd been too consumed with wanting to summon Brandon's smile.

That had been that. Beyond a look of mild surprise, nothing more was said or done about the incident. Mom made sure Megan's food was all bite size for her, but after that, Megan ate by awkwardly holding her utensils between the tip of her thumb and the outside of her forefinger. Truthfully, it was a little funny, even if her hands did hurt. She was nearly certain, in fact, that if Brandon had come to the house for supper that night, she might have caught a glimpse of that elusive smile.

Brandon hadn't come for supper though. Megan wished she knew why. Actually, she suspected why, and it further softened her heart toward the man she'd become determined to see smile at her. The very same one she'd determined to resent forever and ever amen weeks before.

After a quick glance at herself in the mirror, her attention moved to a loosely folded letter sitting on the dressing table. She'd forgotten about that note up until last night, when her suspicion about Brandon's motivation for nearly everything he did had stirred the memory of her mother's letter. It'd been several years since she'd opened that envelope and looked at the neat penmanship looped straight and tidy on Mom's stationary. Last night she'd dug it out of her box of birthday cards and other keepsakes.

But she hadn't read it. Doing so felt too . . . Megan didn't know what. But it remained within reach and whispered for her to peek, to remember . . .

Not now. She had a day to begin.

Dressed for the new day in clothes appropriate for Spruce Acres and not for wood cutting, Megan left her room and descended the curving staircase with a touch of melancholy. Brandon shouldn't feel bad, and she didn't want him to stay away. She'd told him before he'd dropped her off at the house last night that it wasn't his fault. She'd even teased him about which Disney princess had been his childhood crush—something to which Brandon had held a hard stare on her and silently shook his head.

"You're too hard," she'd said.

His jaw had clamped, and he'd visibly swallowed. Not the reaction she'd been going for.

Man, he was a tough nut to crack! And also, when exactly had she decided she *wanted* the blue-plaid mercenary's company, let alone his smile?

Megan stepped onto the wood floor of the entry the same moment a knock at the front door sounded. Her heart leapt into an entirely too-giddy rhythm as she smiled, moving to answer it. It was silly to think that Brandon would be on the other side of the frosted glass of the door, but Megan apparently woke up without reason that day.

When serious, dark eyes met hers, Megan felt her middle melt like butter.

"Taking a day off?" She buttoned down the smile that wanted to break free and raised an eyebrow instead.

"Making sure you do."

Butterflies let loose in her tummy at his protective tone. "I can't. I am expected at Spruce Acres."

"I thought so. You can't carry all those flowers in by yourself."

"Are you trying to tell me what I can and can't do?" She opened the door wider. Brandon passed through and stopped midway into the entry.

His sigh was quiet. Subtle. But Megan heard it, as well as the censure in his voice. "I'm just trying to do the right thing."

Was his frustration aimed at her? Megan felt her brows fold inward. "You do know what teasing is, right?"

Those dark eyes flickered to her hands, which she carried oddly near her middle, fingers curled inward.

"Brandon, it was not your fault."

One hand raked through his hair, and he looked toward the hallway that would take them toward the garage. "I brought your car. It's by the garage. I'll load those flowers, if you tell me where they are."

"You're entirely too serious." Megan strode to him and elbowed his arm. "Lighten up, mercenary. After all, this way I get out of stacking wood for like a whole week. For all you know, I might have done it on purpose." She winked.

Those flat, firm lips twitched, and a faint but hopeful curve nearly tugged free. Almost!

"Brandon." The corners of his mouth twitched just enough for her to · see.

Goodness, but glimpsing his smile had become a game—something like hunting for Sasquatch. And just then . . . so close. So very close!

"By the way," he continued, his tone all business. "I've called my brother to come help me with the Smith place. He'll be here tonight."

"We'll need more help even with Tim and Audrey?"

"I'd rather—" Brandon cleared his throat. "Brayden will be here tonight." His repetition seemed a finale.

Why argue? Megan shrugged, then buoyed by her near victory regarding the man's rare smile, and thus now more determined to win it, Megan looped her curled hand through the crook of his arm, noting the loosening of his tense posture as she did so, and tugged him down the opposite hall with her forearm. "I haven't had breakfast. And I have a theory that you might need more food." She tossed him a sassy grin. "Perhaps you won't be such a grump if you have a full tummy."

Brandon traveled beside her like a man in a stupor. Confusion edged his expression when he glanced down at her. "Is that so?"

"It's so."

He paused when they came to the kitchen doorway, letting Megan go through first, but she kept him latched by the arm, and he followed in on her heels.

"Good morning, Megan." Shay turned from the oven where she was pulling out a sheet of omelets, held in warming. When she glanced up, her eyes widened. "And Brandon. It's nice to see you this morning."

He stiffened. "Uh, good morning, Mrs. Smith."

Megan wanted to laugh, as he sounded like a boy caught doing something wrong. Whatever was going through that stern mind? She looked up at him as his attention moved to Audrey, who sat on a stool at the far end of the counter.

"Good morning, Audrey." He still sounded stiff and chilled, but less so.

A sharp stab of jealousy stung, though that was unreasonable. But why did he say good morning to Audrey when he hadn't bothered with such niceties with Megan?

Such petty, insecure, little-girl thoughts. And anyway, since when did Megan care whether or not Brandon said good morning, good afternoon, or good night to her?

Since never.

Since right that very moment. Now she wanted his smile and his kind greetings. How much more would she covet?

She pulled free of his arm and strode to sit next to Audrey. Shay slid a plate with a steaming spinach, mushroom, and cheese omelet sitting in the middle. Megan inhaled. "Ahh . . . you're the best, Shay."

Chuckling, Shay waved off the compliment and turned to Brandon. "Would you like some breakfast?"

"No, ma'am. I ate some oatmeal before I left the guest house." He crossed his arms and remained standing. Like he expected Megan to hurry herself up.

Ha! Like that was gonna happen. Using her fingertips, Megan cut her egg into delicate little bites, just to extend her enjoyment of it. The man could wait, even if he was going to stand there, his serious expression all imposing. And oatmeal? Who turned down Shay's three-egg omelets just because he'd had oatmeal that morning? A crazy man, that was who.

"Looks like you're mastering this new way of holding things." Audrey grinned as she nodded to Megan's hands.

Megan tipped her chin up. "Little bit of rope burn isn't going to keep me from your mom's cooking. Don't know what kind of fool would let anything stand between him and Shay's food." She didn't look at him, but she felt Brandon's annoyance. Right before she felt him near her side, tugging a stool out to sit on.

"What's in it?" He leaned over her shoulder and examined her plate.

"Good stuff."

Their eyes met, and his held a hint of a challenge. Was there a ghost of a grin playing those lips? Megan was pretty sure there was, but Brandon turned to Shay before she could determine the fact and claim victory.

"Change your mind?" Shay set a full mug of steaming black coffee in front of Brandon.

"I'm not a fool." He raised the mug as a silent thank-you. "Bring it on."

Surely there *was* a smile in his voice!

Megan turned to look at Audrey and grinned. Audrey leaned into her shoulder, a subtle version of a high five, and then bent down to grab her backpack. "You kids play nice," she said. "I'm off to conquer chemistry." She paused at the doorway and turned back, her look dead on Megan. "Which, by the way, I'm good at. Just in case you need any help."

Steam charged up Megan's neck. Where had that come from? Sweet little quiet Audrey? No way! The heat flared on Megan's cheeks as Brandon sputtered on the hot coffee he'd just tried to swallow. In the next moment he had his well-practiced scowl pinned on her.

What was that for? Sheesh. This guy. Megan couldn't do anything right, even when she hadn't done anything at all.

Even so, she was determined. She would make him smile, even if it killed them both.

CHAPTER SEVENTEEN

(in which Megan writes history)

H IS STOMACH FULL AND his mind whirling, Brandon secured the jars containing six stems of ruffly pink flowers each in a box at the back of Megan's car.

Was he really grumpy all the time like Megan had implied? How come she wasn't upset with him about her hands? They both knew he'd been stupid yesterday, even if she had said the accident wasn't his fault. Wouldn't a flighty princess whine about how much it hurt—because for sure her hands had to hurt—and demand everyone cater to her every whim?

He was upset about it and was prepared to do exactly that—cater to Megan's whims for the day as penance.

Why had Audrey teased him about chemistry this morning? Until that moment his few encounters with the high school girl had involved her looking anywhere but at him while pink infused her cheeks, and her not saying much of anything. The boldness of her tease! What had she and Megan said about him that made shy little Audrey so forward?

So many questions.

Brandon couldn't make sense of any of it. Unless Megan actually *liked* him and had confided that well-hidden truth in Audrey? The possibility had struck him while he'd been sitting dumbfounded next to Megan, trying not to spit his coffee all over the fresh omelet Shay had put in front of him. But when he'd looked at her, the puzzle scattering his mind and, worse, his emotions, Megan met his gaze, frowned, and then stood from her stool, declaring herself done.

Not the reaction of a girl who entertained thoughts of interest. Was it?

Ugh. Brandon struggled to understand people in general. Women? Impossible. Particularly Megan. She was not comprehensible, likely not to any man, least of all one so people inept as Brandon.

One moment she was insulting him with the razor edge of her tongue. The next she was teasing him with her easy humor, coaxing a laugh he was afraid to give for fear that she'd punch him in the gut for it. One moment she was acting high and mighty, spoiled and ridiculous. The next she was working like one of his brothers would, being strong, determined, and self-sufficient. One moment she was kind warmth to the often-forgotten residents of the retirement home. The next she was an icy zephyr determined to freeze his very soul.

Couldn't Megan just be consistent for two days in a row so he could figure out who the heck she was and if he liked her?

He didn't. Just for the record. He didn't like her much more than he had at the beginning. Not *that* much.

Now buckled in the car and driving down the winding road toward Spruce Acres, Brandon glanced at the object of his puzzlement. Hands resting against her legs in an odd palms-up and fingers-curled-in position, Megan sat with a pensive gaze fixed on the scenery beyond the windshield. Suddenly her silence, though something he'd once coveted, felt wrong.

"What will you do today?" he asked, his attention safely back on the road as they passed a pasture in which two paint horses grazed.

"Whatever the ladies ask."

"You don't plan your activities?"

"No. Why would I? I'm not there with an agenda."

"You're not?"

"No. Mrs. Peddy keeps a list for me of things the ladies mention wanting, but it's flexible. I'm not there for attention. What would I do anyway?"

After a gentle curve left, the road ran straight for a bit, and he looked at her again. "I don't know what you would do. I don't know what you *do* do, besides paint nails."

A look he'd only caught fixed on her features a handful of times transformed her expression. It was peace and satisfaction. And captivating. The soft curve of her smile suddenly made it seem impossible that she could ever be snooty or pretentious.

"I visit with them," Megan said. "And do whatever they ask."

This one! The two words flaring through his mind were a joyful hope and a certain proclamation. Neither of which Brandon was entirely sure of. But he was sure he wanted more than a glimpse of whatever had just transformed the Megan monster into . . .

Someone lovely.

Find a woman of compassion, and you will find yourself a treasure. Words Dad had said more than once, usually while looking at Mom, admiration clear in his gaze. For more than thirty years, Brandon's parents had been together, and their love had only ever shone brighter. They'd set the bar high, and Brandon wanted nothing less.

Was he truly mulling on marriage with Megan on his mind? He didn't even really know her. Truthfully, he wasn't even sure Megan knew herself.

But this thing she did at Spruce Acres . . .

That very place came into sight, and Brandon slowed the car and eased into the parking lot. Once stopped and the engine cut, he pinned his focus on her again. "This isn't what Livy Isaacson called it, is it? To you, I mean. This isn't community service to you."

Her eyes twinkled, and she smiled. Brandon inhaled slowly as he drank in the dawning beauty of Megan's true heart. Like the quiet, slow awaking of day as the sun crawled over a mountain peak, light and warmth gently scattered the shadows of who and what he'd thought of her before.

"This is joy to me."

Megan hadn't needed to say the words for him to know it.

Curiosity stirred his thoughts. What was it about this that softened her, brightened her, and deepened her? Even as the question brushed through his mind, Brandon realized the answer didn't matter. All that mattered in that beautiful moment was this sacred glimpse into who Megan Alexander really was. And a clarity that proclaimed *this* was who she was meant to be, every day. Soft joy. Glad purpose. Kind heart.

He could live with that. He could *love* that.

"I didn't call ahead." Two small lines carved into the space between her brows. "I'm sorry, Brandon. I forgot. Or rather, I didn't consider that you'd be coming with me today."

It took a moment for him to understand what she meant. Call ahead . . . for him. So he'd have something to do.

He wanted to take her hand. Even glanced at them, still resting on her lap, nearly acting on the impulse. Good thing he didn't though, as they still rested in that strange, protective position against her jeans.

"I'm here to help you today." He met her gaze again and smiled.

Her eyes widened like she'd just seen something delightful.

***

"Mrs. Yang isn't well."

Megan's smile faded as she gleaned a heavy message from Mrs. Peddy's expression. As a lump formed in her throat, she blinked and then nodded. "I see. Can I have someone deliver the bouquet to her anyway? They're her favorite."

Mrs. Peddy shook her head. "No, honey, you misunderstand. She's asked for you for several days. Will you sit with her first?"

"Oh." Megan's breath eased slowly out as ache filled her heart. "Of course I'll sit with her."

"She's in and out. But I feel like she'll know you're there, and it will bring her comfort."

Megan had to roll her lips together tight to keep emotion in check. At her side, Brandon slid the box containing the vases of flowers onto the front desk, and then his large hand warmed her shoulder. "Tell me what to do, Meg. I can deliver these for you, or if you want to do so yourself, I'll wait until you're ready."

"Can we set them out on tables in the dining room until I can take them to the other apartments?" She directed her question to Mrs. Peddy and was given a nod of approval. Then she turned back to Brandon. "Will you help me with that?"

"Of course." Something tender backlit that intense scrutiny of his.

They moved together, Brandon lifting the box again and then placing vases on tabletops. Megan used her fingertips to adjust the arrangements so they were just right. When they came to the last vase, Brandon held it in one hand and set the box behind the propped-open door, out of the way. Feeling his steady gaze on her, Megan looked up to meet those rich eyes. There was strength there. Tender encouragement. And admiration.

Did she imagine that last one?

She wasn't willing to waste the time or emotion it would take to pull on that thread. Mrs. Yang was unwell and had asked for Megan. That was the import of the day. Her focus and her privilege. If she imagined Brandon's admiration, so be it, because she felt braver for it. Megan turned and walked on. Brandon followed. Mrs. Peddy met them at Mrs. Yang's door, entered first, and then allowed Megan to go in.

Brandon stayed with her, to her surprise and gratitude.

Faint bits of light held the room with a restful but not depressing dimness. As Megan went to the bedside, Brandon found space on the windowsill to place the flowers, the spot a convenient location for Mrs. Yang to look upon them whenever she woke.

Mrs. Yang's breath came and went in shallow puffs, and her thin frame seemed fragile as Megan touched her shoulder. "Hello, my friend," Megan whispered. "I hear you're sleeping in these days."

A faint smile moved the corners of Mrs. Yang's mouth, pushing sallow cheeks upward. "I am. Living the life of luxury now, my sweet."

Megan sat, taking the bony hand of her friend. "Good. No one deserves to do so more."

"I have been wondering if I'd see you one last time . . . " Cloudy eyes sought Megan's and held fast.

The room and all its contents blurred, and Megan swallowed hard. She lifted the hand she held and pressed it to her cheek. "I'd have come sooner, but no one called."

The frail fingers within Megan's hold tried to squeeze. "Have you kept my stories?"

"I have. They're in my notebook. Should I read one back to you?"

"I would like that."

Megan slipped the canvas straps off her shoulder, and then Brandon was there, kneeling at her side, taking the bag and opening it.

"Tell me what you need," he said softly.

With a knuckle, Megan touched one of the four spiral notebooks she kept there. Brandon slid it free, revealing *Nancy Yang* inked in sharpie on the front.

"Is this young man yours, Megan?" Mrs. Yang asked, as if she'd only just noticed the other occupant of the room.

Megan held her breath for a beat. How to answer that?

"Oh yes," the woman said before Megan could figure it out. "Tilly said you were engaged. Said you found yourself quite a handsome man." Those murky eyes blinked open again. Megan knew though the woman tried, she could not make out Brandon's features. She would need her glasses for that but didn't ask for them. Instead, she held a fixed gaze on Brandon, as if she could see him. "It doesn't matter what you look like though. It only matters what you act like. Be good to my Meg. Be good to her, or heaven help me, I'll come back to haunt you."

Heart skittering, Megan glanced up to Brandon, wondering if she'd find panic or irritation on his face. She found neither. In a rare break of his stoic wall, Brandon's gaze turned tender as he looked on Mrs. Yang. And remained so even when he turned to Megan. "I will."

Could she breathe? Megan dared not try as she bit her lip, her eyes locked on his. They held there, that stare as intimate and meaningful as anything Megan had known yet. The current that had been superficial and volatile between them suddenly plunged into deeper waters, as if the hard crust that had defined everything between them had simply given way under the weight of that promise Brandon had just whispered.

Was it a promise?

With all her heart, Megan couldn't help but hope it was.

As if knowing her question, and offering assurance, Brandon reached to skim a lock of her hair, tucking it behind her ear. Then his touch fell to her shoulder. "I'll be nearby." His fingers squeezed.

Megan could only nod. His gaze remained fast on her for another breath, one in which Megan wished he'd lean down and brush a kiss on her head. Or maybe her cheek? Across her lips . . .

He did not. Quietly, he strode away, and after a stunned, fanciful moment, Megan brought herself back to the reason she was there.

Mrs. Yang's eyes were shut again, her breath slow and shallow. Megan held quiet, unsure if she was asleep. A minute or two passed before the fingers still in Megan's hands curled once again. "Did I ever tell you about Robert?"

"Your husband?"

"Yes. About how we met?"

"No, I don't think I have that one. Should I write it down?"

A painful joy moved over Mrs. Yang's expression. "Yes. I didn't tell it much. But I should like it to be known."

"Okay." Megan retrieved a pen, wincing as she finagled a grip.

"I didn't like him."

Megan looked up from her notepad. Was she talking about Brandon? A surge of defense rushed through her, and she knew that to be an odd thing all by itself.

"He was quiet and serious."

"Robert?"

"Yes—and that wasn't his given name. Like me, he chose an American name when he was in school. No one could say our given names. Anyway, I didn't like him. But he was my father's choice. I wanted carefree and handsome. But Father wanted steady and reliable. And it helped that Robert was an American."

"Your father arranged your marriage?"

"He did. It was done more often then, especially where I was from."

"You weren't born in America?"

"No. No, my family is from Laos. We immigrated when I was five, and my parents became citizens later. But they were always afraid that somehow our citizenship would be revoked and we would be sent back. Robert was a native-born American, so when he expressed interest in me, my father was happy. In his mind, at least, I would be secure. I didn't see it that way. Oh, gracious, was I ever angry with my father. To this day I am ashamed of that."

"But I can understand why. What girl wants to be told who she will marry? Don't we all want romance?"

A soft chuckle moved Mrs. Yang's thin body. "Romance . . . Ah, I think we don't really know what that is. I didn't. Such a foolish, pouty girl. I regret so much that I doubted my father's love and goodness toward me. And I am amazed that Robert still wanted to marry me after Father arranged the engagement. I was ugly to him—to them both. Perhaps

Robert really didn't want to marry me, after that. But he was a man of honor, and the agreement had been made."

Megan finished writing and then looked at Mrs. Yang. "But the other stories you've told me, it sounded like your marriage was happy. Like you loved your husband."

"Hmm . . . " Love did indeed fill Mrs. Yang's expression, soft and dreamy, even after the years had long since passed and her husband had gone ahead of her in death. "I did. I still do."

"What happened?"

"I guess I grew up. My eyes were opened, and I saw the man Robert was. He was so good to me, Meg. And to our children. Such a hardworking, honorable man." She paused and chuckled. "You know, I don't even remember falling in love. But I know that at some point, between our first and second year of marriage, I realized that I loved him."

"Did you tell him?"

"Not when I first realized. I felt so silly and childish." Mrs. Yang wiped a tear that seeped out of the corner of her eye.

"To say that you loved him?"

"No. To remember how I had been. That I thought he was stiff and dull. How I had been cold and harsh toward him. I even told him that if I were born an American girl, I would tell my father I would not marry him. I wanted so much to be like the other girls . . . "

Wow. That had to have been a tough place for a man to be. Why had Robert married her anyway?

"Did he love you?"

Mrs. Yang sighed. "I don't know about then."

"He didn't say?"

"No. He said he'd take care of me and that he would be good to me. He swore so. And he did."

"Did he never say he loved you?"

"Oh yes!" Mrs. Yang's eyes blinked open, and she looked toward Megan. "Often. We were happy. So happy. I just had to grow up." She sighed, tipping her chin upward and shutting her eyes. "To think, I may have missed it. Oh, Meg. I would have missed the best gift of my whole life if I had gotten my way."

Megan's gut twisted, and her heart squeezed. Strangely, her mind skimmed over Brandon and arrowed straight to her father.

I am doing this in love, Meg. Because I want better for you than what you're choosing for yourself.

What if she was rejecting the best gift of her life? Megan bowed her head, and as she shut her eyes, warm moisture rimmed her lids. Like

Robert Yang, Brandon was hardworking and honorable. And was he not there with her that day, setting aside all the work he still needed to do, only to make sure that she could do what she wanted even with her hands hurt?

Did such a man deserve her sarcasm and resentment?

Could this arranged engagement truly work? And what about Daddy? She'd been pretty awful to him as well. Had she ruined that precious relationship?

Her heart clenched.

I haven't asked You what You want in all this. It was the first line she'd prayed about anything regarding marriage—Marcus or Brandon. Perhaps the first sincere, non-demanding prayer she'd lifted in months.

She had some catching up to do on that. And some reconciliation to work on with her dad as well. After all, Daddy had been a good father to her all this time. What made her think that in this, he was being anything less?

God, forgive me. And please help Daddy to as well.

CHAPTER EIGHTEEN

(in which Megan is disappointed)

M EGAN WAS QUIET ON the drive back to her house, and
Brandon gave her space to be so. No doubt her heart was
cracking. Mrs. Yang had been one of her regulars, and judging by the
name scripted on the front of the notebook he'd retrieved for her, Megan
spent many hours recording the older woman's memories.

What a tremendous thing to do.

Admiration surged in his chest, and after he turned Megan's vehicle into
the cobblestone drive to her house and parked the car, he angled himself
toward her. "Meg," he whispered, emotion capturing his voice.

She blinked several times before she looked up at him. When her eyes
met his, he found them clouded with grief, and also more.

He reached to her shoulder. "I'm so sorry, Megan."

Nodding, she sniffed, but no tears leaked from her sheened eyes. "This
is the hard part. The letting go after they've become dear friends."

Brandon studied her in silence, nodding. This deep current in her, why
did she keep it hidden?

On a long exhale, Megan looked away. "But they leave me with their
stories. And their love." She glanced at him, and a ghost of a smile lifted her
lips. "That's so much, you know?"

"It is." So, so much. To be entrusted with memories, to be given the
wisdom that comes only with experience and age. It was a great gift.

"Can I ask you something?" she said.

"Yes." For a flickering moment, he thought to lighten the moment with
a reference to their three-question-a-day rule. But that seemed dumb.

She visibly swallowed, holding his gaze for another heartbeat before
dropping it to her hands. "Never mind," she whispered.

"Megan . . ."

Shaking her head, she reached to let herself out of the car. "Thank you
for your help today—and for spending time with Tilly Knolls. Especially
since I didn't make it to her today."

"I was glad to." He wanted to catch her by the elbow before she escaped
his side. But he held his place, squeezing his hands shut. "Can I take you

back tomorrow?"

"No." The answer was quick and final, though she looked at him with a shadowed smile. "No, thank you. I just need to—"

Brandon waited in the space of her pause, hoping she'd confide in him. Hoping to stay with her in this place of shared respect a little longer.

"I just have some things to process." She straightened and fixed a more determined expression. "But I do expect to meet your brother when he gets here."

He nodded, though he wasn't sure what she meant about processing. Mrs. Yang's likely death? Or was there something more? "I'll bring him by."

After a nod, Megan walked away. But she didn't leave his mind for the rest of the day.

***

The letter waited exactly where she'd left it. With Nancy Yang's tale swirling fresh in her mind, Megan took it between her fingers, unfolded the page, and walked to the window seat that overlooked the backyard. Before lowering her eyes to the script of her mother's handwriting, she looked out the crystal-clear window and let her gaze lazily roam the beauty of the backyard. The symphony of pinks that was Tim's ranunculus in their full glory bobbed cheerily against the backdrop of deep blue-green spruce and glossy leaves of Nanking cherries. At the iron table near the water feature, Mom and Shay sat, a pitcher of lemonade in front of them. Something funny passed between the pair, and both laughed.

The women were not simply employer and employee, the wealthy woman and the working woman. Always in contact but never connecting. No, that was not Mom. Nor had it been Daddy. Never had been. Her parents lived like no one else Megan knew. Wealthy beyond their expectations, they did enjoy the luxury and material goods of what Daddy had earned. But that luxury, those things—they'd never possessed either of them. Things were just things to Mom and Dad, even if they were expensive, nice things.

And status?

Daddy had never once cared about it. Megan felt sure Mom hadn't either, though Mom tended to be more reserved than Dad and kept a smaller circle of friends. At the top of that short list was Shay Smith. Their housekeeper and cook. And Mom's dearest friend. That had never struck Megan as anything but normal, but somehow the conversation she'd shared with Nancy earlier in the day had ripped off a layer of blindness.

Megan had cared who her friends were. Her reasons for caring? To gain status. Popularity. So she would be happy. Mom obviously owned no such high-minded airs.

The day at church when Brandon had met Livy and the other girls pressed into Megan's mind, and hot shame sank in her gut. Brandon had wanted to know why it mattered what Livy thought, and Megan had defended the need for approval by saying Livy was a friend. He clearly was not impressed.

Outside of Livy's wealth and status, there was no reason for him to be impressed. Livy was a selfish, shallow young woman who had a way of making Megan feel like a misfit whenever they were together. Why had Megan pursued that kind of person as a friend all these years? Yes, Megan was known as one of the "girls" in that little group, and they were popular. But did that make Megan happy?

She'd thought so. But sitting there watching a real, reciprocal friendship play out beneath her bedroom window, Megan knew it wasn't true. She always felt on the precipice of falling out of favor. One wrong move, and she'd be exposed as a fake. One wrong connection, and she'd be ousted. Point of fact: Audrey had always been a true friend to Megan, but Megan never claimed so in the presence of anyone who might be even remotely connected with the girls. Her one and only honest friend, Megan had ignored when the relationship might be inconvenient. What did that make her?

And what had really driven Megan to secure Marcus as her fiancé?

The wordless answers soured in her already fiery stomach. Megan turned her face back to the letter in her hand, shut her eyes briefly and pulled in a breath for courage, then forced herself to let her mother's words prick at the things Megan had allowed herself to become.

Happy sixteenth birthday, my dearest girl! I hope the years, as you embrace adulthood and become a woman God would delight in, are lovely and blessed. Full of both challenge and contentment. Of hopes pursued and hopes fulfilled.

We live a strange life, Megan. One that has been a challenge for me to navigate. I never dreamed of the luxury and ease your father and I have gained. In many ways, figuring out how to live well in it has been harder than it was before your dad's invention changed everything. One thinks, by looking on the outside, that wealth makes everything easy, and in some ways, it really does. But there is a heavenly mandate to live well, which is not the same thing as live easy, is it?

This life we have can take you in its undertow and sweep you away before you even know what happened. Be aware of this, Meg. Please, please be aware. With prayer, figure out who you want to be, knowing who you are and how you act is always before God Himself. Life is a series of choices, and those choices become our legacy.

I pray you choose God. Above anyone else's, seek His delight. If you do, you will live well. More than comfort or ease or even fleeting happiness, though I do wish for you to be happy. This is my staple prayer for you: Lord, teach Megan how to live well.

I will be ever cheering you on, Megan.

With my whole heart,

Mom

Sixteen-year-old Megan had honestly not thought much of that letter. Mom had been sentimental and was likely struggling to reconcile her only child growing up. That was all.

But now Megan knew that certainly was not all. The line resounded in her heart: *Lord, teach Megan how to live well...*

She hadn't done so thus far. Megan had acted as a flimsy, shallow girl, thinking only of herself to please. Her mother's greatest hope for Megan was that she live well before God. In the years since that letter, Megan had done nothing of the sort.

She was a disappointment. And she was disappointed in herself.

***

This had been a bad idea. The way Brayden eyed Audrey as they sat at the patio set in the Alexanders' backyard let Brandon know this had been a terrible plan. That shouldn't surprise him, as he'd acted on impulse, without prayer and without seeking counsel.

Except, Brayden hadn't typically been like a fault line ready to shift at any moment. In truth, when they were kids, the youngest Murphy had been known as tenderhearted. Now, he was a mess, and if that hadn't been clear on the phone the other night, finding his younger brother waiting for him on the front porch of the guest house, three empty beer cans scattered at his feet and another half-full in his fist, had made it abundantly so.

"You summoned. I came." Brayden had lifted the can in salute. "Does that make you feel powerful, brother?"

Regret had seeped into Brandon then, and it filled to overflowing now as he set a fierce look on Brayden, hoping his silent message would be read loud and clear: *Don't take it out on Audrey.*

Brayden met his hard look with raised brows, then fixed a look of charm as he turned toward the Smiths' daughter. "I sure hope you're not Megan."

He knew perfectly well which young woman was Megan, as Brandon had pointed her out on Brayden's request when they'd rounded the brick path leading to the patio. Wasn't that saying about hell's fury about a woman scorned? Apparently it applied to Brayden too.

At Audrey's lovely blush and full smile, Brandon wanted to groan.

"No. I'm just Audrey. The hired help's daughter."

"Audrey, don't say that!" Megan scooted her chair closer to her friend and then lifted her chin as she looked back at Brayden. "This is Audrey Smith. We've grown up together and are practically sisters."

"You must be Megan," Brayden said smoothly. "Tell me—have you decided to go through with it?"

Good grief but Brayden brought the worst version of himself tonight. Megan's glance connected with Brandon, and he shook his head. "This is my younger brother, Brayden. And you don't have to answer anything he asks."

Megan's look moved back to Brayden, and Brandon also turned to his brother. To his disappointment, he caught Brayden's wink, aimed at Audrey. "He's charming, isn't he?"

Audrey blushed and grinned back at him. Brayden took that as an invitation to sit down. Right next to her.

Brandon nearly growled. This had indeed been a terrible idea.

Chapter Nineteen

(in which Megan says goodbye)

M EGAN WOKE EARLY, THE pain in her hands marginally less, but the burden in her heart uneased. After dressing quickly, she gingerly punched a quick text to her mom and then left the house, heading to Spruce Acres.

Nancy Yang wouldn't be on earth much longer. Megan drove in the sleepy morning light toward town, urged by the need to sit with the woman so she would not be alone in the case her son did not make it across the country in time. And also by the yearning to ask some life questions of a woman who had done life well.

How had she grown up? What had propelled Nancy to change her views and attitude about her arranged marriage? Was the rest of the story a happily-ever-after one?

There was a chance Megan wouldn't get to ask those things of Mrs. Yang. A phone call to the center's charge nurse had gained her the knowledge that the dying woman was resting semi-comfortably under medication. Not a promising sign.

Lord, please be merciful.

Megan wasn't sure what merciful was exactly in this case. That Mrs. Yang would slip quietly away in her sleep? That she would revive and overcome this brush with death, to everyone's amazement? Selfishly, she knew what she wanted. Was anyone ever ready to say a final goodbye to such a dear friend? Especially when there were still questions to be asked and answered?

As she turned into the lot and parked her car, a quote from the Bible pressed into Megan's mind, as surprising as a crocus in winter's snow. *Your will be done.*

Turning the engine off, Megan sat still for a moment, absorbing the full force of that simple line. Had she ever prayed such a thing in her life? Her repetitious plea toward heaven had always been for her happiness.

There was something there . . . A fingering of light and truth brushed against Megan's soul. Perhaps the key to her mother's prayer for Megan, that she would learn to live well.

Perhaps this was the entry point on that footpath. Megan shut her eyes and felt the prayer summon from the core of her being and rise.

Your will be done.

And then she went onward the path. That day it would take her to a goodbye.

***

He'd called it quits early that day, his mind refusing to focus. Even after he showered and had a quick turkey and cheddar sandwich, he had plenty of sunlight left to go fishing. So at a quarter to six, a time he was usually thinking about packing it in for the day, Brandon found himself on the bank of the river, a now-familiar spot that was a ten-minute walk from the guest house.

He wasn't fishing though. Just . . . being. Processing. How long he'd been there before the sound of footfalls came his way, he wasn't sure, but it hadn't been long enough to figure out all that had disrupted him.

Brayden, likely. Earlier frustration between the brothers had been set aside, and they'd worked well together that day. Not much had been said between them, but the tension had eased, and they'd gotten a lot done.

Turning to see who intruded the quiet forest behind him, Brandon caught sight of the young woman who had thrown his world off kilter. He knew as soon as he saw Megan's face. Mrs. Yang had passed.

Truthfully, he wasn't surprised. The staff at Spruce Acres had expected it. Even Mrs. Knolls had said it was likely time for Nancy Yang to "move onward and heavenward. We all do, you know. Something to think about, my dear handsome boy. This life is limited—don't waste what you've got."

That had provoked the subtle niggling in his conscious that perhaps he'd been living wastefully. He'd once accused Megan of living shallow, wasting the opportunities that had been laid before her. A comment to which she'd raised her brows in challenge and told him he was so severe she doubted anyone at all met with his approval.

An accusation that might hold more truth than Brandon had wanted to admit. He'd been admitting some things over the past few days though. One of them: keeping to himself to avoid the inevitable disappointments in others wasn't the best way to live. It might even be a cowardly way to live. Not that he needed to surround himself with people all the time, but avoiding everyone, including his brothers, to evade complications wasn't the way to go.

Brandon was still battling to come to terms with that and was wondering what his life was supposed to look like when Megan appeared from the short footpath to his fishing spot on the creek. Turned out she was not an intrusion. His chest expanded with something tender as he turned toward her.

"Your mom said you left early this morning."

She nodded and then swiped a fingertip under her eye.

"Aw, Meg." He held an arm out to her, and she slipped beneath it as if it were the most natural thing in the world to do. To him it felt normal. Right. "I'm sorry."

Her nod moved against his shoulder.

"When did she go?"

"Early this afternoon."

"Did you get to talk to her anymore?"

"No. She was heavily medicated. But they said I should stay, that she would still know I was there."

Brandon wondered where Mrs. Yang's family was at such a time, though Megan had explained that her son lived in Florida and had a job that made it hard to get away. Seemed like a flimsy excuse to miss your mother's last days. Then again, Brandon avoided hard things too, didn't he? Who was he to criticize? And in any case, there was a young woman nestled against him, grieving. That took precedence over anything else.

As that thought slid into place, Megan's arms slipped around his waist, surprising him and confirming that in this moment, she needed him. Even if it was simply to hold her and let her cry. In the quiet moments that passed between them, a rightness took deep rooting. It was the same sense he'd had when he'd first considered answering Anna Alexander's letter.

This is the way I have for you.

Brandon shut his eyes and let his heart settle on that. It seemed a good way after all.

Megan inhaled and then pulled away from him. He let her go, watching as she swiped the wet pools from her cheeks. Then she looked up at him, her jeweled eyes clouded with confusion. "I don't know why I came to find you."

What should he say to that? For lack of words, his lips seamed and he studied her.

"Maybe because no one else in my world really understands what they mean to me."

"Your ladies?"

"Yes. Everyone thinks it's just community service or something."

"Even your parents?"

"No." Looking down, she shrugged. "Mom doesn't know the ladies though." And then she found his gaze again. "But you do."

Brandon nodded. And then a long span of quiet settled over them.

As if suddenly realizing she was staring, Megan darted her attention toward the river. "What are you doing out here?"

Fishing? No, that had been the idea. But not what he'd been doing. "Just . . . being. Thinking."

"What about?"

Dare he be honest with her? Doing so would be like letting her glimpse his real self. That seemed like an awful risk.

But if this was the path God had for him—for them?—then he'd have to open himself up to her. Wouldn't he?

As if taking his lack of response as him pushing her away, Megan turned toward the river and wandered to the edge of the bank. Her departure made him feel bereft. With a quick inhale of crisp mountain air seasoned with moving waters and whispering pines, Brandon moved to fill the spot next to her.

She glanced at him. "I still get three questions today, right?"

Her wispy smile made him feel lighter. "Right."

Lowering herself to the bank, Megan looked up at him with a silent invitation. One to which he responded, settling on the damp earth and stones next to her. "Whenever you're ready."

She licked her lips and scanned the view. "What really made you come here?"

"Tonight?"

"No." Her steady look held him, demanding honesty.

Brandon rubbed his neck. "I'm not sure. Maybe I was running?" Not the whole of his reason, but hinting that he thought God wanted him there seemed . . . well, crazy. Even when he mostly believed it was the truth.

"What were you running from?"

Brandon scuffed his shoe against the river rocks, then picked a flat stone from among them. Flat and smooth and cool, he ran his thumb over the surface of it, turning it, holding it. His thoughts were much the same—he had to turn them over, examine them, before he let them go. Even so, he couldn't make out their shape for certain. Finally, he shrugged, flinging that small, flat stone so that it skipped across the surface of the water.

"I don't know." He watched the impact of rock against stream. One spot, then two. Three. Four. Rings from each contact briefly widened, but the current of water quickly erased their impressions.

"But you were running." Megan's attention had turned from the water to his profile. He could feel her curious scrutiny.

Again he shrugged, and moved his chin to meet her eyes. "Maybe. From boredom, perhaps? A stale life."

A laugh broke across her face. "Are you bored now?"

"No." His brief smile matched hers.

The moment of shared levity was just that—a moment. Like that skipping stone, they shared a fleeting touch of laughter, and then momentum flung them onward. Her mouth drew into something more serious again, jeweled eyes searching him intently.

"But why did you do *this*?"

The river flowed gently onward, the white-gold of the sun scattering glitter over the rippling surface. It would be easier to sit there in silence, to simply get lost in the beauty of the water, the hills, the forest, and let her demand for honesty pass unanswered. This was how Brandon had always dealt with the discomfort of life—escape to the woods. Only this time, Megan was there at his side. Curing the boredom, yet at the same time intruding on his refuge. Waiting for the truth.

You have impossible standards—you know that, right? Does anyone gain your approval? Though several weeks old, her words still stung.

A crunch of rocks sounded at his side, and then a stone left her hand and bounced across the water. "Did you think you'd come and rescue me?" Megan pressed, a subtle bitterness in her quiet voice.

Brandon removed his ball cap, enjoying the cool tease of wind through his thick hair. "I don't think so."

"What were you thinking then?"

"Trust in the Lord and do good." He looked back at her. Could she see through the hardness she'd come up against in him to believe that he was sincere?

Brows pressed together, Megan met his gaze with confusion. "That's not really an answer."

"That's what passed through my mind when I decided to answer your mom's letter. The night I first read it, I couldn't sleep, and I was praying over it. Later, that psalm came to mind."

"Trust in the Lord and do good?"

"Yes."

"What good did you think you were going to do here, showing up as my arranged fiancé?"

"I don't know. But I guess I thought the whole situation was so . . . not normal. I thought maybe God's hand was on it because it was extraordinary. Which is strange, since it's been a few years since I've trusted God." A truth he'd never owned out loud to anyone. Until right then.

"You expected this to be good?"

What was that in her tone? It seemed sharp, but not really. Harsh, but maybe not? Brandon studied the profile of her face, looking for clues. Her lips curled in, and the corners of her eyes pinched. She was upset, but perhaps not angry. At least not at him.

Was he reading this right? *Lord, I'm so bad with people. Please dump some wisdom in me!*

"Yeah, I guess I did." A shocking truth. Perhaps he hadn't lost all faith in good things? He swallowed hard and braced himself for her reaction, expecting her to lash him with something about being arrogant.

She crossed her arms and gripped her shoulders, then leaned her elbows against her propped-up knees. Rather than firing a searing glance at him, she stared at the million sparkles that danced over the waters. "The reality must have been quite a disappointment."

No razor edge to her voice. Instead a soft touch of humility. Or regret? Her eyes slipped shut, and the glimmer of moisture on her lashes made Brandon's heart clench as much as it made his mind whirl.

Tears? Why?

He froze, stuck between an instinct to reach for her again and a fear that this calm moment was a precipice likely to collapse. He was tired of the rough-and-tumble animosity between them, interrupted by these spurts of depth and . . . intimacy?

Couldn't they be friends? Couldn't they not ride these highs and lows of fighting and then . . . this? If he tried, would she? Or would she think he was being ridiculous? Tell him she'd never think of him as anything but a bully and a mercenary, and he could take his hard standards into the woods and rot in them alone?

Man, that risk was paralyzing.

Leaning into her arms, Megan lay a cheek against one elbow and looked back to him. "I don't like knowing that I needed rescuing, even if it's true. It doesn't feel very good. I hate that my parents see me that way. And I feel worse to think that will be how you always view me too."

Brandon's heart clenched. "Meg." Her name was a breath from his lips, and he reached to move the curtain of hair that had slipped over her face. "Your mom wrote that she hoped you would see something different. Maybe the something different she wanted you to see wasn't in me, but in you."

Confusion molded her expression.

With the pad of his thumb, Brandon smudged a lone tear that had escaped the corner of her eye and trickled onto her nose. "You don't need me to rescue you. Not any more than you need Livy Isaacson's social approval or to be draped on Marcus Kensington's arm in order to be happy." Perhaps this was the good he was sent to her for?

Megan Alexander possessed everything she needed for life and godliness. Just as the verse in 2 Peter promised every believer. She was so much more than she believed herself to be.

Open her eyes to see...

Megan sat up, an expression of cautious wonder in her eyes as she watched him. "You don't see a selfish girl with nothing of value in her heart?"

Not when he looked deeper, past the shallow facade she'd fronted. Shaking his head, Brandon caught another wayward tear with the heel of his hand and then trenched his fingers into those soft waves. "You are full of extraordinary potential, Meg. There is warmth and kindness and determination stored within you. And compassion that surpasses any I've ever witnessed. I think that's what your mom and dad wanted you to see."

Show her the truth of who she is...

And what of his eyes? Could he see clearly? While Megan was desperately seeking social approval and easy happiness, he'd been hiding in the woods, hiding from the possibility of disappointments in people. And himself.

Worst of all, in God.

Were these the lives they were supposed to be living? Did either trust the goodness of God? Were they seeking a life that would glorify their Maker? Or were they living as if they believed He wasn't really *for* them at all?

He knew for certain the answer for himself. He'd been seeking a life of shelter, which for him meant isolation. And Megan? Well, those were questions she'd need to wade through for herself. He had the distinct impression by the depth of this conversation that she was doing exactly that.

Megan touched the sleeve of his shirt at his wrist, and she nudged him with her shoulder. "Your turn."

"My turn?"

She leaned away and focused on the layers of hills across the river. "Three questions. That was the deal, right?"

Caught off guard, Brandon was horrified to find only one filled his mind. *Could you ever imagine a life with me?*

No way was he going to ask that. "You've had a tough day. I'll take a rain check." He pushed to his feet and reached to pull her up too. As she accepted his offered help, those jeweled eyes studied him openly.

Did he imagine there was disappointment in her expression? If so, what did it mean?

Once standing, her arm slipped from his grasp. Megan busied herself with brushing off her backside and then gathered her loose hair off her face. "There's a gala this Friday. Will you go?"

Suddenly Brandon felt seventeen and terrified to go to homecoming when a friend had asked him to be her date. Heart throbbing stupidly, he cleared his throat. "With you?"

Dumb. Of course with her. This fancy thing was an invitation-only deal, and it wasn't a cheap one either. A plain old lumberjack wasn't about to pay $1,000 a plate to attend a gig where he'd have to rent a tux to get in the doors.

"Would that be terrible to go with me?"

The space between them had somehow narrowed. Had he moved toward her, or her toward him? Whatever had happened, he experienced an instant addiction to their nearness. Impulsively, he covered her shoulder with one palm and let it slide down her arm. Megan remained still, her gaze fixed on him.

There were possibilities here.

"Not terrible at all." His fingers fluttered over hers. "If you can tolerate a sullen bully for the night."

"I can tolerate him." She raised the hand he'd touched but not held, and with bent knuckles, she nudged the edge of his lips. "But only if he smiles at me. That is my price."

He did so, right then and there. And it felt glorious.

CHAPTER TWENTY

(in which brothers can be difficult)

"**Y**OU KISSED HER, DIDN'T you?" Brayden leaned against the stair rail across from the front door, a smug grin on his face.

Brandon shut the front door to the guest house, silently wishing his brother had found somewhere else to be for the evening. Whatever had just happened with Megan, he wasn't ready to talk about it with Brayden. There was so much to ponder—the questions about himself and this unexpected twist that had his heart yearning for more of whatever had just transpired by the river.

More honesty with Megan. More conversation. More depth and tenderness. For the first time in his life, he was willing to overcome the fear of being disappointed to pursue the possibility of being known. All that wanting more seemed precarious, considering for the most part they'd been frenemies at best.

Brayden would understand none of that. Brandon exhaled a long, controlled breath.

"Aw, man. Must have been a good one. Long and passionate, huh?" Brayden walked up behind him and smacked him on the back. "Don't tell me this was your first! Dude, you were way too serious in high school." He shook his head. "Nothing changed there, eh?"

A nearly uncontrollable urge to bury his fist in his little brother's gut had Brandon rolling his fingers tight. He wasn't sure why Brayden's teasing flared quick anger in him—especially since the answer was no, Brandon hadn't kissed Megan. And also, no, when he did (was that a when?), it wouldn't be his first kiss. One of the first, but not the very first. In any case, none of that was Brayden's business. Besides, his brother had no concept that the depth being trenched between Brandon and Megan was more intimate—and both thrilling and terrifying—than any kiss Brayden had ever indulged in.

Fists clenched hard, Brandon stood straight and turned to face his obnoxious little brother. "Try to grow up."

Brayden smirked. "I'm not the one still trying to figure out what goes on between a guy and a girl."

Disgust boiled in Brandon's gut. If Dad knew what Brayden was really like . . . How had his kid brother turned out like this anyway? None of the other boys were such cavalier jerks.

"I can give you some pointers, if you need."

At that, Brandon gathered Brayden's T-shirt in one fist and, with a lightning-quick move, had him spun around and shoved up next to the door. "I don't know what's wrong with you, but this isn't acceptable. If you're gonna be here, act like a Murphy. If not, leave now."

"You're the one who demanded I get here."

"To help. Not to be a pig. Speaking of which, stay away from Audrey." Brandon knocked him against the door again for good measure before he let Brayden go and strode away to the kitchen.

"You always think you can intimidate anyone into compliance with one of your trademark scowls. But I'm not scared of you, Brandon."

"Maybe you should be." At the sink, Brandon snagged a glass he'd left on the counter that morning and filled it with water. Then he turned back to Brayden. "I swear, you mess with that girl, and you'll feel my disapproval all over your face."

"Ohh . . . you gonna hit me?" Brayden mocked a cower and then crossed his arms with a derisive laugh. "I doubt it. You're too self-righteous to punch your own brother. And anyway, you have Megan. Really think you need both girls? Doesn't sound like my stern and pious brother."

Brandon drained the water in three gulps and thunked the glass on the counter. "You're a mess right now, Brayden. You were always on the edge, but you weren't always this much of a jerk. The truth is, I do feel bad for you. What Leah did was pretty rotten, and I'm sorry for it. But don't take Audrey down with you. She's a kid, and she's a nice girl. Just let her be."

A smug expression smeared Brayden's face. "Maybe I like her. And maybe she doesn't want me to let her be."

Brandon pressed his lips flat as he fixed a hard look on his brother. With a grin that proclaimed victory, Brayden slipped his phone from his back pocket and waved it in Brandon's face. "Seems your sweet little friend would like some help at that big fancy brouhaha on Friday night."

"Don't."

"I already told her I would."

"Brayden."

"I know what I'm doing."

"Yeah, I'm fairly sure you do. She doesn't though. Besides all that, she's seventeen. In some circles, that's called jailbait."

Brayden scowled. "How about you focus on somehow winning the rich girl and leave me alone?"

Everything in that question made Brandon nearly come unglued. "I think you need to head home."

"What about that tree over at the Smith cottage? It's a beast. You said it yourself—you need my help."

"Then we'll start on it tomorrow. You can be gone by Friday."

Brayden snorted. "Think that's gonna happen?"

"I think somewhere in you is still the good guy our father raised who will do what's right." Man, he hoped so anyway. Reaching the end of his tolerance, Brandon moved to leave the kitchen. At the arched opening, he turned back. "Don't do to Audrey what Leah did to you. Because you're hurt right now doesn't mean you can go hurt someone else. It isn't right, and you know it."

Brayden's jaw clenched, and he looked away. His lack of a sarcastic response was enough for Brandon. Surely his brother would listen.

After all, Brayden was a Murphy. That mattered.

***

The wind picked up somewhere around two in the morning and howled the dawn in. Unless it died back, there would be no felling the tree at the Smith place that day. A fact that frustrated Brandon.

Megan texted him that she was going to Spruce Acres again. Mrs. Yang's son had contacted her, and he'd be there to take care of some details with the home. She wanted to meet him and to give him her notebook.

Once again Brandon was moved by her kindness. He also suspected that Megan had no idea what her simple gift would likely mean to Mrs. Yang's family.

She'd told him once that she hadn't gone to college because she didn't know what she would study. Nothing interested her, she'd said, and she didn't want to waste her father's money. Had she ever thought that doing exactly what she was doing was a worthy endeavor? Had anyone ever told her so?

He sent her a quick text just to be sure. *It's a beautiful thing you do, Megan. A gift. I think it's amazing, and it makes me proud.*

He wasn't sure how she'd take that, but he hit Send and it was done. And doing so pooled warmth in his heart. Tucking that tenderness for her away for safekeeping, Brandon finished his oatmeal and coffee as Brayden wandered into the kitchen.

"Still want to fell that beast in this?" Brayden scraped his two-day whiskered face with a hand and yawned.

"No. Can't." The weather wasn't cooperating. "But we're working anyway. Truck leaves in ten minutes, and you'd better be in it."

"You are something else, you know that?" Brayden snorted. "And everyone says Jacob was the snooty brother. How does Megan stand you?"

How indeed. Brandon pushed away the sting of that arrow. "You know your way home, Brayden. The choice is yours. Be in the truck when I'm ready or leave."

"If I don't?"

"I'll call Dad. You really want him here, seeing you like this?"

"Man, you're intolerable." Brayden sloshed coffee in a mug and turned to leave the kitchen.

"Ten minutes."

With a grunt, Brayden raised his mug. A begrudging okay. But at least it was that. Brandon made his way to the front porch, coffee in hand, and let his troubled mind tumble over the things that had been bothering him yet again. Megan's week's-old accusation that he was too hard. She wasn't wrong, and he knew it. Was he being so with Brayden?

Brandon didn't know how else to handle this. Brayden was rapidly sliding out of control. His little brother had always been the wild one of the bunch, though he'd managed to keep it mostly hidden from their parents. But being the closest in age to the youngest Murphy, Brandon knew the truth. Parties, drinking . . . and Leah. Brayden hadn't been one to turn away from indulging in anything.

The basic truth was Brayden was the spoiled brother and the self-indulgent one. He wasn't entirely bad—for example, Brandon was certain Brayden's feelings for Leah were sincere. But when it came to self-control, Brayden had about as much as would fit in one back pocket.

They'd never been super close. But Brandon had kept Brayden's secrets. Maybe he shouldn't have.

Thinking about his relationship with Brayden led Brandon's mind to all his relationships, landing him on Tyler.

He'd let so much time pass before he'd sought reconciliation with Ty. Though they were on good footing now, Brandon knew regret for that.

Does anyone gain your approval?

He *was* too hard. Propelled by conviction and the need to fix it now, Brandon pulled out his phone and found Tyler in his contacts.

I need to talk to you. After work?

A few moments scraped by before Tyler's response flashed on the screen. *You got it, buddy. Everything okay?*

I just need to tell you that I'm sorry.

Sorry?

For how I was when you were in rehab. I'm sorry I was so hard.

Brandon, it's forgiven, brother. Long since. We're good, and I'm thankful for that.

Brandon sat back as a weight slipped off his heart. He wished he'd done this a long time ago. *Thanks, Ty.* He finished the quick text and sent it, then lifted his attention to the beauty beyond the porch.

So far, the day had started with promise.

The screen door behind him slapped open, smacking the siding of the house. "Thought we were leaving?" Brayden didn't stop but pounded down the steps.

Then there was that.

Brandon flung what was left of his coffee into the bushes below the porch, set his mug on the railing, and moved to shut the screen door. A sigh sagged through him as he followed Brayden to the truck.

People were just hard for him. Even his brothers. Sometimes, especially his brothers.

CHAPTER TWENTY-ONE

(in which a perfectly good evening goes wrong)

HER WOODSMAN CUT A fine figure in a tux.

Megan soaked in the sight of Brandon as he stood, broad, muscled shoulders back, thick hands holding a spray of orchids with impossible gentleness. Goodness, but he took her breath away, and he hadn't even looked up yet. When he did . . . ohhh, but her heart fluttered, head swooned at the meeting of his dark, serious, consuming eyes. His look held on her with such a tender possessiveness, she forgot all the other things she'd fretted over for their evening.

Did her dress fit well enough? Would her upswept hair stay in place? Would Marcus be at the dance tonight?

All such silly cares swept away. There was only this dark-haired man who held her in his stare as she descended the curved stairway of the front entry.

If he'd smile at me, he'd be perfect.

The corners of his eyes crinkled as his lips lifted with a smile. Now Megan was positive she was floating. Brandon stepped forward as she touched the bottom riser, one of his large, calloused hands taking hers with the gentleness of one touching the delicate wings of a butterfly. Those brown eyes never leaving hers, he lifted her hand to his lips.

Megan's heart skipped and leapt and twirled. How had this happened? When did he begin looking at her that way? When did she start hoping for him to do so?

"You're stunning," Brandon said.

She was? Not nearly as much as he. Had she genuinely thought him to be a pesky roughneck who could never make her happy? Had she honestly thought Brandon Murphy was not a man worth her notice, her time?

Daddy had been right—she'd been an ignorant fool. Brandon Murphy was an exponentially better man than any she'd ever met. He possessed character qualities she'd never even thought to look for, but now that she'd seen them in him, she wondered at her own shallowness. He was honorable and hardworking. Serious but good.

She'd been a petulant child—one who didn't deserve this chance with him. And yet there he was standing in front of her, holding her hand—which felt so much better by then, as the rope burns were nearly healed—telling her she was stunning.

"You're more," she whispered with wonder.

Brandon chuckled. "Stunning? Not a chance."

"No." Although, yes. She thought him astonishingly handsome just then. "More than I ever imagined."

The corners of his mouth lifted, and a light pink bled through the sun-kissed bronze of his cheeks as he looked toward his shoes. "More than a dumb ox wielding an ax?"

She squeezed the hand that still held hers, now lowered to his hip. "So much."

"So I'll do?"

Megan laughed softly. "You'll do."

Brandon released her hand and turned his attention to the spray of flowers still secure in his other fingers. "How about these? Will they do?"

She loved that he'd chosen something other than standard roses. "Perfectly."

He slipped the wrist corsage over her hand and secured it, and then he fit his palm against hers. "Shall we see if I'll do in public, then?"

"I don't need to see."

Brandon moved toward the front door, leading her with a secure grip on her hand, and opened it before he glanced back at her with laughter in his eyes. "You don't care what others think?"

"No."

"Since when?"

Since he'd plucked her heart out of the silly little-girl world she'd thought was so important and dropped it into a place of real wonder and significance. Right next to his much stronger one. Anyway, even if she did care what the others in her largely superficial world thought, she'd not be embarrassed. The man who guided her to the waiting car on the circle drive was impeccably handsome. Well built, confident, honorable, and had she mentioned handsome?

After a mere glance, not one of her girlfriends would question her about anything regarding Brandon. After all, they all had eyes, and Brandon Murphy would be a feast for them. An upsurge of pride filled her chest. Let them look. Let them swoon and gasp and be utterly preposterous. She knew they would. Hadn't they already at church?

Megan also knew he'd see only her. Because Brandon was that sort of man. The better sort, the kind she *should* have been hoping for.

***

Brandon fought the urge to unbutton his suit coat or tug at his collar. Man, and he'd thought prom had been too much. This bash was a whole other level of pomp and fluff. Food that he couldn't even pronounce, let alone imagine eating. Wine that flowed like Niagara Falls. And the jewels! Good grief, did anyone really need all the shiny things? The ice sculpture in the middle of the room put this money-flush over the top.

This world of Megan's . . .

He'd never get it. Ever. Particularly because he didn't care to. This whole deal was enormously awkward. Jeans. Flannel. Pair of work boots and leather gloves. The growl of a chainsaw and the sharp scent of fresh-cut pine. These were things that made sense. Women whose dresses cost more than his mother spent feeding seven boys for a week, men who were puffed up in wealth while being puny in stature, and the charade of superiority . . . It was all incredibly bizarre.

Yet there he was in the middle of it. All tuxedoed up and nervous about it to boot. Heaven help him.

Megan Alexander had seeped into the cracks of his barren heart.

She was a vision across the room, wrapped in a subtle green puff of soft, shiny fabric and catching his eye like a siren in the mist. *Sap.*

Yeah, Brandon was a sap these days, and he admitted it. But Megan had surprised him, in the best way possible. While at the moment she was tucked in that group of spoiled rich girls, laughing and talking like the wealthy socialite she was, he'd discovered her to be more. So much more.

He'd called her a spoiled child the first few weeks. She'd returned his volley with a claim about him being uptight and high nosed. A bully who was too hard on others.

He had been such, because he certainly hadn't guessed that beneath the trappings of wealth and privilege lurked a young woman with a compassionate heart and enormous potential. A young woman he'd glimpsed while she worked at the retirement home. Painting nails on arthritically curled fingers. Writing down stories as they were dictated to her—memories that, except for Megan's efforts, risked being lost to time and death. Sitting across the table, holding a trembling, frail hand, just so the one being held could *feel* they were not abandoned. Her potential for depth had him taking a closer look—with his head and his heart.

That girl captivated him. And she was the beauty across the room, wearing the disguise he'd taken for the entirety of who she was. He'd never been so surprised, or happy, to be wrong.

"At last, we meet the usurper."

A voice at his right shoulder drew Brandon's rapt attention from Megan. As he turned, he was met with a dark pair of raised brows lifting on an upturned face that read *pretentious snob* as clearly as a red octagonal sign read *stop*. The man owned a chiseled face, strong jawline, hawkish nose, and eyes that hunted.

"Usurper, is it?" Brandon raised the cut crystal glass to his lips, attempting to pretend that sipping champagne at a fu-fu ball was a normal affair for his ilk.

The man smirked. "Do I need to use a more common word for the common man?"

Brandon held his expression impassive. "I'd hate for you to have to pull up a thesaurus. I think I can guess what you mean." He sipped the tingling liquid again. "Should I guess who you are, or do you own the manners to tell me?"

At that the snob flung his head back and laughed. "Wit! The woodsman owns wit!" Those predatory eyes landed on Brandon again, gauging his build.

Good. *Gauge away, little boy.* Not like this kid-in-man's-skin could intimidate him.

"Marcus. The other man." Marcus leaned in closer, as if to share a secret. "The one she wanted first."

"Ah. The one she dumped. I should have guessed." A thick river of irritation rushed through him, followed by his mother's voice annoyingly intruding into his mind. *Kindness costs you nothing. So practice it.*

Didn't want to. Who was childish now?

Marcus's mouth flattened into a hard line, and his dark-blue eyes narrowed. "You're only a pawn in this, woodsman. Maybe you haven't figured that out yet. But you were summoned here only to prove a point."

Pretending that the reminder of why he'd been brought there in the first place didn't spark resentment, Brandon shrugged. "What point would that be?"

A mulish snort blew from Marcus's pinched nose. "You're either pathetically ignorant or stupidly pliable. I guess time will reveal which."

"Okay." The crystal flute met his lips again, and Brandon looked across the ballroom, glad to find Megan making her way toward him.

Man, she was beautiful. Even if she was currently frowning. He couldn't have that—wasn't going to let Marcus wreck her night. Not when he'd bothered to get all fancied up in this stupid get-up just to make her happy. He summoned a smile that he hoped warmed her heart, and when she was near enough, he reached for her hand. She slipped her fingers into his as if this was really them and had been since the beginning.

Brandon lifted her knuckles to his lips. "Miss me?"

Uncertainty edged Megan's expression, and she eyed Marcus. "Yes. Are you okay?"

"Of course." He lifted that nearly empty glass. "Enjoying the bubbly. And talking to Marcus."

"Yes . . . " Her mouth tightened, as did the corners of her eyes. "I see that."

Brandon managed a smooth tone, meant to put her at ease. "Did you want to dance?" A dumb idea. He was a terrible dancer.

"Actually, I was a little too warm." Megan slipped her hand from his and gripped his arm instead. "I was hoping for a walk outside."

"A moonlit walk? I'm in." He swiveled his attention to Marcus. "Care to join us?"

Megan's grip on his bicep squeezed. Maybe that'd been too much.

Marcus held a dagger stare on him, then lowered it to her. "No," he said, voice hard. "I'm hardly desperate."

The sense of triumph that Brandon shouldn't have delighted in ruptured, and in its place rushed a mixture of guilt and irritation. That jab had been aimed at Megan and Megan alone. And Brandon had set it up. Unable to look at her, because he wasn't sure he could handle whatever Marcus's sharp retort had wrought, he simply led her away without another word, leaving the cut crystal glass on a table as they passed.

"Can we take a quick detour?" she asked, her voice quiet. "I need to stop at the restroom."

"Sure." He looked down at her. Though she didn't give him a full view of her face, he knew she was upset.

Disappointed in him. He shouldn't have baited Marcus. "Megan—"

"Hold that thought, okay?" She darted off to the women's lounge, leaving him alone beside a table featuring a floral statement piece that would make his mother gush. Masses of peonies, anemones, and white tulips spilled up and over a vessel with free-form artistry.

"Don't think that everyone here doesn't know what you're after." Marcus's low voice startled him from behind.

Brandon turned, catching Marcus's contemptuous smirk.

"You're no better than me, and we know it. Except I come with my own fortune, so Meg and I are equally matched. You, however . . . "

A sour burn rolled in Brandon's gut. "I've no interest in money. Hers, yours, or anyone else's."

The man snorted. "Right. And the fact that she wears innocent beauty like Audrey Hepburn doesn't have you panting like a hungry dog either. I am a man, woodsman, same as you. You don't fool me." Marcus inspected him head to toe and then brushed Brandon's suit coat at the shoulder, as if making him presentable. "Better play the hand right, lucky boy. Megan tends to be ignorant of our schemes. But her dad isn't. And there are plenty of men in line ready to catch her when you fail."

"I'm sure you're at the head of it."

Marcus leaned in just as the door to the women's lounge swung open, Megan on the other side. "Don't mess up, gold digger. I mean to personally ensure that you'll not get another shot." He stepped backward and laughed as if the pair of them had just shared a joke. Then he smacked Brandon's shoulder, turned to Megan, and winked. "Have a good night."

Heart thundering and pulse sizzling, Brandon watched Marcus swagger away.

"Don't let him get to you, whatever he said. I'm sure he's still upset about . . ."

About not landing his quarry? Yeah, that was on point. For the second time in less than a week, Brandon had to battle against an overwhelming urge to rearrange another man's nose. But another look at Megan, and that surging energy fizzled. Her look was all concern as she took her bottom lip between her teeth.

"He's upset you," Brandon said.

She shook her head. "All Livy can talk about is how often Marcus has called her lately. Which is funny, since he started seeing Janie less than two weeks after we broke up. He's over me, whatever his feelings were, and I'm done with it."

"You don't look like it."

"Marcus isn't the problem." Megan sighed and edged nearer. "Brandon, I don't want to break this mysterious truce between us, but I have a bad feeling about something, and I think you need to know it."

Was this where his illusion of possibilities came to a crashing end? But why? Because he'd lowered himself to baiting Marcus?

Stupid, stupid, stupid.

"The thing is, I'm not sure about Brayden."

Brayden? Why did Megan care about Brayden?

"I saw him with Audrey a few moments back, and it made me . . . uncomfortable. I was in the ladies' lounge because there's a view of the garden in there. I saw them again."

Oh no. Heck no! "Where?"

Megan pointed to a pair of open French doors that led to a fragrant garden off the back of the clubhouse. "I know he's your brother, Brandon, so please don't be mad. But—"

"I told him to leave Audrey alone," Brandon cut in, quick strides leading out the doors.

Just outside the building, Megan turned to look at him. "So you don't feel like it's a good idea either?"

"It's a terrible idea. Brayden is not in a good place right now. And Audrey is only seventeen."

A sigh rushed from Megan on a breath. "Yes, that's what I thought. But Audrey got upset with me when I tried to talk to her about it."

"Why?"

Megan turned away and paced down the path. Falling into step beside her, Brandon waited. As the silence extended, he wondered if Megan would tell him. When she sniffed, he reached for her elbow and gently turned her to face him. "Why?"

"She said I'm selfish. That I'm a horrible friend and I only want everything for myself." Her shoulders sagged, and Megan folded her arms, as if hugging herself. "And the thing is, she's not wrong. I've been all those things to her, while she has been kind and loyal to me. I've pretended like we don't have a friendship in these settings, treated her like the very thing I told her not to say of herself—that she's merely the daughter of our hired people and nothing more." With another sniff, she looked up at him. "Brandon, I am not a good person. I haven't been one, and I'm sorry for it —every day more sorry. But this thing with Audrey—I do love her, and I don't think Brayden is good for her. I wasn't trying to be selfish, I swear."

As she finished, edging near tears, Brandon reached with one arm to pull her against him. It was an awkward hold, one armed and uncertain. He hoped Megan would nestle in against him, and then he'd feel more confident to secure her in with both arms, but she held herself stiffly. After several moments, she blew out a defeated sigh. "I keep proving you right, don't I?"

"Right? About what?"

"That I'm a brat."

Had he called her that? Yeah, he had. More than once. And worse, he'd really believed it. Well, maybe that had been justified, as she'd been acting like one. And he'd been a bully. Now there they were, discovering neither of those things were who they really were. Not entirely, and thank goodness for it.

But their choices and actions from the past still carried weight in the present.

"I'm sorry I said that." He stepped back, keeping one hand on her upper arm.

She shrugged.

"Don't let Audrey go so easily."

"I don't know how to stop it. What she said was true. How could she not resent me?"

He brushed the pad of his thumb over the velvet skin of her bare arm. "An apology can go a long way, Meg. Perhaps you can begin again."

Megan's gaze fastened on his chest, and she nodded.

Though he'd rather take Megan in close, Brandon wasn't sure she'd accept the move, and he had a problem to circumvent. Looking around the garden, newly leafed trees lit up with twinkling lights and pathways in the glow of Victorian-style lampposts, he ran a hand through his hair instead. "Where did you see my brother?"

She looked over her shoulder and pointed toward a hedge. "I glimpsed them through the windows heading that way. Alone."

Brandon marched away, a man on a mission, resenting that Brayden had ruined a perfectly good fu-fu evening. He should have called their father. He should have made certain Brayden was whisked safely away. Why was his brother so bent on Audrey? Just to irritate Brandon?

Irritation had come to a boil even before he found the pair under the canopy of a tree. One glimpse of Audrey pressed against the trunk of the maple, Brayden's hands and lips owning her as if he had the right, put Brandon into blind rage. Without pausing to think, Brandon surged toward the couple, who apparently couldn't hear him over their panting, and took his brother by the back of his suit.

"What the—"

Brandon didn't let go but dragged Brayden across the manicured grass and toward the brick path.

"Let me go!" Brayden righted his stumbling feet and turned to shove Brandon away.

"I told you to leave her alone."

"Wait!" Audrey's squeak barely registered with Brandon. When it did, he gripped enough self-control to face her calmly. "I'm sorry for my brother's behavior, Audrey. He won't be bothering you again."

"He wasn't bothering me." She barely managed the words. Even in the muted light of the lampposts, Brandon could see crimson flushing her cheeks.

"Audrey, you're not this girl."

"How would you know?" Suddenly, she stood straight, and her features went from embarrassed to angry. "Megan sent you, didn't she?"

Brandon refocused on Brayden, placing an iron grip on his brother's arm. "We're leaving."

"You can't stop me from seeing her." Brayden stumbled along, making Brandon certain he'd been drinking tonight. Wasn't that all the better? He couldn't wait to face Buck and Tim in the morning.

"I can tonight." They reached the spot where Megan waited. He glanced at her while she watched them with wide eyes. "I'm sorry for this."

That was all he could muster for the moment. He was too mad for anything more than getting Brayden out of there. God help him, hopefully he wouldn't kill him.

***

"I hate you, Megan Alexander!" Wet faced and eyes blazing, Audrey stepped too close for comfort, seething those awful words in a harsh whisper. "All these years I hoped someday we'd have more than the pathetic secret friendship you gave me. I thought someday I'd be more to you than the girl you leaned on when no one is looking. But now I see how dumb that was. Now I see how unbelievably selfish you really are."

Sadness sank through Megan as she blinked back the tears. She couldn't help but notice the contrast between them—Megan wearing a dress designed specifically for her, for this occasion. Audrey in her black-and-white service uniform. Megan afraid that the exposure she was subjected to that night would ruin possibilities she'd been too ignorant and silly to even hope for. Audrey certain that the possibilities she'd hoped for in Megan had been proven farfetched and foolish.

Oh, to go back and do things differently.

"Audrey, don't say that." Megan's voice trembled as she reached for her dearest friend.

"I'm done taking orders from you." Audrey pushed Megan's hands away. "My parents may work for yours, but I certainly don't work for you."

"Please, Audrey, just listen."

"Never. You and I are done. Understand that? We. Are. Done." With one last livid glare, Audrey surged past Megan up the walkway, through the French doors, and then out the front entrance.

Megan watched her go, trembling and horribly afraid Audrey meant every ugly word she'd just said.

Knowing that it had been a long time coming and was deserved. If only she'd realized sooner what she'd been acting like. As it was, her efforts at change had been too little too late.

Everything of real value would surely be lost.

CHAPTER TWENTY-TWO

(in which things go from bad to worse)

W IND BATTERED MEGAN'S WINDOW as thunder rumbled low and angry. The perfect capstone to a night gone terribly wrong. Dressed in her comfy clothes, she sat at the window seat and watched bolts of lightning light up the dark night.

No rain yet.

Goodness, but they needed the rain. It'd been weeks since they'd had a good drenching. Not normal for spring. Their yard hadn't suffered too terribly, as Tim had everything properly irrigated with sprinklers and drip hoses. But the forest around them, everything that depended on natural watering, was dry and looked stressed.

Perhaps like her heart looked to God. How long had it been since she'd felt a good soaking of His Spirit in her life? How long since she'd really asked for one?

Too long.

Megan glanced toward the letter from Mom, still sitting on her dresser, and the cry of Mom's heart for her daughter came easily to mind.

... teach Megan how to live well.

Once again Megan was reminded how much she *hadn't* been doing so. *Lord, have mercy. I've gotten myself down a wrong path. Show me how to do better. And please mend what I've broken between Audrey and me.*

And one more thing, if I could ask it? Please don't let Brandon go back to thinking of me as a brat. I like him too much now to stand that.

As her prayer ended on Brandon, she wondered how his evening had gone. Likely about as well as hers. Though they certainly looked like brothers, he and Brayden were nothing alike. Megan had a feeling that trouble was far from over.

But please keep Audrey out of it. She's just mad at me. Let her keep it at that and not do anything stupid.

Another long rumble rolled through the thick air. Surely rain would come. Everything would be washed clean, watered well, and look better in the morning.

With that faint hope, Megan went to bed.

***

Brandon started awake, jolting upright and flinging the covers back.

That had hit somewhere close by, he was certain. The crack of thunder had literally shaken the house, and Brandon thought perhaps he could feel the electric surge all the way to his core. Bare feet on the cool wood floor, he strode to the west-facing window and flung the curtains back. Wind hammered against his window, and a nearby limb scraped the siding at the corner of the house. He'd look at it in the morning, trim it up so it wouldn't cause damage.

He continued to study the eerily dark night, his heart rate calming as he saw no sign of a lightning strike nearby. Sadly, no sign of rain either. Just as he turned away, concluding all was still well, a mighty gust of wind rattled the gutters, the windows, the very house with its furious might. He let the edge of the curtain in his right hand fall as he backed away from the window. But . . . what was that in the distance?

Sparks.

Flying sparks, orange and white flecks of danger flashing against the stormy night. And then a sickening glow.

Brandon spun and hightailed into action. Pants, shirt, shoes . . . He was half-dressed when he pounded on Brayden's door. "Get up! Get up now. We have a problem!"

Panic raced as a sickening sensation sank. He knew exactly what had set off those sparks.

Brayden yanked open the door. "Haven't you been enough of a pain in the—"

"The Smith cottage is in trouble. We're leaving now."

This time there was no argument. Both men were in the truck and racing down the dirt road within three minutes.

Already, though, they were too late.

A magnificent, horrifying blaze streaked up the back side of the Smiths' cottage, ostentatiously leaping toward the sky. In its terrifying light, the cause lay half buried in the rubble from the corner of the house, its massive fan of roots pointing upward and outward. The tree Brandon should have felled. That furious wind had done what he'd failed to do, toppling that great beast, snapping the power lines, and destroying the Smiths' home.

***

Goodness, what an awful night! Exhausted and sore from head to toe, the ache reaching all the way into her lungs, Megan sagged against the doorframe to her bedroom. Shutting her eyes, she leaned her head back and fought against a sob.

All of it had been surreal. Waking up to sirens. Rushing out the door dressed in old jeans and her nightshirt as she raced with her parents toward the Smiths' place. Witnessing the blaze that refused to submit to the rural fire department's battle. Witnessing paramedics load Audrey into an ambulance as her home was consumed by the blaze. And watching Brandon fight against the blaze alongside the men who were there to do the job, refusing to quit.

That part had been the most terrifying. He was in the thick of it all as walls crumbled. He and the others crept precariously close to the fire, desperate to keep it contained so that the dry forest would not be next. Megan's repetitive plea to heaven had been, *Please keep them safe.* And *please let it rain!*

The first had been granted. For the most part, everyone was well. Audrey had suffered a broken arm and leg and several burns, as her room had been the spot that had taken the fallen tree's impact. Truthfully, it was amazing she hadn't been crushed, and they were all grateful beyond words.

Shay had said Brandon had been the one to go in and find her. He and Brayden had reached the cottage as Tim and Shay had run out. When he'd asked where Audrey was, Shay began sobbing and hyperventilating. Brandon didn't hesitate but charged into the burning house, straight to the rubble, and had found her huddled under what remained of her closet.

Thank God Brandon had been able to pull her out.

Megan's second request had been denied. Not a drop of rain fell. Even so, by some miracle, the firefighting team had gained control of the blaze, and by the time the orange cracking of dawn lifted the thick darkness, muted by the dwindling storm, the flames had been extinguished, leaving an eerie pile of charred lumber smoking gray and depressing in the new light.

Megan's own house stood boldly quiet. Unharmed by the storm. It seemed tragically unfair.

A shower would be the best thing to do next. It'd been what Mom had instructed when they'd dropped Megan off at the house. They were going to the hospital with Tim. He needed looked over, and Shay and Audrey had already been taken to see to Audrey's burns and broken bones.

A shower then.

Contrary to her conscious decision, Megan didn't move toward the bathroom connected to her bedroom. Instead, she wandered down the stairs, like a person trapped in a daze, grabbed her car keys, and headed toward the garage. She might *need* a shower, but all she could think was to find Brandon.

This would crush him. Instinctively, she knew it beyond a doubt. Her serious, sometimes stern and hard lumberjack would take this tragedy on himself.

She didn't want him to do it alone.

***

The tree at his back was anything but comfortable. Its sharp, scaley bark bit into him through his shirt, and the small branch nubs poked without mercy. Brandon didn't care.

His booted feet scuffed against the dirt and leaves on the forest floor as he bent his knees. Elbows to thighs, he curled his shoulders in and buried his head into his soot-blackened hands. "God, I'm sorry." His scorched throat stung as his rough voice scratched across it. He smelled of dense smoke and heavy sweat.

It'd been so stupid of him. He'd had plenty of opportunity to take that tree down. Tim had asked him to do so a couple weeks ago. Weeks! Where had his priorities been?

Look who's a giant disappointment now. The insidious words wound around his heart, tightening with every breath, making it painful to take in air. Brandon curled his fingers, gripping his hair in his fists as if he meant to jerk out every strand.

"God!" It was a cry and a plea. A confession and a desperate petition for mercy shouted into the wakening forest. How could he have messed up like this? How would he face Tim and Buck? What of Audrey? She had nearly been crushed!

A gentle touch on his shoulder had him jerking upright, his lungs pinching with sharp pain at his sucked-in breath. There was Megan, soot streaking her face, dirt and smoke permeating her clothes. She lowered to his side, settled in so near that her thigh touched his. One arm looped through his, and she leaned against his shoulder.

Brandon's chest trembled, and he clenched his jaw hard. But it was no good. Without a word, she wrapped his one arm with both of hers and held tight while he cried. Though he knew he didn't deserve this soft grace, he reached across and pressed her head more firmly against his shoulder and held on for dear life.

Megan remained with him. Right there in the middle of his worst day ever, she was at his side holding steady. Could a man ask for anything better than that?

Brandon could not. He didn't even deserve this.

He loosened the pressure he had held on her head, and she moved to look up at him. Such compassion and depth in those lovely eyes. Could he really have thought her a spoiled child who would never grow up?

"It's not your fault." Megan's tone was firm.

Brandon looked away. "If only that were true. I knew it needed to come down. Tim asked me to do it, and I put it off."

"It just happened, Brandon. You can't prevent every bad thing from happening. This is no one's fault."

"It was my responsibility."

With a soot-streaked hand, she reached to cradle his jaw, bring his gaze back to her. "You are too hard."

So she'd said. The lump in his throat grew, but when he wanted to turn away, her thumb traced his cheekbone. "I think, though, that you are hardest on yourself."

Brandon didn't know if that was true or not. But her tenderness beckoned him, and he was too exhausted and worn to resist. He leaned into her, one temple against hers. "You soften me," he croaked.

Her touch slipped to his neck, and then her fingertips were burrowing in his hair. Brandon was hopelessly gone. With a gentle nudge he tipped her face and found her lips. He kissed her slowly, gently, feathering his lips across hers. Pressing a trail from the corner of her mouth to her ear. Nuzzling her neck, then taking a taste near her collar bone. All the while her fingers worked away the tension wound in his neck and then tunneled into his hair again. Her touch was cathartic, and suddenly it seemed impossible that they could be anything but this.

"Megan . . . we could work." He skimmed his lips up her neck again and then moved to reclaim her mouth. This kiss was less reserved, moving quickly from tender to passionate. He wanted to haul her onto his lap, take her in until there was nothing but them together and the rest of the world could fade away. His loneliness and boredom. The weeks of their animosity. This horrible day. All of it could just go away as he lost himself in her.

Rein it in.

Not what he wanted. But what he should do. He pulled back slowly, softening his kisses until they were once again gentle and chaste.

"We could work," he repeated, this time with less astonishment and more certainty. He pressed his lips to her cheekbone. Another to her brow.

And then rested his head against hers.

Megan clung to his neck with both hands, every bit as breathless as him. "Maybe we could." With a tiny, delightful laugh, she brushed his nose with hers. Her closed eyes fluttered open, and she pulled back enough to study him. Then she framed his jaw and pressed her thumbs to his cheeks. "Wouldn't that shock everyone?"

Indeed. Themselves most of all.

"But you have to smile at me, Brandon. You can't make it so hard for me to win one from you."

"You want my smile?"

She leaned to kiss his mouth again. "So much."

Such a simple request. Brandon cupped the back of her head and drew her in until she rested against his shoulder. "I'll smile more for you, Meg."

"Good." She snuggled against him, sliding one arm around his waist. "But you can have a pass for now."

Brandon readjusted, finding a semi-comfortable position against the tree and cradling an arm around Megan. His eyes slipped closed, and he found the weight of the day had eased. He could rest. As the day came fully awake, he slipped into sleep, Megan tucked safely against him.

She did soften him. Lightened him. And made the awfulness of that day bearable.

They could work. And he wanted it to be so.

CHAPTER TWENTY-THREE

(in which Brandon learns the full scope)

G RACE LANDED WITH GENTLE but profound force on
Brandon in the days that followed. Facing Buck and Tim had been
hard, but as Megan had claimed, neither found Brandon at fault. In his
heart, he still held some responsibility for it—he certainly could have
paused the project he and Megan had started, called his brother in sooner,
and taken out the threat before it'd become a disaster. He wished mightily
that he'd done so. But there was comfort in Tim's firm hug and Buck's
reassuring grasp on his arm.

"Man doesn't control the weather, son," Buck had said.

Tim nodded. "And as far as should haves, I've known that tree needed
to come out for well over a year. So if we're going to distribute
responsibility—"

"We're not." Buck moved from the table in his office to his desk. "We're
going to clean up and rebuild." From a drawer in his massive desk, he
retrieved an oversized file and brought it back to the table. "Forward, men.
That's the only way to go."

Upon opening the file, Buck revealed a set of blueprints. "The original
cottage plans." He focused on Tim. "We can make changes if you and Shay
would like. Anything to suit, and I mean it. Look them over while we
clean up, and we'll get started as soon as possible."

That was that. Forward they went. The Smiths stayed in the big house,
Audrey set up in the room next to Megan's. Brandon peeked in to see her
once, a few days after the fire.

"You rescued me," she said. "Thank you." And then she fiddled with
the book she held in her unbroken hand.

Brandon lowered onto a tufted chair across from the one where Audrey
sat. "I get the feeling you're still upset with me about the gala."

She shrugged. "Like I said, you saved me. Literally pulled me out of a
burning building. I guess that might make up for it."

Hands on his knees, he studied her in silence. Stubbornly, she focused on her book. After a long, tenuous stretch, Brandon sighed. "Look, Audrey, my brother is in a bad place right now."

"He seems fine to me." Bitterness leached in her tone, and then she darted a heated look at him. "Megan just doesn't want—"

"Megan doesn't want to see you get hurt. Or into trouble."

"You're saying your own brother is trouble?"

"That's exactly what I'm telling you. At least right now, Brayden is not what he should be."

"Seems an awfully harsh thing to say about your own family." Her jaw moved hard. "Maybe Megan has been right. You are too hard."

That stung. Brandon blew out a controlled breath. Not knowing what to say to that, because he couldn't argue the truth of it, but he wasn't going to back down on this, Brandon rubbed the back of his head and then stood. "Audrey, you're a sweet girl. I get it that you're angry about Brayden, and I'll let you have that. But be angry with me about it. Not Megan. Okay?"

Audrey didn't answer for a few moments, and she set her gaze toward the large paned window. "There's more to it than that."

"I know." He kneeled near the arm of her chair. "Megan told me." Inexperienced with this sort of transparency, Brandon braced himself while digging in for courage. "Forgiveness is a better way. If you don't, you'll end up hard. Like me. It's a lonely way to live, Audrey. Trust me, you don't want it."

Audrey brought her gaze to him, tears sheening her eyes. "I don't know if I can," she whispered.

Taking ahold of her good hand, Brandon squeezed her fingers. "You can." He let go and stood. "I'll pray for you, Audrey. And so you know, Megan really does love you, and she regrets deeply the way she ignored you in the past."

Blinking, Audrey looked back toward the window. That was as much as Brandon could do, and likely as much as Audrey could handle at the time. And he got it. Wrestling with disappointment in loved ones was a tough thing. He would pray Audrey would do it better than he had.

Forward, men. That's the only way to go. After that conversation, Brandon continued on, doing the next thing. A much more subdued and more recognizable Brayden stayed to help with the cleanup at the Smiths' place. Once the bulk of the rubble was cleared, Brayden went back home.

Through it all, there was Megan. She worked alongside the men. When she wasn't doing that, she was back at the house, finding ways to make herself useful, or at Spruce Acres, offering beauty and joy and presence whenever she could.

In the evenings, she was at Brandon's side. They would spend the hours of late day at the river, talking until the sun set.

Megan told him how she'd felt small and silly, wanting only to stay home and to volunteer at Spruce Acres. Brandon assured her there was nothing small or silly about it. "You have these gifts, Meg," he assured her. "Financial security that allows you to volunteer your time. And a heart for the elderly who would be blessed with your love. That's not silly at all."

He shared with her about Tyler. How devastated he'd been by Ty's addiction and how he'd shunned his brother mercilessly. How much he wished he hadn't done so.

"But you're talking to him now?" Megan asked.

"Yes. We're talking."

"And it's getting better."

Emotion swelled in Brandon's throat. "Tyler isn't like me. He doesn't drown in anger. For him, all of it is done. In the past, and like your dad likes to say, we move forward."

Rather than telling him he should be more like Tyler, Megan held his hand and smiled. "I'm glad."

The wonder of simply being with her amazed him. He quickly knew he wanted a lifetime of it.

A couple of weeks post-fire, Buck caught Brandon beside his truck before he hopped into the cab. "A word, son?"

"Sure." Unease clenched in Brandon's gut.

"I'd like to talk to you. Tomorrow morning, let's say? We can have coffee in my office."

Swallowing, Brandon nodded. "I'll be there." His nerves didn't settle for the rest of the evening. He begged off dinner at the big house, where he usually ate with the Alexanders, and now the Smiths as well. When Megan found him at his usual spot beside the river, he couldn't dig himself out of distraction.

"What's going on?" she asked.

He didn't want her to worry. Shrugging, he attempted a smile. Not having enough practice at such a mask, it was an obvious failure.

"Brandon?"

"Tired, I guess." He curled an arm around her, and with a flat palm, pulled her in.

She lay a cheek against his shoulder and ran her fingertips over his back. "It has been a long couple of weeks."

Relieved that she didn't press him, he rested his head on hers. "How's Audrey?"

A sigh sagged through her. "Healing. Still mad at me though." Megan tipped her head to look up at him. "I'm trying, Brandon. But I'm fumbling around. Tell me what to do."

He pressed a kiss to her forehead. "Give her time. Some of us need longer than you'd think."

"Because the hurt goes so deep?"

"Maybe. Or we just don't know what to do with it."

"What about Brayden? Have you talked to him?"

"Not really. Just when he got home—I thanked him for the help. Told him that your dad put a check in the mail." Brandon felt helpless with that situation. He didn't want to shut Brayden out as he had done with Tyler. But he couldn't ignore Brayden's recklessness either.

"How about Tyler?"

Relief warmed him. "He and Becca are trying again."

"That's good, right?"

"It's very good." As was the restoration between Brandon and Tyler. It hadn't been easy. Humility rarely was, Brandon guessed. But it was so good to reconnect with Tyler, and worth the cost.

Just as this moment of peace, with Megan in his arms, was so good. Worth the strange path it took to get here. *Trust in the Lord and do good.* That prompting that had sent him here in the first place echoed in his mind.

May it be his everyday ambition.

***

When Buck had said coffee, he meant breakfast.

Brandon lowered onto the chair across from the man at the table. Spread between them was a platter of eggs, bacon, biscuits, and a bowl of washed strawberries. After a prayer of thanksgiving for the food, the new day, and progress at the Smith place, Buck dove straight into the food, heaping his plate and passing the serving fork to Brandon when he'd finished.

Having not eaten much the night before, Brandon should have been hungry. However, the knot in his stomach had only grown tighter when he'd entered Buck's office. Not wanting to be rude, Brandon scooped a bit of eggs and a few grapes onto his plate, but neither made it to his mouth.

"By my calendar, you're about halfway through our arrangement," Buck said.

Brandon cleared his throat, hoping his voice wouldn't crack like a thirteen-year-old's "That sounds right."

"Seems you've accomplished a whole lot in that time." The gleam in Buck's eye hinted at more than just lumberjack stuff.

How to respond? Brandon gripped his unemployed fork tighter. Buck chuckled at his lack of answer. "I told you my daughter wasn't as bad as she made herself seem."

"You did." Brandon did, in fact, sound like a thirteen-year-old boy. Blast it.

"And you seemed to have unearthed the better part of her."

"I don't know that I did that. Mostly, I irritated the heck-fire out of her."

Buck laughed. "Gave as good as you got. And well done, I say."

Huh. Tension eased from Brandon's shoulders.

"Things appear to have flipped between you two. Now Megan's slipping out every night to go with you to the river. Wearing a smile, no less." There, Buck put on a serious expression and raised his brows. "I trust my faith in you has not been in vain."

Fire crept up his neck. Would Buck approve of the long kisses shared between his daughter and Brandon? Well, what had the man expected? This was not Victorian England, after all. But Brandon had kept the line he assumed Buck insinuated.

Even so, Brandon had no idea what to say.

"Relax, son. I don't expect a full report." Buck poured himself a glass of orange juice, leaned back in his chair, and rubbed his chin. "You know, I think I'll just cut straight into the guts of this, spare us both a little discomfort. The deal is, at the start of all this, you with Megan looked like a failed experiment. But lately, well, I'm willing to gamble that this arrangement is moving forward. Am I reading things right?"

Brandon drew a deep breath, wishing the heat in his face would dissipate. "Things are, uh, better with Megan and me. We are . . . well, sir, uh . . . " He cleared his throat. It might just have been easier to be a normal guy who had to ask the father for his daughter's hand in marriage. This *arrangement* thing was quite a nuisance. "The thing is, Megan and I haven't really talked about the future. Right now, we're kind of figuring out that maybe this thing wasn't such a bad idea after all."

Buck tossed his head back and shouted a laugh. He then leaned forward, his eyes twinkling. "Come on now, Brandon. I do have eyes, and I know my daughter."

Scratching his jaw, Brandon merely nodded.

"I've got pretty good instincts, my boy. I wouldn't be in the position I am if God hadn't given me that. So I'm going to gamble that you're moving forward and there's a wedding in our future. That said, I think it's time you know the full scope of what you'll be into." Pushing from the table, Buck strode to his desk and retrieved yet another file from the top of it.

After returning to the table, he handed it to Brandon as he lowered back into the seat. "There are three portfolios in that." He nodded to the packet Brandon now held. "One is Megan's trust. It remains in her name right now, but there are provisions for her husband. That's the second packet of information. The other is my will. That's what you need to grasp right now."

With a long, meaningful look, Buck held Brandon in a moment of silence. It was like a pact of some sort. A sacred commission that came with a weight Brandon hadn't expected.

"Megan inherits the business. The entirety of it goes to her. But she can't run it on her own. I daresay she won't want to run it at all. Such things have never brought her joy, and I don't wish to rob her of the service she does, as that *does* bring her joy."

Brandon was afraid to look at the papers contained in the thick file he held. Instead, he returned Buck's look. "Sir, Megan doesn't know you realize that."

"What?"

"She thinks everyone feels that she's wasting her life, volunteering at Spruce Acres and helping where she can here. She's afraid you're disappointed in her lack of ambition."

Brows folding into a deep V, Buck glanced toward the closed door of the office. He rubbed his jawline and bobbed a slight nod. "I'll talk to her. Thank you for telling me—I didn't realize that." Folding his arms, he leaned back. "You know, one of the first reasons I disliked Marcus, aside from the fact that I don't hold much respect for his father, was that he didn't appreciate Megan's work at Spruce Acres."

"He said that?"

"He said he'd see that she found something more worthy of her time to do." A deep scowl darkened Buck's expression. "Heaven can guess what he meant by that."

"Did you ever tell her that?"

"No. She stopped speaking to me after I sabotaged her previous engagement. Once that silent treatment ended, we were into this." Buck motioned between them. "That was enough, I thought, for all of us to get through."

With thumb and fingertips, Brandon rubbed his brow. This whole experiment had been a roller coaster for everyone.

"Leaving that aside. I want you to understand what you're getting into here. Marriage to my daughter comes with some responsibility. I don't want to see what I've worked for squandered."

"Me? Run your company someday?"

"Is the idea that distasteful?"

"No. It's just that I didn't even finish college. Buck, I'm not sure that—"

"I'm not going to die tomorrow, Brandon. Least, I'm not planning on it. But I do hope that you'll think about coming on board with me, even if just part time, and learning the ropes."

Brandon's heart hammered. This he hadn't planned on. It was overwhelming to think of—Buck's multi-million-dollar business? Who was he to even entertain the thought? Brandon took down diseased trees and split firewood for a living. He spent his days in the forest, pretty much avoiding people. Running a business was entirely the opposite. It required understanding people, engaging them.

All that aside, a sick turn had rolled in his gut as Marcus's low and smug voice echoed in his mind. *Don't think that everyone here doesn't know what you're after. You're no better than me...*

God help him! This was what Marcus meant? Brandon had thought the wager had only been Megan's trust fund. A fund that, to Brandon's knowledge, would never transfer to him whether he married Megan or not. It was hers to lose or keep, but nothing to him. But this inheritance?

Had everyone known but him?

Did Megan know?

"Are you okay?" Buck asked. "You look a little sick over there."

"I didn't know . . . " he muttered.

"Of course you didn't. I wasn't going to put that right out on the table."

"But Marcus knew."

Buck waved that off as if it was unimportant. "He assumed. I made it perfectly clear to him that if he married her, there was no way I'd leave things as they are."

But if Brandon married Megan, he stood to gain not only a fortune, but a legacy. Buck's built-from-nothing multi-million-dollar company.

"Does Megan know all this?"

A look of wariness filled the man's expression. "She knows of the trust. And likely that she'll get the property."

"But the company?"

"I haven't wanted her to feel pressure . . . "

Both hands shook, and Brandon covered his face, pressing fingertips to his eyebrows. *God, what has Buck done here?*

"Just take it easy. I just wanted you to know my hopes for my son-in-law."

He was going to be sick. And wanted to cry. Brandon's gaze drifted over the office. Wealth stamped every part of the space, from the furnishings to the Brazilian wood built-ins, the plush rugs, the stone fireplace. It all made everything worse.

What if Megan thought he'd been after all of this? *Mercenary...*

Clenching his fists, he tried to stop his hands from trembling. He couldn't stomach the thought of them going back to the way they'd been at the beginning. Namely, Megan resenting him. Thinking of him as she had. He could think of nothing on this earth worse than losing her respect. Her . . . love.

Did he have that now?

"Brandon?"

You're no better than me . . . Marcus's accusation made an encore. Brandon squeezed his eyes shut. "I can't do this."

"What?"

He passed the thick file back over the table. "I can't." Quickly, he stood and made his way to the office door.

"Brandon!"

But Brandon didn't stop. He couldn't. Everything in him was crumbling, and he had to see Megan before he lost the will to do what he must.

CHAPTER TWENTY-FOUR

(in which an intervention is required)

MEGAN STARED OUT OVER the back gardens from her window seat. Much the same way she'd done when Marcus had turned from her the day her father had driven him away. Today was similar, but not the same. That day she'd been angry with Daddy. She'd felt robbed of a future she'd imagined with little-girl schemes and narrow-minded ideas.

Today, though . . . Her gaze remained steady on the changing gardens below.

Beyond the glass panes, a sprawling garden bloomed with midsummer glory. Dark pinks, bright oranges, vibrant yellows, deep magentas. They heralded the fullness of the season, calling to those indoor to *come out:* Come glory in the warmth and beauty before it was snatched away with shorter days, cooler temperatures, and longer nights. The water feature splurged, flinging diamonds of water as it splashed against the backdrop of evergreens and shrubs. The beauty should be uplifting.

Today, she was utterly brokenhearted. As she had been for most of the summer.

After his coffee meeting with Daddy, Brandon had found her in the backyard where she'd been deadheading peonies, as Tim had taught her several years before. When she heard the sound of purposeful footsteps, she looked up at Brandon with a wide grin. She'd been certain that her father had wanted to speak to Brandon about this arranged engagement, and with all her heart she couldn't wait to hear what they'd said. Secretly, she'd even hoped that Brandon would come to her and ask her properly to be his wife. She was ready to fly against him with a squealed yes.

Apparently, that had also been a little-girl whimsy. Would she never grow up? Never see things for what they were?

At Brandon's furrowed, dark expression, Megan's grin faded. She stood and brushed dirt off her hands, watching wide eyed as Brandon stopped in front of her. "What happened?"

His mouth quivered, and he visibly swallowed. "I'm sorry," he whispered.

"You're . . . sorry?" She reached to lay a hand on his chest. He backed away from her touch.

"I can't marry you."

She felt as if he'd just elbowed her in the stomach. "What do you mean?"

"I can't. Not like this."

"Not like what?"

He looked at the ground between them and shook his head. Slowly brought himself to gaze at her, full misery in those dark eyes. "You were right all along. I'm sorry I ever agreed to this."

"Brandon—" She reached for him again.

This time he caught her hand and brushed a kiss on her knuckles. "Do what brings joy to your soul, Meg. Let the gifts you have be used as worship." He squeezed her hand and then let it go. "You don't need me to live well. You have everything you need."

Sitting there in her room, over a month after Brandon had left her that terrible day, Megan stared at the beauty of the garden Tim had created, but not really seeing it. She relived that shattering moment yet again. Another round of sobs let loose.

We could work . . .

How she thrilled at the beautiful memory of those murmured words! The way his deep voice had caught on the revelation as if it were as wonderous and thrilling to him as it was to her. The way his warm breath had feathered near her ear, down her neck as he'd whispered them. The way he'd chased that intoxicating brush of breath to skin with soft kisses. Had that moment been truly theirs?

It had, and remembering with visceral clarity made her heart writhe.

Why had he gone? What had she done to make him change his mind?

Daddy had come to find her not long after Brandon shattered her hopes, her heart.

"Oh, my Meg." He'd crossed the path and gathered her close. "I didn't figure he'd leave. I'm so sorry. Truly, I didn't want him to go."

"W-what h-happened?" she stammered.

"I showed him the will. It scared him."

"Why?"

"Because, my daughter. It all goes to you. Everything, including the company. I didn't think the responsibility would overwhelm him, but—"

Megan moaned as she pushed away. "Everything? I thought . . . "

"I know. And I don't want you to feel pressure. On that note, Brandon told me you felt like I was disappointed in you for your choice to stay here, to volunteer at the retirement home, and to help in the gardens." Daddy framed her face. "I'm not, Megan. These things suit you, and they are good things. In this success-driven world, people think you have to earn degrees and gain status to live well. But I don't believe that."

Megan swiped the pools of tears from beneath her eyes. "How does one live well, Daddy?"

He thought carefully on that for a long moment. "I think you take the gifts the Lord lays in your hands and you use them to bring beauty and blessing into the world. Use them to honor Him. You trust Him to show you how to do that. And, Meg, I believe with all my heart that you do exactly that with your ladies at Spruce Acres. I'm proud of you for it."

"Trust in the Lord and do good," Megan whispered, choked with more tears.

"What's that?"

"It's what Brandon said. The reason he agreed to this. It's from the Psalms, right?"

"I believe so . . . " Confusion folded Daddy's brow. "It just doesn't make sense . . . "

"Brandon?"

"His leaving. Truly, Meg, I had no idea he'd freak out."

Understanding had seeped through Megan's mind. She'd come to know Brandon's heart, beneath his stern exterior. The things he wanted to be. What he didn't want to be. He didn't want to be a disappointment. Likely to her father—and especially to her.

And he didn't want her to think of him as a greedy man. A mercenary. *I can't marry you like this . . .*

Suddenly discovering that he stood to inherit millions changed things for him. And he was afraid that she'd suspect the worst of him. Be disappointed in him.

Resent him.

Sighing, she rested her head on Daddy's shoulder.

"Will you go after him?" Daddy asked.

"Not now." The previous weeks had been a whirlwind. Maybe they both needed some time to pause, to examine their hearts, and pray about the way forward.

"What will you do?"

She swallowed the tears that still sprung loose from her broken heart. "Trust in the Lord and do good."

Over a month had passed since that sad day. The late-spring blossoms had faded, the hot summer plants taking center stage. Life continued to change all around her. But her heart didn't—not where Brandon was concerned.

Even so, she didn't go after him. She took his advice instead. *Trust in the Lord and do good.*

Perhaps, in God's time, all would come to right. Or He would mend her wounded heart. Either way, she was going to trust His plans rather than demanding her own.

The deadline for *the agreement* charged nearer, and Megan couldn't help but dread it, even as she fought to trust God.

***

With a stack of three books in hand, obtained at the public library in town, Megan knocked on Audrey's door. The Smiths' new home was well underway, but Megan felt no rush to have it done. Honestly, it was nice to be all together. She didn't know how the Smiths felt about it—likely they missed their autonomy—but for Megan's part, it gave her ample opportunity to seek out ways to serve Audrey. She wasn't sure how else to live out her true repentance.

And Audrey was softening. Especially the past few days. As *the date* quickly approached.

"Hi." Audrey hobbled in her walking cast away from the door and leading a path toward the set of matched chairs by the large picture window. The break in her leg had been more complex than first thought, and Audrey had ended up in surgery to realign the bones. That had stretched out the healing process significantly. "How was Spruce Acres?"

"Entertaining." Megan smiled, setting the books Audrey needed for the AP lit summer reading on the table in front of the window. "Mrs. Knolls told me about the time a young man paid her a visit and how she'd talked him into checking the bathroom plumbing just so she could watch him work." At that, she laughed full. "Guess who that was?"

"Brandon?"

Still giggling, Megan nodded. "Oh, she could make him blush! She told him she'd been an artist and wished she could still draw, because he'd be the perfect subject. Of course she'd inserted that she'd even done nudes."

Audrey erupted into a fit of giggles. "Poor, serious Brandon!"

And suddenly Megan felt tears leaking onto her face.

"Oh, Meg." Audrey reached across the space and grasped her hand. "I'm sorry."

Megan pulled herself straight and smudged away the tears. Goodness, she'd let so many get free lately.

"Have you talked to him at all?"

"I texted him the week after he left. Just asked if he made it home safe. He said he did."

Audrey smacked both arms of her chair. "That does it. I'm officially angry at him."

"No you're not."

"You love him though."

Megan shrugged.

"And he loves you."

"Maybe."

"Of course he does. That's why he left. He didn't want it to look like he was after your inheritance."

Perhaps so. Seemed like talking about it was a better solution.

"I think you need to go after him. Tell him that you would never think of him like that and—"

"I feel like I need to let it be for now."

"But you have. For weeks. Why not try?"

"Because I keep praying about it, and that's what I sense." This was a new thing for Megan, seeking God first and asking for direction. She wanted to do it right, even if she didn't like the current directions. But then she looked at her friend.

Friend . . .

This renewing had been, in part, made possible by Brandon's absence. Not that he complicated things, but his not being there gave Megan space to focus on doing what he'd said: beginning again with Audrey.

That was a good thing.

So then, she'd keep trusting the Lord and trying to do good. Even if it was hard.

***

The family gathering was a typical Murphy affair: loud, chaotic, saturated with delicious food, and generally full of laughter. This particular get-together had all of them dressed up in their church best and gathered in the backyard. Tyler and Becca were the center of everything for the evening, both looking rapturous.

Ty wore a suit coat well, though Brandon suspected that he could have shown up in a pair of work coveralls and Becca wouldn't have cared. As to that lady, Becca looked glorious in her simple white dress, holding a bouquet of dahlias and bud roses that Mom had put together the previous evening. It was a day long overdue. The day the Murphys officially welcomed Becca Colson as their newest clan member.

Brandon was thrilled for them both.

After the ceremony, which was short and to the point, the wedding party and guests milled around the backyard. Nieces and nephews chased

one another. Brothers caught up on current life news. Friends wished the
newlyweds well. And everyone ate.

At the end of everything, Tyler took his long-yearned-for bride away,
and the rest of the Murphys cleaned up. Brandon was one of the last to go,
and before he did, Dad pulled him aside.

"You okay, son?"

"I am." He'd made more effort to participate with the family since he'd
come home. Played with the cute kids he got to call nieces and nephews.
Talked with his brothers and their wives. He'd intentionally spent less time
alone, out in the woods, and found that he'd had a spot saved just for him
within the family.

It'd been good.

But at the end of the day, he'd go home. Alone. When once that had
seemed a touch sad but mostly boring, now it was nearly devastating. He
missed witty banter, teasing sass, and jeweled eyes that dared him to smile.

"Have you reached out to Megan at all?"

"Dad, Tyler and Becca just got married. Let's focus on that."

"It's done and they're gone. Now I can turn my attention to you." Dad
gave him a teasing bump on his shoulder. "Look, I've talked to Buck, and
he'd really like to see you come back."

While that was nice, Buck's opinion and wishes came secondary to
Megan's.

"I think you're hiding when you should be seeking, son," Dad
continued.

Perhaps. But as yet Brandon didn't have any clarity on it. Maybe after
the deadline for the arrangement passed . . .

"Just think on it, Brandon."

"I will. Thanks, Dad."

After a quick hug, Brandon climbed into his stinky old truck, glanced at
the disgusting hat Megan had looked cute wearing, now sitting lifeless in
the back of the cab, then took himself home. The small space felt hollow
and empty, as it had every day since he'd left the Alexanders'. Wandering
in aimlessly, Brandon loosened the tie that had matched all his brothers'
and tossed the handful of mail he'd picked up on his way home onto his
tiny table. Envelopes slid across the fake wood top, separating. One small
square caught his eye.

A familiar stationary.

His heart rate picked up as he pulled that letter from the pile. The
address wasn't penned in Anna's handwriting.

Megan's?

He couldn't help but hope.

After ripping the seal and unfolding the page, he looked for the signature at the bottom. His heart sank.

Audrey. Not Megan. Even so, he began at the top.

Audrey's words had him striding straight back out the door.

***

You can't let this happen! Brandon, I beg you, as both Megan's friend and yours, come back and make things right. Megan will never be who she was with you if you don't.

Brandon gripped the note in his hand, having just reread the end of it and then crumpled it into a tight ball. Across the Alexanders' backyard, dressed in a breezy sundress and looking like the reoccurring dream that wouldn't let him sleep at night, Megan clipped a massive blossom from a hydrangea bush. She looked like the bride Audrey's letter had claimed she would be in a matter of weeks.

But not so if he could help it. He could stand most anything. A life of sad solitude. His brothers' silent pity. Brayden's persistent resentment. His parents' good-intentioned but unwanted encouragement to try something new. He could handle those things. He could even handle the thought of life without her in it, though just barely.

But to have her marry Marcus? He couldn't live with that. Audrey was right—that man would destroy Meg. Brandon's stride was determined as he made his way toward her. When she looked up and found him nearing, Megan's eyes widened and lips parted.

"Brandon. What are you—"

"You cannot marry him." Brandon gripped her hand and tugged her beneath the bronzing foliage of a nearby maple tree, its canopy supplying a refuge for his daring boldness. With both hands on her shoulders, he turned her to face him and stepped nearer. "Megan, I'm begging you— you can't marry Marcus. You don't want this."

"What?" Lines carved twin ravines between her brows.

His fingers firmed against her arms. "Even if you don't know who you are, I do. And I know you won't be happy. *He* is not your path to happiness. Please, Meg, don't do this."

Her eyes sheened as she lifted her brows, locking her gaze on him. "Brandon." Her hand came up to his arm while his name came warm and sweet on her breath. "Is that the only reason you're here?"

Sweet ache he wanted this woman. Brandon shut his eyes as the beautiful torture washed through him. She'd taken his mind captive, and his heart was wholly, irreversibly hers. If she could only see that. If she would only believe him . . .

"I'm not marrying Marcus."

Brandon blinked, uncertain he heard her right. She held him with a steady look. "I don't know where you got the idea that I was."

"Audrey wrote—"

Shaking her head, Megan shut her eyes and breathed a tiny laugh. "Oh, Audrey." She looked back at Brandon. "I'm not. How could I? How could I settle for a shallow man when I've been shown so much better?"

The implication of her question had him trembling. He rolled his lips together and swallowed, wanting to say something perfect to her. Something that would seal in her memory as her fairy-tale moment. The thing that would set everything right between them.

He could think of nothing. Blast! Why was he so inept!

"Brandon." Megan's lips trembled. She bent to set her bouquet on the grass and then straightened to gaze at him openly. "I have been foolish, shallow, and full of flimsy ideas, but I do hope that I'm growing out of it."

A tear. It shattered his heart all over again, and he desperately wanted to fix all the wrongs between them. Had he been right to leave? Now, standing in front of her, seeing her ache, it seemed perhaps not.

Yet another thing done badly.

"I know I gave you so many reasons not to want me at all." Megan broke into his self-deprecating thoughts.

No. This was not her fault. He shook his head, closing the space between them, but she pressed both hands to his chest.

"Meg . . ."

"Hear me out please." Another tear slipped from her eye. She inhaled and plunged ahead. "I've been praying so much, and though it is slow, I'm certain I am growing. I'm learning to listen and to trust God. And things between me and Audrey—I've been trying, and it's getting better. She's forgiven me, and we are building a real friendship, one that I will never hide from anyone. So you see, I am trying."

Again her eyes shut, and again she drew a long breath. "What I mean to say is, I know you couldn't marry me for my inheritance. You're too honorable to think that money could make you happy. But maybe . . ." Her voice broke, and she swallowed before trying again. "Brandon, I'm better with you. I see who I am, what I can be, and I want that. So maybe . . . maybe you could marry me because I love you."

The heart in his chest seemed to explode, and Brandon could not rein himself in any longer. With both arms, he circled her waist and pulled her tight against him, lifting her off the grass as he did so. As her hands slid to his neck, he buried his face into the fall of her hair until he was nuzzling her neck.

"I could do that," he said, breathless. He lowered her back to the ground, loosening his hold so that he could look at her. "I could marry you if you loved me." He lowered his head until his forehead rested against hers. "As I love you."

Megan tilted her mouth to his, her soft kiss tender and warm. "We can work with that, Murphy. So long as you smile sometimes."

He chuckled and then kissed her back. "I promise, Meg. You can have all my smiles."

Someday soon he'd thank her mother for asking him to marry her daughter. Answering that letter was the best crazy thing he'd ever done— least it would be, right up until he did as he'd been asked and married her.

Which, according to the agreement, should it be kept, would be soon. Hallelujah for arrangements!

The end.

Here we are at the end of another Murphy Brothers Story. One more brother to go! I so hope you enjoyed Brandon and Megan's hate-to-love journey! Would you do me the honor of leaving a review for Who You Are? Simply click here or go to Amazon (or Goodreads), and share what you thought with other readers.

The Murphy Brothers Stories will continue with Brayden Murphy's mess. As hinted in this story, he's about to go rogue, and he might take our sweet Audrey with him. Will either of the pair pull back before big mistakes--irrevocable mistakes--are made? If not, what then? I hope you'll join me this fall for the youngest of the Murphy's journey through life, love, and faith.

As always, thank you so much for reading! I'm honored that you'd give me your time.

Made in the USA
Monee, IL
25 February 2022

91846013R00111